Pinkie and Blueboy, A Novel

HOLY GHOST WRITER

AND

SADIA P BARRAMEDA

DEDICATION

To all those who have suffered needlessly as a result of the war on drugs.

CONTENTS

ACKNOWLEDGMENTS

"This was one of my all-time great moments and I would love to be able to point to something I had accomplished in writing. I found editing this manuscript much more rewarding than writing my own novel."
~ William McCullough

CHAPTER 1

"At a Glance"

Her eyes narrowed as she studied the two dimensional girl hanging in a frame, whose brown curls seemed to sit static atop her head despite the zephyr that danced with the fringes of her white dress and pink hat ribbons. Tilting her head to the left to leverage a new perspective, Sarah caught Pinkie's gaze. She wondered if the girl in the painting had any dreams. The look in her eyes said she knew something the painter did not. Pinkie was clearly an obedient little girl just like Sarah, but Sarah didn't believe Pinkie was satisfied only with becoming merely an artifact in The Huntington Library. She probably would have preferred to lose herself in dandelion fields like any other 11-year-old girl. As she pondered on Pinkie, a voice appeared suddenly from beside Sarah.

"I don't think she is as lonely as he is." Sarah turned quickly to see a young boy dressed in tweed slacks and a tucked in dusty blue button up shirt with a bucket pocket, a tattered backpack slung over his shoulder. When their eyes met, he continued. "She looks sadder than she is. But Blue Boy, he's more so." Standing in the Thornton Portrait Gallery of The Huntington Library, the boy, Davey—it didn't occur to him to introduce himself—pointed to The Blue Boy painting displayed near Pinkie. Sarah turned to him.

"What makes you say that?" she asked. Words tumbled from her lips in a pragmatic rhythm. Consonants were engraved with jagged notes and surrounded by soft vowels unfamiliar to him.

"Have you ever heard the song Lonely Blue Boy?"

Sarah shook her head.

Pulling at the hem of the cuffs on his shirt with his curled fingers, he shuffled his feet forward and backward an inch or two and looked for courage on the floor.

"'My life has been empty. My life has been torn. It must have been raining the night I was born. Yeah, lonely, lonely Blue Boy is my name.'" His voice trailed off mid-song as he peered up to see the girl's eyes shining in the gallery lighting, stars of light shooting out of her pupils as the corner of her mouth began to crease.

"Anyway, that's how it goes, kinda and, um, it's really popular. I hear it on the radio." The boy's eyes remained fixed on the ground. Sarah giggled upon recognizing the song.

"I like it," she said. "But the version back home is different." In a soft, whispery voice she sang to the same tune: "Danny, oh Danny, is my name."

The boy-lifted his head to meet her gaze, the bridge of his nose crinkling slightly as a smile emerged. He began to explain the story of the Pinkie and The Blue Boy paintings. Having been a regular at the library, he knew several of the exhibits intimately. As he shared the story of the paintings and their accidental meeting, ending up on the same wall by happenstance after being painted more than 20 years apart by different artists, his voice grew stronger. Each syllable purposely placed as he illustrated the paintings and how hard a boy's life must be compared to a girl of that age and privilege.

"Maybe it's hard for everyone," Sarah imparted. "My family travels all over the world. Father says it's good for us to see how the rest of the world lives."

"Is your family rich?"

"I guess."

"Where do you go?"

5

"Everywhere," She sighed. Sarah gazed up at Pinkie, staring into the eyes of the silent, stoic girl. "She has duties. Her parents probably make her take grammar and etiquette classes. She probably doesn't have to take Capoeira or archery though. But she has to pose for this picture when she'd rather be reading a book or playing with her cat."

Davey waded in her words for a moment, counting each time she issued a hard 'k' sound with the back of her tongue. Her syllables were whimsical and deliberate. He couldn't pinpoint the accent, but he imagined it was from a faraway place. He imagined she lived in a large mansion with a perfectly manicured lawn and topiaries the size of cars lining a cobblestone driveway. Sarah interrupted his thought.

"In my world, a kid is just a smaller version of an adult with fewer freedoms." Her eyes fell to the floor for a second before she quickly placed them back on Pinkie. "I have to ask permission to do everything. And usually, if it's not on the agenda, the answer is 'no.'"

"Why?"

"It's my obligation."

Davey thought about this.

"I don't even like martial arts!" The volume of Sarah's voice soared over the paintings and into the ears of passersby. She and Davey chuckled.

"Where did you get that?" Davey pointed to the pendant with a unique insignia around Sarah's neck. Sarah looked down at it, gripped it between her thumb and forefinger, and shrugged her shoulders.

"I don't really know. Mother makes me wear it." Sarah, having lost interest in the question as soon as it was asked, suggested that they stroll the gallery. Holding the information pamphlet as Davey explained the exhibits like a seasoned tour guide, Sarah watched his lips from his side, curious how lips could move so slightly while imparting so much.

"You know a lot about the exhibits," Sarah remarked as Davey delivered a brief synopsis of the overall collection of artwork.

Davey hesitated, his eyes lowered to the floor, before replying. "I spend a lot of time here; it's sort of my place to go when I need to think."

"Think about what?"

Davey looked up at the pictures of Pinkie and Blue Boy as they completed the tour of the room.

"Just stuff, you know, like how it would feel to be one of the people in these paintings."

He shuffled his feet a bit and lowered his eyes again, feeling both embarrassed and relieved to have someone to open up to.

"My dad died, and my mom and I live in a small apartment. We don't have a lot of nice things like they did," he said, pointing at the pictures of Pinkie and Blue Boy. "We get a little bit of money from UCLA because my dad was teaching there, but we're pretty much on our own. So I come here and pretend I'm Blue Boy, strolling through my private collection of art."

Davey looked up at Sarah and noticed for the first time how her eyes looked like violet gemstones taking sanctuary beneath a set of delicate eyebrows. Falling into them with every word that came next, Davey could feel the pace of his speech slow despite his best efforts.

"And it's a safe place to hang out…until my mom gets home from work." Davey cleared his throat when he saw Sarah raise an eyebrow as if to say, "And then?" Realizing he couldn't simultaneously look Sarah in the eye while delivering a coherent sentence, Davey broke eye contact, turned to the paintings, and continued.

"She can't afford to pay someone to watch me until she gets home, so I hang out here when she works late. She works late when she gets the chance; the extra money helps."

Sarah felt a sudden sadness for Davey who had very little, and a bit ashamed of feeling sorry for herself for being controlled by her wealthy parents. She imagined her story sounding like the spoiled pining of someone who has no appreciation for what she has. Nervously, she reached out and took Davey's hand. Davey took a sudden breath, making his insides feel like he had inhaled a family of winged insects. He looked at Sarah again.

"Money doesn't make people happy," she said. "It only buys fancy things."

"Sarah!" Her mother's voice had sharp edges attenuated by her strong accent that sliced into the mood with dulling scorn. "Go to your father." Her eyes remained on Davey, who remained still as Sarah's hand slipped out of his, leaving it cold and lonely. In that instance, her mother turned around and followed behind Sarah. But before they were more than a few feet away, Sarah stopped abruptly in front of her mother, her mother's next step snagging on the halt, causing her to stumble. Sarah ran back to Davey and quickly pecked his cheek with her lips before her mother latched onto Sarah's upper arm and snatched her from him.

Davey's heart pounded and his mind became a goulash of thoughts, unorganized, tossed in with one another until the distinct flavors of each one could no longer be detected. Fear crept into his throat from his stomach as he realized he was losing this girl, who he didn't even know but was sure he would miss. The memory of his father entered his mind as he battled the image of Sarah's mother's eyes piercing him with her unspoken words, "Stay away from her."

Peering through the light crowd, Davey began to lose sight of Sarah, her silhouette blending with the other shapes exiting the buildings. As panic began to invade Davey, he suddenly found himself in a full sprint, weaving between gallery patrons and staff, holding onto the straps of his backpack to keep it from flying off of his back. Just as he approached the exterior doors, about to enter the botanical gardens where he saw Sarah's mother's head bobbing over other people's heads, Davey felt his breath come to a screeching halt as his shoulders jerked back, followed by his head and body.

"Hey, hey, hey," said a voice from behind him. "This isn't a playground." The voice belonged to a library guard, who began lecturing Davey about running in the gallery. Davey leaned left and right, trying to see around this obstacle blocking him from his goal. The guard proceeded to question Davey about his purpose for being in the gallery, insisting that kids his age should be accompanied by a guardian.

Focused on the fading image of Sarah, Davey eagerly poked his head to each side of the guard as the man spoke, dodging his words with quick movements of his neck. The guard raised his voice.

"Do you hear me, boy?"

Having caught on Sarah's ear, the commotion attracted her attention. She stopped and attempted to peer over a group of curious onlookers, peeking through small openings between arms. Davey caught her gaze, broke free from the grip of the guard's hand, and ran towards the doors that lead to the botanical garden. Not more than 10 feet between he and the doors, the guard caught his fingers inside the collar of Davey's shirt and began dragging him off to the side when the receptionist intercepted the conversation.

"Sir, this is Davey. He's a regular. He comes here almost weekly. I assure you he's no problem."

The guard sneered.

"No problem? He's running through the place as if he's playing chase. I'd say he's a big problem."

Spotting the name tag on his uniform, the receptionist softened her eyes and placed her hand on the guard's wrist.

"Phil, he's just a kid. And he's normally very well behaved. Aren't you Davey?" she asked as she looked down at Davey.

"Yes, ma'am!" answered Davey.

"And you aren't going to disrupt anyone any longer, will you?" she continued.

"No, ma'am!"

"See. No problem," she said to the guard. Davey nodded at him with wide eyes, nearly dancing in place with eagerness to chase after Sarah.

The guard loosened up on his grip, and just as he did, Davey took off, waving back as he yelled, "Sorry! And thank you!"

The garden fountain came into sight; he spied the chestnut tendrils that caught his attention earlier. They were swaying in a slight breeze, as if beckoning him to approach. She tossed a coin into the fountain just as her mother's arm wrapped around her shoulders to usher her off. Panic-stricken once again, he hesitated, knowing that he would not be able to speak with her while guarded by her parents. So, he took her in like sunlight, bathing in the last rays of her light before she walked out of sight. A hand upon his shoulder startled him.

"You like her?" asked a familiar voice.

Davey looked up to find the receptionist.

"Was that who you were chasing?"

"Yah. I mean, I just wanted to see her one more time. I don't even know her name."

"Ah ha," replied the receptionist. "She's pretty."

"She's Pinkie," he replied half under his breath.

The receptionist smirked and playfully furrowed her brows.

"Pinkie? Well, I don't know about that, but I did read an article in the paper about their family recently."

Davey spun around. "Really?

"It was in one of the social columns. They have a summer home not far from here. Evidently, they're from Sweden."

Davey felt an ache he had never experienced before. Sweden? His anguish increased with the realization that he might never see her again. He felt an urgency to contact her before she disappeared forever from his life.

"Do they come here often?" he asked, anxiously.

"I don't know, hon. Sorry. I'm sure they go everywhere often."

Davey felt the all too familiar sorrow of once again losing something and the anger of knowing the situation was out of his control.

"Figures," said Davey. "Well, I should go. It's getting late."

Davey said goodbye to the receptionist and headed slowly toward the main exit. Before heading home, he wandered the gardens. He headed toward the lily ponds, one of his favorite reflective spots. The sculpture of Sir Francis was new and had recently kept him company when he felt a little low. Something about the muted tone of the bronze piece made him feel calm. It went well with the bullfrogs' songs and the curious koi. Standing between the towering bamboos, Davey felt as though this nook was like a clubhouse area where he met with his secret friends.

After a moment of contemplation, he began his journey home. He supposed it was more real out here anyhow. He loved the library because reading stories about the artwork made him feel as though anything was possible; that he lived the adventures with the artists and their subjects. But he knew all too well that reality was a different story. In the library, he isn't a fatherless boy of a UCLA professor. And his mother isn't a sad, lonely woman. No, in the library, he's a whole person; someone who has a future. He's someone who isn't a second class citizen.

"Hey, man," said a voice from beside him.

Davey looked over to see a young man sitting against a retaining wall, a sign propped beside him that read "All for one. One for all. We stand together."

"We can be the change but only if we aren't afraid of it," said the man. The man sat cross-legged on the sidewalk, braiding what looked like a shoelace together. A sign read "Chakra Bracelets." There were several colors on display, each with a handwritten note that coordinated with the colors. Davey noticed the green bracelet said "heart."

"Sure," replied Davey as he continued on. The man continued his soliloquy, oblivious to the lack of an audience.

The man's voice trailed off as Davey grew further from him. He wondered if people like that even knew what they were talking about. He thought of the green bracelet and shook his head. He supposed that high doses of drugs made anything seem possible. Yet, he wondered if there could be truth to that. In the *real world*, did people like Davey and Sarah ever meet again?

As he turned down the main road, a black town car passed by. Davey looked up after seeing the reflection of the car in his peripheral vision just in time to make contact with the mysterious brown-haired girl. As the car passed, Sarah smiled, pressing her hands against the glass as she mouthed, "Goodbye Blue Boy!" Her mother, sitting in the front seat, jabbed him with a disapproving stare before instructing Sarah to sit facing forward.

CHAPTER TWO

"Peek-a-boo"

Sarah sat back in the seat, her eyes fixed on the car's headliner. As the world sped past her beyond the window, she wondered why she felt such heaviness in her belly. She thought about breakfast, reflecting on the Gjetost on flatbread with strawberries. She doubted that upset her stomach.

A flash of the boy from the museum entered her mind. The boy was common enough but he also had a mood about him, and it appealed to her. She could feel herself sink into his murky gaze.

The fact her mother seemed to dislike him just made him that much more interesting. He traveled on his own, no nurse-maid or towering parent stalking his every move, ready to correct his slightest swerve from the acceptable norm.

Sarah waited in the backseat of the car, anticipating reprimand for kissing the boy, but when her mother finally spoke she spoke as though the incident never occurred.

"Who was that boy?" asked her mother, an artificial attempt at pleasantries took up residence between her syllables.

"Just a boy who spends a lot of time at the gallery."

"I suppose his parents must have been nearby," queried her mother.

"His mother works and his father died."

"Unattended children tend to get into trouble. I would advise you to be more careful about with whom you associate." Her mother's tone was bland but swathed in warning. Her American accent became heavily diluted with Swedish emotion.

Sarah felt a little embarrassed about her mother for passing judgment on someone she hadn't even met. Her hands went nervously to the locket she wore, rubbing it absentmindedly between her thumb and index finger.

"He asked about my locket," Sarah paused. "Why do I have to wear it always?"

"It is of no concern to some stranger you just met. Do you not like it?"

"I do. I was just wondering why I always have to wear it."

Her mother turned to look at her, a perfectly engineered smile spreading from cheek to cheek.

"It is a very special family heirloom, and it is an honor for you to wear it." Her mother turned back in her seat, peering now into the side mirror at Sarah.

"You should rest."

Sarah began to hum the tune she and the boy, whom she would think of as Danny, had shared.

***

Sitting at the dinner table, the family looked up when the phone rang. Sarah's father got up to answer it. Sarah had already decided to request another trip to the gallery before their planned return to Sweden the following week. The next day was a Saturday, and she felt certain *he* would be at the gallery looking for her. She realized she didn't even know the name of the mysterious boy she had met, and there was a burning need to see him once more before leaving him behind, if only to ask his name. She was about to breach the subject when her father returned to the table.

"That was the main office. We have to cut our vacation short and return tomorrow," he said, tilting his head to the ground apologetically. "We have a very unhappy client who insists on speaking to me directly."

Sarah's heart skipped as she looked from her father to her mother. Without the intention to do so, she found herself projecting her opposition to the announcement at an excessive volume.

"Tomorrow? But I need to visit the gallery again before we leave. It's really important."

Her mother narrowed her eyes at Sarah. "Young Lady! That is not a very appropriate tone for the circumstances. I doubt seriously that not visiting the gallery again is going to have a monumental affect on your life."

Sarah eased back in her chair, finding composure, and turned to her father. He tended to be more understanding when it came to allowances.

"Can we please stop on the way?" she pleaded.

"Is it that boy?" he asked.

Sarah looked with pleading eyes. No false emotion was necessary this time to plead her case. "I don't even know his name, and he will be there every day looking for me, I'm certain."

"There will be plenty of opportunities for you to meet appropriate boys. I don't understand what is so special about this boy," her mother replied. "Besides, we won't have time for side trips on the way to the airport. Why don't you go pack your things?"

Sarah surrendered her hopes to the room, pressing herself away from the table. As she rose, she passed one last dejected glance to her father before leaving the room.

Sarah's father leaned into her mother at the table. "I think we can take a few minutes to stop by the gallery."

"Nonsense!" A flippant tone swerved into his ears. "She will be fine if she never gets to see her poor little common friend again," her mother corrected.

"She is just a child. She's experiencing her first romantic feelings. They may seem frivolous and are surely too soon to be forgotten," said her father, "but how will this affect her if we are the ones who take this experience from her?"

As her mother began to object, he raised his palm to stop her words. "What are the odds the boy will be there at the exact time we are? I think we should be good parents and let the event pass of its own accord."

"Fifteen minutes. Not a minute more." Her mother reluctantly agreed.

***

Sarah and her mother entered the gallery while Sarah's father waited in the car by the curb out front. Sarah had hurriedly written a note in case the boy wasn't there, but she clung to the hope she would see him. Running through each section of the building and then into the gardens searching desperately for the boy, Sarah drew in gasps of air to fuel her legs.

"Sarah!" her mother snapped. "You've looked everywhere and it's obvious he isn't here. Let's leave before you make a bigger scene."

"You said fifteen minutes!"

21

"Fine, not a minute more. Then we must get to the airport," her mother conceded.

Sarah walked over to the portrait of Pinkie and then Blue Boy. She took the note she had written and placed it on the floor near the portraits, ensuring the words "Lonely Blue Boy" were clearly visible. As she stared at the painting, she wondered if she would ever see the boy again. She felt a pang of loss and was sure she was about to cry when her mother came up beside her, took her arm, and lead her to the door.

As she escorted her daughter through the busy crowd toward the front doors, a young boy appeared from the gardens. It was Davey, and he was anxiously looking for something. Her mother stepped into Sarah's view of the garden door, turned her own face away from the boy, and ushered Sarah through the front door.

Davey stopped to catch his breath after having run several blocks from a bus stop to the gallery. The room swirled around him. He was certain he would run into Sarah. A sense of dangling from a tightrope by one finger engulfed him. He had been wrong, and as a result, he was losing grip. As his thoughts focused on disappointment, Davey watched as a maintenance worker bent down and picked up a scrap of paper, tossing it into his debris can.

***

Davey lurked around the gallery most of the day. Sarah appeared several times in his peripheral vision and in the faces of passersby. Each time, his excitement was followed by a hollow feeling as each turned out to be a mirage. Just as he decided to give up looking for her, his friend Lisa, the receptionist, noticed him and waved for him to come over to her desk.

"Hello, Davey," she said.

"Hi." Davey approached the desk with slumped shoulders.

"I noticed you haven't been yourself today. It wouldn't have to do with the young lady from yesterday, would it?"

"Have you seen her today?" Davey asked in anticipation.

"We've been pretty busy since opening this morning. Saturdays, as you know. Was she supposed to meet you here?"

"No, I just thought maybe…"

"Didn't you get an address so you could keep in touch?"

"She kinda got called away pretty fast, and I didn't have time to get any information about her except that her name is Sarah. And I only know that because her mother called at her when she came to take her away."

The receptionist pressed her lips out into a pout as if to mimic his plight. Then, one of her eyebrows took flight on her forehead.

"Hey, I'll bet the article I read is in one of the papers in the recycle bin; they don't get sent out but every two weeks if you think you might want to try to find her."

"You think?" yelled Davey. "Would it be okay if I looked?"

"Well, go find the maintenance guy and see if he will let you take a look around."

"Thanks!"

Davey made a beeline for the door marked "Employees Only."

The maintenance man on duty eyed Davey as he came in through the employee area door.

"Hey!" he called out. "Are you supposed to be back here?"

Despite feeling nervous, Davey over-rode his anxiety and approached the guy wearing a brown uniform with the nametag "Doug" on the left breast.

"Miss Lisa said it might be okay with you if I look through the recycle newspapers for an article I need."

Doug looked appraisingly at Davey.

"What's your name?"

"Davey," he replied, attempting to sound surer of himself

than he felt.

"Well, Davey, I'll tell you what. You make sure that every scrap of paper gets back in the bin and you can dig as long as you want, at least until 6 o'clock because that's when I get off."

Doug showed Davey to a metal bin in the back of the building. The lighting was dull but Davey remained undaunted.

"Thanks," he called out to Doug.

Doug threw a simple wave behind his head as he walked away.

Davey dug through piles of papers: old gallery listings, catalogue drafts, and incomplete business letters straining his eyes, trying to locate all the newspapers among the various other paper products. He pored through dozens of papers from a week's worth of trash and slowly scanned every page of every social column section he could find.

Finally, the words "Swedish Socialites" peered out from beneath a sheet of tissue paper. Davey reached for it, unfolding the edges of the page and began reading the article about two influential people who called Sweden home, at least part of the year. Davey thought this could be the information he needed to contact Sarah.

The article mentioned several powerful people who resided

in the surrounding area, but only one caught Davey's eye. The article mentioned a couple with a daughter named Sarah. *It had to be her.* There was no address, but they were reported to live in a small community just north of the library. Davey tucked the article in his pocket and hurriedly placed all the paper he had removed back in the bin. As Davey started to leave, his excitement overwhelming him, Doug shouted, "Hey, you missed something there! Everything back in the bin before you go."

Davey turned back, picked up a small note on folded paper, and tossed it back in the bin. The words "Blue Boy" were clearly visible as it settled among the other papers.

***

It didn't take long for Davey to locate an address for the family mentioned in the article. All it took was a call to the community's post office. The town was quaint and it was no wonder the woman at the post office was more than willing to discuss the prominent people living among regular people, taking refuge in small crowds.

The postal lady provided Davey with the California address and assured him his letter would find the family-He wrote to Sarah, trying to keep his hand steady so as to come across as calm and mature as possible. His quivering fingers wrote that he wanted to see her again if she could arrange it. He took the letter to the local post office the following Monday morning. The mailbox became

Davey's most frequented spot from that day on.

**

Sarah's mother sorted through the morning mail in their Östermalm, Sweden home and came across an envelope addressed to Sarah at their California address from a boy named Davey. She hurriedly tore the letter into four pieces before tossing it in the trash. Over the next month, four more letters had been forwarded from California, all to Sarah from that common boy. They, too, were treated with the same disregard.

CHAPTER 3

"New Traditions"

Days had grown longer again. They had made it through the long hours of winter, finally approaching the much-celebrated summer solstice. Having spent all twelve years of her life in Sweden, Sarah thought that she should be used to the cold and long, dark hours of winter. School ski trips and weekend sledding with friends made winter days more bearable. Still, Sarah kept dreaming of the California sunshine.

All through fall, she had tried to convince her parents how splendid a Christmas trip to California would be. All of her attempts were thwarted by the argument that a Swedish Christmas was much nicer: the mulled drinks, snow-shoeing, Christmas festival, and snow on the ground. "California is not for Christmas," her mother stated matter-of-factly. However, Sarah's persistence paid off, with a promise to return in the summer.

***

Placing the hot coffee press in the middle of the table, Sarah's mother joined the breakfast table.

"You know, our summer holiday is only one month away."

Sarah's stomach was immediately filled with flutters of excitement as she pictured everything she hoped the summer would be.

"Well, should we stay in the same area as last time?" asked her father.

"I think we should," Sarah interjected sheepishly. "Because … well, do you think we could go back to some of our favorite places this year?"

"You sound like you have something particular in mind," her dad teased as he winked at her.

"Well, I'd kind of like to spend more time at The Huntington Library."

Her mom raised her eyebrows. "I certainly hope this has nothing to do with that boy you met last year."

Trying to sound as casual as possible, Sarah replied, "There were just so many good things to see."

"We can all decide together later," said her father. "But I have one stipulation. I don't want us to get lazy in our exploration of other cultures. Let's not stay at the beach the whole time. We should either venture south to Mexico or up to Canada for a week or so."

"My vote is Vancouver," her mom threw in, beginning to gather the breakfast plates. "Sarah, Honey, why don't you head upstairs and get changed out of your nightgown. You can come with me to the market this morning."

***

Finally, everything had come to a close for the summer. Another school year was gone, her ballroom dance classes concluded with a grand recital, and everyone was on holiday for a month. Sarah couldn't believe that they were heading back to California and was sure that if destiny were on her side, she would see the boy she had nicknamed Danny–the one she had associated with the "Blue Boy" painting. Thinking about their meeting every day since that hot summer morning, she felt affirmed in her feelings for him. She dared not share with anyone, though; not even her best friend, Linnea. She had thought about it many times, but it all sounded silly out loud. She had even said it out loud in front of the bathroom mirror: "I met this boy last summer that I haven't stopped thinking about …" Okay, that didn't sound so crazy. But then: "We didn't actually speak … and I don't know his name … or really where he lives … or how I'll see him again." Now, it was getting crazier. "But I'm sure we will see each other again because it was a magical moment. It was indescribable. The way we connected, it was as though we were encircled in a bubble, reading each other's hearts and minds." That was the part where she was sure of what she was saying, but she knew it wasn't possible to share that with anyone.

***

A strike in the Charles de Gaulle Airport had left the family panicking to reach their connecting plane on time. Sarah had held her hat on her head with one hand and her mother's hand with the other, all racing through the airport together. Two planes, a little running, a long wait at the luggage carousel, and a rental car pick-up later, they were settling in at their beach house, the family's home base for the next month.

Per her father's desire and her mother's input, they would be leaving for one week to explore Vancouver, Vancouver Beach, and the Squamish area. Per her suggestion, they were able to get a vacation house a little further up the coast and closer to L.A., where her parents promised they would visit The Huntington Library at least twice. Sarah had easily convinced her father of this based on the argument that they should spend one entire day indoors to review the new exhibitions, as well as one day outdoors. He had eventually been able to convince her mother to go along with the idea, once again pointing out that it was not likely the boy would be visiting the same two days.

"Can we go to the library tomorrow?"

Adam chuckled at his vivacious daughter. "We just put our suitcases down! What if we find some dinner and rest before making any plans?"

"And Sarah," her mother chimed in. "We need to let our bodies rest for a few days to get used to the time change. You won't be able to enjoy the library so much when you're falling asleep standing up."

She knew there was no point in arguing this one. And really, they were right. The family would spend the next few days reading, sleeping, and watching the waves to synchronize their time zones. Their meeting was in the hands of Fate, anyway.

The freckles on her mother's pale complexion were becoming more prominent after a few days under the sun. Sarah was beginning to feel antsy about getting out to do something, and her parents had finally deemed them all rested enough to do so.

"So then, what will our first day trip be? I can already guess what you're going to say, young lady," joked her father. "Let's get this child back to The Huntington Library before she has a meltdown." Sarah was happy she didn't even need to say anything. Feeling like a bit of a nag for the last few days–or really months–she had been trying very hard to hold her tongue and not be a pest. Now, she tried to show her appreciation for their consideration by restraining the whims of a giddy, foolish schoolgirl.

Her mind raced with thoughts as they drove to the library; this time, a shorter drive. Would it happen? Would he be there? Would they recognize each other? She had grown enough in the last year that she no longer fit into the white sleeveless dress with the pink sash that she had on before. That morning, she had chosen her outfit with great consideration, but the main item of attention was her hat. She had it with her again, so perhaps he would recognize it. After a few audible sighs and groans of displeasure, she had picked something out: a similarly long and whimsical dress, but this time in pink with an old-fashioned collar and cuffs on the short sleeves. Instead of waiting on her mother this morning, they had been waiting on her.

Pulling up once again to the grand estate, she had not yet decided what would happen if Davey was there. Different scenarios had played through her head: she would be standing in front of "Pinkie" once again, and he would come up behind her, gently spinning her around to look into his eyes. Or perhaps they would see each other in the corridor, eyes locking as they drew closer to each other. He would say, "I've been waiting for you." She would return the sentiment. Whatever romantic scenario raced through her mind, she knew one thing was important: they had to find a way to keep in touch. There had to be a plan to see each other again. She was sure that he would want the same.

As her dad put the car in park, Sarah closed her eyes and drew a deep breath.

"So, what is it today, inside or outside?"

"It's a beautiful day to be outside," her mom commented. "Why don't we check if there are any special programs going on before we decide?"

Sarah followed behind, her eyes wide and attentive, on the lookout for any boy around her age. Since she was the one who had begged and fussed about their visit, she attempted to remain engaged and enthusiastic throughout the visit. However, she was so focused on finding the boy that nothing else mattered. It was a treasure hunt, and he was the prize. When the end of their day in the gardens arrived, she tried to hide the disappointment in her face. A mother can always tell her child, though.

"Was it not as beautiful as you remember it being last year?"

"Oh, it was. I can only dream of having a garden like that one day."

"Then why don't you look as excited as I expected you to be?"

"I don't know. Maybe it's leftover jetlag," she shrugged.

"Well, are you excited about seeing the new exhibit

in a few weeks?"

"Yes!" Once more, her eyes lit up with hope.

Anyone would have envied the family's summer holiday. They maintained a similar schedule to the previous year: relaxing on the beach, enjoying different foods, shopping, and typical tourist to-do items. British Columbia had fulfilled their desires for spending time outdoors, and their cabin had been a stark contrast to the suburban L.A. location they had stayed the rest of the time. Although they ended up going back to The Huntington Library two more times, Sarah was disappointed after each visit.

Feeling as though she was given a special third chance, she came up with a plan in the event of his absence. When her parents suggested that they attend the exhibit opening one day before their return flight, Sarah prepared a special note to leave for the boy. She was absolutely convinced that he must be visiting, as well, and that they were only missing each other by days, hours, or minutes. On a small piece of paper, she wrote:

> *To The Boy in Blue,*
>
> *I have been waiting to see you since last summer. Though I have visited the library three times, each time hopeful,*

Fate did not bring us together. If you find this note, please write. My address is:

Baltzarsgatan 22
11340 Stockholm

Sincerely yours, Sarah
The girl from The Thornton Gallery

Having tied a pink ribbon around the carefully folded paper, she tucked it safely into a vase of flowers on a small table near the painting of Pinkie, leaving one corner visible.

"Well, were you just as infatuated with your second trip to California as your first?" her father asked. Their three brown suitcases were stacked once again on the trunk, ready for the long flight back to Sweden.

"Indeed. There seems so much to do, and the sun seems to shine in a special way," she replied with a sigh for dramatic effect. Her plan was to coax her parents into making this trip a yearly tradition, but she didn't want to push too hard just yet. Slow and steady over the next months was the plan of persuasion.

CHAPTER 4

"Peanuts, Cracker Jacks, and Signs"

David's first year of middle school had gone better than he expected. His quirky disposition was widely accepted as interesting and unique, save for a few obligatory jerks. He had gone to dances, joined the yearbook club, and caught the eye of a few young ladies. Girlfriends were casual at best, largely due to awkward and undeveloped flirting techniques. Still, the girl he had met in the Thornton Gallery that day almost one year ago hadn't left his mind. He had grown from a Davey into a David for the most part, but a portion of his heart remained embedded in memories.

His summer tickets to the Huntington Library were already purchased, and David had checked the list of programs available that would give him a valid excuse to visit the library often. He was feeling very grown-up these days, having just turned 13. He didn't mind the thought of going to family events on his own, especially if it meant a greater chance of seeing the girl with violet eyes once more.

The year's last school bell rang, signaling summer freedom for the next two months. The halls were a flurry of activity as kids spilled from every classroom like a flood of salmon upstream. David went to his locker to finish clearing out the various paraphernalia and wrappers that had gathered before joining the buzz of excitement outside.

"Hey, Little Bro!"

David was looking around, trying to decide between joining his friends for a soda and heading home.

"Hey, Big Man!"

He turned around to see his brother, Wayne, waiting to hand him an end-of-the-year celebratory candy bar.

"Hey, you're here."

"Yeah, Big Man. How does it feel to be done with the first year of middle school?"

"Good, I guess. Are you home for the summer?"

"Nah, I'm staying at UCLA again to work a camp, but I have two weeks to hang out with you and Mom. I asked Olivia if she would come for a weekend, too. She's not sure."

"Cool." Because Wayne and Olivia had been rather close as siblings, especially through their father's death, David always felt like the odd sibling out. He was much younger, a lot different from them, and never really got the feeling that they cared too much about him. Perhaps feelings of jealousy had sprung up as their mother began to baby David more in the absence of their father.

"You wanna walk over and get a milkshake to celebrate, or would you rather I beat it so you can hang out with your friends?"

"A milkshake sounds great," David replied with unconvincing enthusiasm.

As they walked in silence towards the soda fountain a few blocks away, David turned to give one last glance back at the school, basking in the glory of another year done. Though he felt he could finally say his age with a slight puff in his chest now that he was officially a teenager, David still felt as though he should be growing up faster—that he was older than his physical maturation. He wished he could zoom past the next few years until he reached adulthood. Did everyone else feel this way? They continued to pass by small clumps of happy teenagers hanging out on the sidewalk.

"Hey, I've got a surprise for you."

"A surprise?"

"Yeah, well, I figure I've missed your birthday a few times and that maybe we need some brother time. What do you think?"

"Sounds good. What are we going to do?" David was actually thinking in his mind that he hoped it didn't interfere with any of the plans he already had.

"We, little bro, are going to a ball game!" Wayne stopped and excitedly pulled two tickets out of his pocket. "The L.A. Dodgers, buddy! We have two tickets a few sections up from the home team dugout for next weekend. It'll be great!"

"Wow, I've never been to a ball game before." David's show of enthusiasm was once again slightly unconvincing.

"Yeah, I figured it was something you and Dad never got to do, so I'm making it my brotherly duty."

David wasn't opposed to going to a sporting event; it was just that he never had. Maybe he would like it. The ideal scenario of two brothers sharing a warm baseball afternoon with Cracker Jacks in hand contradicted his fear of a boring afternoon spent with a brother who didn't really want to be with him, who instead would spend his time flirting with any pretty girl around them. He hoped for the best and actually did look forward to being inside the large stadium for the first time.

David came out of his room to join the breakfast

table on Sunday morning, already dressed.

"Hey, did you make a sign for the team?" Wayne nodded at the poster rolled up in David's hand, which he hadn't previously mentioned or shown to anyone.

"Uh, you'll see it when we get there! Let's go!" When David found out that the Dodgers were playing the Philadelphia Phillies that afternoon, and that it was going to be a big rival game, he figured it would be one of the afternoon games broadcasted on national television. He had decided to use it as a chance to get a special girl's attention.

David found the noise and bustle of the stadium a lot more fun than he expected. The boys had each gotten a box of Cracker Jacks, a bag of peanuts, and a Coke to enjoy. David felt it was really unlike anything he had ever been to—so many people, so much excitement, and so much noise—all there because of a game that was actually kind of slow. He made the note to himself that maybe he would start watching baseball more often. The brothers didn't talk much; Wayne was up and down in his seat, occasionally shouting and spilling some of his peanuts. Whenever Wayne would stand, David would grab his poster and hold it up high.

"To Sarah, (Pinkie at Huntington Library)

Meet me there July 10th at 1:00 p.m.

Blue Boy"

His goal was to keep it concise enough and hold it up as many times as he could if there was any chance that she would see it. He had tried to think of some dramatic way to draw attention to himself during the game, but he couldn't think of anything that wouldn't get him grounded, therefore diminishing his chances of seeing her at the library at all. He figured this chance was just an added bonus; a hope.

"Do you have to hold that sign up all the time?" Wayne irritably questioned by the end of the fifth inning.

"I really want to see this girl again."

"You know most people make signs that say, 'Go Team!' or they say something about a player or something mean about the other team. Like that guy over there—," he pointed.

David didn't respond, but rather continued to hold his sign.

"Well, are you going to tell me about her at least, if you want so desperately to get her attention? I didn't know you had turned into such a romantic."

David was shy about sharing too much. He didn't see a point in trying to explain too much about their dramatic meeting without words; how they knew nothing about contacting each other, really, yet he was sure that Fate would bring them together again.

"She likes a lot of the same things that I do," was all he could say.

David would have no way of knowing if his sign would be successful until July 10, but he wondered every day if she had seen it—if she would make it to the library. When that day finally arrived he spent the bus ride there trying to decipher his feelings. Was he nervous, or excited? Was there a way to calculate the odds of her being there? What he did know was that he prepared to wait all day for her in the Thornton Gallery.

He had prepared himself as much as he could. That morning, he dressed and packed himself lunch to eat on the bus ride there. A book, notepad, and pencil were also in his bag, as he planned to sit in the gallery for the remainder of the afternoon until the library closed.

He looked at his watch as the bus pulled over at his stop. Perfect. It was almost noon on the dot. He still had the mile to walk but figured it would give him time to be there early, just in case. He kicked a small stone all the way, concentrating all of his energy into asking the universe to coordinate their meeting, if such tactics worked. He wasn't sure he believed it, but he was willing to try. Adding a quick prayer to God before entering, David greeted the familiar faces at the front desk and headed to spend the next hours in the gallery.

Every twenty minutes, he looked down at his watch, trying to keep himself occupied and distracted in between. One o'clock passed … then two o'clock … and all the hours passed until it was time for the library to close. He couldn't help but feel disappointed, hanging his head slightly as he said good-bye to front desk staff on his way out.

David thought about it all the way home. He was no less convinced that Fate would have them meet one day. He would still be visiting the library frequently in hopes of a chance meeting, and he would simply have to keep thinking of ways to get her attention. He quickly grew frustrated by the limitations of his age, sure that he could do more if he was older, wealthier, and could travel independently. Nonetheless, he remained determined. It would happen; he was sure of it. He wouldn't forget her, nor she him.

CHAPTER 5

"New Plans"

By the beginning of October, Sarah had already missed almost half of school due to illness. The cough started soon after they had returned to Sweden but was easily blamed on germs from the airports and planes.

"You never know what you might pick up in those germ-infested places. Everyone is squished together in a tight place, breathing the same stale air for hours. It's a wonder that this is the first time any of us have gotten sick," her mother had commented.

The coughing and occasional fever never ceased, though. Even on the first day of school, her doctor hadn't given her the clearance to attend, and attendance had been on and off the last few weeks since then. On the days she was home, her mother made a tincture of bitter herbs to boost her immunity. It was her grandmother who had mixed together the age-old 11-herb remedy soaked in strong alcohol. Serving it up in a small glass before breakfast, Sarah would just look at it and shudder. The alcohol burned her throat; the taste making her close her eyes tightly and shake her head. She was sure she would never be an alcoholic.

As mid-October rolled around, Sarah's parents were becoming more concerned about her lingering symptoms. The tour of doctors began. Various treatments or medications were prescribed and suggested. Sarah was getting frustrated with the poking, prodding, and multiple doctor visits that didn't seem to produce any results. All they did was keep her out of school. Linnea would bring her any school work that she missed, but when Sarah was able to attend school, she felt like a stranger. She enjoyed school, especially literature class, but she could feel herself growing distant from her classmates. They would laugh at stories from moments she had missed, while she would sit in the back trying not to cough and be a disturbance. Keeping up with the schoolwork was okay, but in her frustration, attending school became less enjoyable.

Despite her suffering, Sarah relished the extra minutes of sleep on sick days. As days grew shorter and temperatures grew colder, staying under the covers became more appealing. It was another doctor day. Her mother was getting especially particular about ensuring she had on plenty of layers of warm clothes—so much so that she wasn't sure her shoes would fit on over the double layer of wool socks that her mother made her wear. Hands tucked inside her muff, Sarah's fingers grasped onto a handkerchief inside, as she was sure she might lose one of her lungs on the way to the doctor.

"A viral respiratory infection," this doctor announced after doing the usual routine of listening to her lungs, swabbing her mouth and take a good look around after demanding to 'open wide and say ah.'

"Well, how are we to be sure and what are we going to do about it?"

"I'll analyze the swab from her mouth, but unfortunately, medicine won't help a virus."

"Well, what then? She's just going to cough a hole in her lungs?" Sarah's mother was getting even more exasperated with doctors than Sarah, and she had taken on this edge with most of the doctors they had recently visited.

"We'll try to find a solution, but first we have to look at the cultures. It may not be something we're familiar with."

Her mom huffed in pure frustration, unsure of what to say while Sarah began to put her layers back on.

"You know, maybe some warm air and sunshine would do the girl some good."

They both looked at the doctor, but with very different meaning in their eyes. Her mother's was one of distrust and skepticism, while Sarah's was one of hope and delight. Sunshine and warmth? That sounded like a good solution to her. She knew it would be a topic of discussion at the dinner table, just as the doctor visits were. Usually, the conversations were full of anxiety. Sarah would sit quietly, poking at her food while her mother complained and her father proposed solutions.

School was growing increasingly uncomfortable, and throughout the afternoon, Sarah's mind drifted to familiar and comforting warmth. When she closed her eyes, she could almost feel the California sunshine on her face.

"So, anything helpful from the doctor today?" her dad asked, serving himself some potatoes and passing them to her mother.

"Well, this doctor seems to think it's a serious viral infection that they may not know how to treat. At least he's honest instead of just throwing more medicine at us." Her mom reached out and touched her arm. Though she seemed to have a tough exterior with the doctors, seeing her daughter sick for such a long time was beginning to weigh heavily on her spirit.

"So, what exactly does he propose?"

"Well, he's going to look at the—"

"He suggested sun and warm weather," Sarah piped in right away, trying not to insinuate anything immediately, but rather looking meekly down at the food on her plate.

Her father's eyes raised in a reply of body language before any thoughts came out of his mouth. "Uh, huh …."

They all sat in silence for some moments. Chairs creaking, ~~Sarah's~~ and the clatter of silverware on plates were the only sounds heard until her father's thoughts became audible.

"Well, Christmas vacation is too far away to see if this is an option. You need to get better sooner than that. I certainly can't go anywhere right now, though. Why don't we wait for the results of his analysis first, and then see about any remedies of sunshine and heat."

"You know, I was thinking," Sarah quietly offered, her eyes fixed on the plate in front of her, "what about boarding school for a year?"

"I can't let you go for a year," her mother responded

quickly.

Putting his utensils down, her father let his chin rest on his fist. "We certainly don't like the option of sending you away, but it is an option."

"Well, let's not get hasty. Let's wait for the doctor to call first. Anyway, we don't know how serious he is about this suggestion. Let's not go changing our lives on a whim."

They finished their dinner without much further discussion, all engulfed in their own thoughts of what a treatment of "sunshine and warmth" might look like.

No one had brought the subject up again until they received the phone call from the doctor. Indeed, he admitted that he wasn't sure about what to do for Sarah. A mixture of discouragement, frustration, and concern filled her mother's heart. From her bedroom that night, Sarah could hear her parents discussing what to do. She crept out of bed in her ruffled white nightgown and sat on the floor, pressing her ear against the door. It was mostly only muffles that could be heard through the thick walls of their home. Occasionally, she could make out words or parts of phrases—mentions of the south of France and visits to doctors in London. After straining for some time to hear what she could, her eyes were eventually drooping and drifting in and out of sleep. She would have to wait until tomorrow to see what kind of solution they would suggest.

After spending another day at home with her schoolbooks and papers sent from the teachers, Sarah was always happy for some change. She had especially been waiting all day for her father to come home, since she knew that dinner conversation would involve whatever their parents had stayed up talking about the last night. The smell of her mother's fish soup filled the house and kept her anxiously awaiting for dinner.

Arriving home later than usual, her father arrived that night with something in hand. She and her mom had already set the table, ready for dinner as soon as he arrived.

"I'm starving!" Sarah played dramatically as he finally walked in the door.

"Good to see you, too," he retorted playfully.

"What's that?" she asked, motioning towards the folder in his hand, decorated with an American flag.

"This is a list of boarding schools in California. I was

at the embassy just now, asking them some questions. Come on let's talk about it over dinner."

By the end of the night, the Lillienbergs had reached a conclusive decision together. Sarah and her mother would leave for California soon. Even if the climate change made no difference, they could continue to see doctors there. Sarah would continue her studies based on what the teachers could give her before they left, and come January, Sarah would be enrolled in the Southwestern Academy boarding school in San Marino, California. Her dad was pleased with its well-established history and international reputation. Sarah was the only one mildly pleased about the solution. Her parents, however, expressed concern and anxiety over the separation. Of course, she had her own nervous thoughts to assuage: starting a new school, in a new country, with new people, without her parents every day. And what if she didn't get better? At the forefront of her mind, though, was excitement and disbelief that she was actually going to be living in California. The agreed-upon stipulation was that Sarah would only attend for the spring semester to allow for healing.

By November, only a few weeks later, Sarah and her mom were giving teary-eyed farewells to Adam, a pile of suitcases heaped around them. It would only be one month until he joined them for Christmas vacation. Still, the challenge of new and sudden plans loomed overhead as the unknown beckoned.

CHAPTER 6

"As the Years Pass By"

The half year at Southwestern Academy for Sarah and the back-and-forth international travel had proven to be a time of changes for the Lillienberg family. Sarah had indeed healed from the respiratory virus—though it was unclear if California had really been the magical cure, or if it had just been happenstance and time.

Despite Sarah's nervousness about the new school, she had made friends easily. By the time the spring semester started in January, the healing process was already well under way, and they had shopped for a new wardrobe to boost her confidence and ease the nerves of attending a boarding school. In the brief months at Southwestern, she had not only developed some close friendships but had developed a passion for writing and theater. Her parents even went to see her perform as Myrtle in the school's stage version of *The Great Gatsby*.

***

Many tears were shed on her last day of the school year in California. Sarah felt as though she had grown up so much in those months. It had been difficult for her parents to let their little girl be away for such a long time, though they were happy to see her better. She knew, then, that she must return to Sweden for the coming year. Yet, she promised herself that she would return to the school, or perhaps an exchange program, for more of her teenage years—when her parents were ready. In the meantime, she would have to settle for their yearly visits to the vacation house. Throughout those six months, she had continually wondered about her chances of bumping into that blue boy she still referred to as Danny. Though they had taken school trips to The Huntington Library and were allowed occasional passes out on their own during a weekend, Sarah still never saw him. She remained convinced, though, that she would see him one day.

***

David had successfully made his way through middle school without too much of the stereotypical trauma that often accompanies the awkward early teen years. He had mostly remained on the fringes—not joining any of the sports teams, band, drama groups, etcetera, but stuck only to the yearbook club. David had always been a boy of perpetual behaviors and was carrying many of his childhood habits into his teen years, including the summer activities at Huntington Library and a mix of comic books and historic novels. With such good grades in math and science, David was automatically enrolled in high school honors classes.

David and his friends were beginning to try new things. Busy with her job at the IRS, his mom started to pay less attention to his activities as he grew older. He was really beginning to feel like an adult.

Their fun was mostly innocent—fulfilling dares for an adrenaline rush. Then, minor trouble began. His first major dare with friends was a stereotypical rite of passage for L.A. teenagers, they felt, deciding the appropriate time would be Halloween. Each of them had picked a different costume: Daniel was Superman, Kenny was a gorilla, and David was the Phantom of the Opera. Acquiring a spotlight, a large fabric, some spray paint, and some ropes, the boys loaded their bikes and the supplies into the pickup truck of Daniel's older brother, who had agreed to drop them off and pick them up at an appointed time. The three boys lay in the bed of the pickup staring at the stars above and laughing about their upcoming adventure as they drove down to the Hollywood sign after dark. They laughed at Kenny's strained efforts to climb into a giant gorilla suit and laughed again as he struggled to operate his bike while impeded by the cumbersome outfit simultaneously trying to maintain control over his share of the materials

Still developing their attitudes of rebellion, the fear of being caught kept them moving quickly. David personally welcomed news coverage but preferred to avoid anything to do with the police. They grabbed the large material, draping it over the sign, and then stood with their spray paint cans looking at each other. They hadn't exactly discussed *what* they were going to paint on the sign. After the lanky teenagers stood there for a while, they finally agreed on "BOO"—an appropriate Halloween-themed prank that couldn't get them into too much trouble, they figured. Each taking a letter to paint, then standing to look up at their handiwork, David and Daniel mockingly put their hands on their hips to let their capes float in the wind.

Their moment of glory lasted only for a few seconds. In the night sky, the sound of a helicopter interrupted the steady drone of traffic from the freeway below, and a bright spotlight was scouring the ground as it headed their way.

"Spread out!" yelled David. "We'll meet at the truck!"

But as David jumped on his bike and sped

dangerously down a steep incline he caught glimpses of Kenny and Daniel right behind him. Frustration filled him as he wondered what the others didn't understand about the statement to spread out. He finally gave in to the fact that if even one got caught the other two would soon be found out anyway. So, he headed for the trees, hoping to avoid the exposing beam of the helicopter spotlight.

David finally decided it was best to steer away from the assigned pickup point until they could be sure they had avoided being followed. They hid among a few trees and stared up at the helicopter as it circled above.

"Hey," said Daniel, that's a news copter.

"Cool," was Kenny's only remark, but his tone displayed his pride in being almost famous.

David wondered if their act would make it on the news. Either way, they vowed that they would be The Three Musketeers throughout their high school careers, seeking opportunities to play pranks wherever they could find them.

***

Sarah was sitting in the lounge of her dorm, twisting

her light brown long hair into pin curls. Some of the other girls were painting their toenails, while another group was sitting in the corner putting together a board for their upcoming presentation. There was only one T.V. in their dorm, so the lobby often became the evening hang-out location, unless one was off courting or trying to catch a date in the school's food court. Sarah had control of the remote, and she was flipping through the channels for any evening sitcoms. She paused briefly, instead, on a news story— "Halloween prank on the Hollywood sign." Sarah laughed to herself at the three boys in costume that the camera showed. By the time the news chopper had caught anything on tape they were only running away from the sign to their escape; looking rather hilarious, Sarah thought, as a gorilla, Superman, and Phantom of the Opera. She imagined in her head that whoever was the Phantom was most likely the most interesting of the three based on his costume pick—an unusual and sophisticated choice.

After finishing a few more years of school back in Sweden, her parents had agreed to let Sarah finish her last three years at Southwestern Academy, to improve her English and expand her cultural experience. She was old enough now that they felt they could let her go. She would happily return to Sweden to enjoy the Christmas over winter break, and her parents would join her at the vacation house in the summer. They had seen how Sarah had thrived there. And they were happy to see her interests in writing and theater take off.

CHAPTER 7

"Happenstance"

It was that time. Sophomore year was when the ambitious students started thinking about university entry, but junior year was when the hallways were a buzz of college discussions: "Where have you visited?" "What are you thinking?" "Where do you want to go?" "In state or out of state?" "ACTs or SATs?"

David found the conversations to be extremely dull, as everyone seemed to exchange the same information over and over again. Along with his weekly visits to The Huntington Library and getting into minor trouble here and there with friends, he had been responsible enough to gather some folders of information from various universities in the area. In actuality, though, he was pretty sure about where he was going.

It all came down to family tradition and finances. David was assured of a full scholarship just as his siblings had been before him. Since his parents had met there and his dad had later become a professor at UCLA, the family was ingrained with loyalty to the university. His dad had been such a well-loved individual that a bust was placed in the history department where he taught before his tragic death. Possibly an accident on campus that UCLA felt responsible for, having justified free education for his children. His mom loved telling the story of their starry-eyed meeting in the cafeteria back on that California winter day in the '50s—"the glory days," his parents always said.

It had been over a decade since that time period, yet many professors and staff members retained the memory of David's father. Both of his siblings had also left their own mark behind at the university. Though it wasn't really discussed at home as a matter of obligation, it was more of an assumption that his choice was already made.

But there was a small problem. David and his friends had not gone unnoticed and their frequent pranks had gotten the attention of the admittance committee. Not all the members were in favor of providing a full scholarship to what they saw as the black sheep of one of their most celebrated university families.

David's mom scheduled their attendance for one of the Saturday visiting days. David had already attended the visits on his own at a few of the other universities in the area, just for good measure and comparison's sake. He was sure that a visit to UCLA with his mom was merely a walk down memory lane for her, since she hadn't been interested in seeing any of the other places with him.

"Ready?" Polly asked as she finished wrapping her red polka dot scarf around her neck. David nodded and finished lacing up his shoes.

"You know, no one is forcing you to go here."

"Look, Mom. It's like a family legacy. I like traditions. Besides, where would I get the money to attend anywhere else? Even after visiting other schools, I'm happy to go to UCLA—if they accept me, of course."

"Oh, well there's no question about that."

Putting the car in park and pulling up her oversized sunglasses, Polly stepped out of the car with an air of owning the place. They were quite a mother-son pair. David had grown into a handsome, though somewhat gangly young man. His mom tended to raise eyebrows for another reason. She had maintained her young figure, and having an office job, her wardrobe was full of dresses and skirts that drew attention from the hem of her skirt down to the heels she was usually wearing. While others parked their cars and looked around for signs of where to go and what to do, David and Polly walked straight ahead.

As they joined the crowd of curious families, Polly was immediately the socialite, connecting instantly with the other mothers to share her opinion as to why UCLA should be everyone's top choice. David sized up the crowd they were to follow, still playing the game he always did—making background stories for all the "characters" of the day. He decided that the girl with long, straight blond hair was a daddy's girl, probably average grades, and based on her build, was a member of the track team—a very beneficial member. He assumed that another boy in the group was interested in the music program at UCLA; based on the look of his hands and his seemingly large lung capacity, he appeared inclined to play a few instruments. David wondered what the others assumed or thought about him.

Since the purpose of his visit wasn't really for information, David allowed himself to soak in the surroundings of the campus and the students. He followed behind, passively listening while his mom whispered and pointed out memories from her past. "That, son, is where your dad and I first kissed. Right under that tree." The show went on, with David happy to appease his mother as she reminisced of days past. Their tour group passed many others on their trip around campus. With his mind already made up, David wondered which of those individuals would be joining him for freshmen orientation the following year. He was particularly interested in the seemingly parent-less group that was touring. "I wonder what that's about," he wondered. 'Maybe a boarding school or other high school trip?' He strained to see if he could make any observations, but they disappeared behind another building before he could focus.

His mom's grasp interrupted David's curiosity, and he was suddenly aware of a man's presence—an old friend of his father.

"David, you remember Professor Ralston?" his mother inferred as the tall gentleman extended his hand to David.

"It's been a long time since I've seen you, young man. Enjoying the visit to your future home?" he asked as he put his arm around his mother's waist in a manner more familiar than David could comfortably tolerate.

"Well, there's no guarantee I'll be accepted, is there?" David replied, rather firmer than expected.

"Don't worry, David," said his mother rather sheepishly. "Don ... I mean Professor Ralston ... has been putting in a lot of effort to get the acceptance committee to overlook your little indiscretions during high school."

David felt a sudden hatred for this Professor Ralston as well as a disgust for his mother he didn't think he was capable of feeling. He couldn't seem to control himself as the sudden realization that his mother was involved with a former close friend of his dead father came over him. Worse, he couldn't block out the image of his mother using her good looks to gain him acceptance into the same university at which his siblings had already excelled. He felt angry, deceived, and even embarrassed that he had to depend on others to get him accepted into the institution that his father's service and recognition should have assured him entrance. His high school pranks—so innocent at the time—now embarrassed him, and he couldn't separate the emotions to put the blame on any one person. He gave a quick, accusing look to his mother and his father's replacement before storming away.

"David!" his mother called after him.

David quickened his pace as he tried to block out his mother's voice, finally stopping far from his mother's site and leaning back against the side of a building, casting his eyes into lightly clouded sky. He vowed never to trust or depend on anyone again, especially those who were supposed to love him.

***

Sarah didn't really need to be visiting colleges yet. She was only a sophomore and still had some time to really worry about applications and college decisions. The world was a lot larger to her than for many of her friends. Most of them were all looking within state, some out of state, but at least 95% of them would stay in the country. She had to decide whether to stay in the U.S. or go … well … anywhere, and a warm climate is what appealed to her. She had become addicted to the California sun and couldn't imagine going back to Sweden or somewhere cold, such as Quebec. She wanted to stay in the area, but at the same time, she wasn't quite ready to limit herself. Since her friends were a mixed group of ages, with many of them starting to seriously narrow down their college selection, Sarah decided to join them on some of the school-organized college visits.

They had already toured the University of Southern California the weekend before. This Saturday morning's visit was to UCLA. Sarah pulled on her short-sleeved floral gown, slipped on some gloves, and laced up the boots around her narrow ankles. As they boarded the bus for her second college visit, she reflected back on the last few years; how they had gone in a way that she never would have imagined five years ago.

"I can't believe you're seriously looking at colleges." Sarah had sat next to Josie on the bus ride there. Josie's family was Mexican-American, giving the girls an international sense of camaraderie.

"It's unbelievable, right? I mean, I still have some months to keep looking and take my tests, but by this time next year, I should have all my applications in."

"Are you sure you're going to stay in the U.S.?"

"Not at all. You?"

"I don't know," Sarah sighed. "All I know is that it'll be somewhere warm."

"Your pale Norwegian skin still hasn't gotten used to the sun!" Josie teased as she held her arm up to Sarah's.

"Come on, I'm Swedish," Sarah opposed. They laughed and continued to discuss plans, pros, and cons, feeling very mature and grown-up in the moment.

Sarah was at the front of the line when it came to the tour, even though it was less pertinent to her than to some of the others. She took in the landscape of surrounding trees and buildings, trying to place herself there one day. As they paused for a moment by one of the buildings, she let her mind block out the words of the tour guide and drift off into an imaginative exercise, looking forward three years as she entered into the university picture. As they continued walking, she noticed that many other groups were touring on the same day. With such a largely populated campus, she imagined that they must do floods of tours all the time. She began to become keenly aware of a strange intuition in her head. Something in her in her gut was telling her that she should be looking for something, though she was unsure of what. She observed passing individuals and the flurry of details in her surroundings. During the last forty minutes of the tour, she couldn't help but be preoccupied with this persistent obsession of seeking someone or something.

In the distance, she saw a woman trying to console what appeared to be an upset boy; possibly her son. She felt a bit lonely for the company of her parents, and the intuition she had been feeling abated as she turned back to her friends.

As they finished their lunch in the cafeteria and boarded the bus to head back to campus, Sarah gave one last lingering stare out the window as they drove away, deciding it must have been a false intuition—or maybe it was a sign that she was supposed to be there? She let it go for the time being, acknowledging that the elusive someone or something would come to her if it was meant to be.

CHAPTER 8

"Putting Pictures into Words"

Sarah sat on the park bench in the courtyard, letting the breeze blow her curls; the ribbons of her hat dancing to the slight rhythm of the wind. Only three more days were left in her junior year at the Academy. She had already begun to pack for the summer holiday, cramming in last moments with friends and studying for exams in between. Some of her friends were packing up for good now, on their way to California colleges. They all had promises of seeing each other on weekends and writing letters, though they all feared the reality that time would fade into new lives and new friends.

She had been going steady with one of the senior boys for the better part of that year. Ever since he asked her to dance at the fall formal, Robert had gone through multiple romantic attempts at winning Sarah's heart. He surprised her with flowers, took her out for a nice dinner, and even organized a serenade on the beach with his friends. After the winter holidays, Sarah finally succumbed to his romantic gestures and agreed to date him.

Now she sat on a bench by herself, wondering if it had

been worth it. Back when she agreed to be his girlfriend, he had promised to return from college every weekend to see her during her senior year. Now the time had actually come for him to leave, but they both agreed that it just didn't make sense. Sarah knew her heart wasn't one hundred percent in it, and she figured it was best to let him be on his way to explore the exciting new freedom of being a college student. Of course, she felt some level of sadness about the break-up, but she had remained practical and skeptical from the start.

The relationship with Robert had never been more than friendship, even though he wanted more. Sarah could never overcome the aching void in her heart. She was constantly aware of how meaningless a relationship felt when there was not even a spark of what she felt when she remembered her brief encounter with 'the boy.' There were no butterflies, no sudden heat in her cheeks; no shortness of breath.

Sarah couldn't help but wonder if her involuntary and impractical infatuation for the young boy from years ago and the romantic fantasy it represented might prevent her from ever experiencing a heartfelt attachment to any man.

Sarah was old enough now that her parents didn't mind her being at the holiday home by herself. This summer, she was having a few of her girlfriends stay at the house for a week after school. Giddy with excitement, they had been making plans to spend hours on the beach scoping out men, going to movies they hadn't seen, and making mixed drinks late at night. It would be a welcome relief from the stress of the last school week.

After the initial summer celebration, Sarah decided to keep herself busy during the empty weeks. Of course she would do the usual with her parents, and this year, one week in Toronto and New York were on the agenda. In between, though, Sarah had felt compelled to do something a little more beneficial with her time than lying on the beach, eating, and shopping; especially now that after some years of yearly summer vacations, they had been to all the surrounding tourist spots multiple times. She decided to volunteer her time, both for her own interest and for the benefit of beefing up her college resume. What had come to her mind first was The Huntington Library.

Ever since that first visit six years ago, she still made it a point to return at least a few times, lingering in the Thompson gallery room with "Pinkie" each time. She had never seen that boy again but still thought about their meeting each time she was there; secretly hoping that they would have a magically romantic encounter once again, face to face, each standing by the respective painting. Though seeing the boy again wasn't her main objective of volunteering at the library, the curiosity of whether they would meet still crossed her mind. Would she even recognize him if she saw him again? Had he ever found the letter she left him? Would he still recognize her? Though she wasn't entirely sure what she was signing up for as a summer volunteer, she was excited to spend time surrounded by art and literature.

After the initial days of awkward uncertainty, Sarah felt as though the serene and inspiring library was her second home. Two days per week, she went to the library to help organize, sort, and clean, as well as direct tourists. The senior English teacher had given a pre-assignment to complete before attending his class in the fall. Everyone was to write a short creative piece; either a non-fictional, momentous time in their lives or a fictional story of how they wished an event had happened in their lives.

After her volunteer hours were over, Sarah would sit in the gardens to work on her project. The recently-planted herb garden had become one of her favorite places to meditate, allowing the potent aromas to enter her nose and clear her mind. She had decided some weeks ago to do a combination of the options for the assignment. She would write about that day, as an 11-year-old girl visiting California for the first time, meeting a young boy at The Huntington Library. To her, it had been a momentous time in her life, during which she first experienced a sense of love. It was a magical moment for a young girl—one she still had not forgotten or hoped would turn into something more one day. She decided to take the reality of her thoughts and emotions from that day and change the story into a narrative of what would have happened had the girl and boy spoken, or had they met again. The story of Sarah and the boy she called Danny filled her with emotions and possibilities.

After only a few writing sessions in the garden, Sarah had already finished the obligatory five-page assignment; however, the first five pages hardly touched on the entirety of the story that she wanted to write. The inspiration that flowed out of her while penning her reflections seemed to overtake her pen, and she had put the story down for a few days, feeling as if there was no way she could fit this story into the designated assignment length. "It's like trying to fit *The Count of Monte Cristo* into 75 pages," she thought.

Sarah continued to wander through the gardens for any divine notice of what to do with the writing. Somewhere between traveling over the Japanese bridge and wandering among the variety of Salvia, Sarah began to wonder if this was a sign of what direction she should be going. The questions of "Where are you going to college?" and "What are you going to major in?" had already started, even though she found it ridiculous that anyone would expect a 17-year-old to have their entire future mapped out.

The Huntington Library had a weekly newsletter that Sarah always read on her lunch breaks at the beginning of the week. It mostly consisted of news about upcoming events or gallery grand openings. The general layout was rather dull; a bland, typical headline, one thick line crossing underneath, and a few columns front and back. Both its contents and its look left much to be desired—more a symbolic gesture that someone made out of obligation than any care for ingenuity and interesting content. Looking over its layout, an idea came to her.

What if she could contribute? The person writing the newsletter couldn't possibly like doing the job, she imagined. If they did, then she felt bad for their lack of creativity anyway. Writing the newsletter would be a great opportunity for her work on her creative side; not to mention it would also be great to put on her college applications. The monotony of filling in line after line of the same generic information made her loathe each time she sat down with a new application. What she didn't mind, though, was writing the essays. Her words seemed to flow from a fountain of imagination. Any essay, regardless of its topic, could be written quickly, usually with a great amount of clever inserts. Perhaps The Huntington Library newsletter could be her new outlet for creative expression. And maybe, just maybe, they would give her the approval to write a summer short story series.

Sarah went directly that afternoon to the head office of The Huntington after her volunteer hours were over. Sheepishly knocking on the door to the president's office, she felt butterflies in her stomach as the strong voice on the other side granted her permission to enter. Sarah held The Huntington Library in such high regard that going to speak with the president sent her nerves on high alert. Fiddling with her hands as she walked through the door, she meekly introduced herself to Mr. Koble. Sitting behind a desk with papers scattered about, his broad shoulders crouched over one particular stack with pen in hand as he looked up to greet Sarah with an almost-smile and friendly "Hello." "Maybe he doesn't look so frightening," she thought to herself.

After introducing herself as one of the volunteers, President Koble seemed to immediately know who she was, standing out in his mind because her age was unusual. Most of their volunteers were older people with extra time—not young students. After a few introductory exchanges, Sarah was put at ease, finding her nerves settling as she realized that his large stature and commanding voice was not a reflection of his softer personality.

Getting on with her questions, Sarah was delighted by Mr. Koble's response. He was very interested in her idea, explaining that finding someone to take care of the newsletter was always an ongoing ordeal. It seemed to be the job that no one wanted and was therefore always done out of lackadaisical obligation rather than any desire to create something worth reading. He scribbled down a name on a piece of paper, giving her instructions to go speak with the individual currently in charge of writing the newsletter. He was more than confident that they would be thrilled to give up their duty for a few months. Sarah was more than confident that she would enjoy taking over the duty for a few months. It was perfect. The butterflies returned as she thanked Mr. Koble and left his office; this time they were butterflies of excitement rather than nerves.

Sarah didn't want to wait for her next volunteer slot and instead returned the following day to settle the newsletter. After asking around for the name scribbled on the paper, she was finally able to track her down in a far room of the mansion, surrounded by stacks of books, frames, and what looked like a giant mess to Sarah. She seemed akin to a mad scientist, surrounded by art clutter instead of beakers and flasks.

She knocked gently on her way in, asking for the "Naomi Rimameek" written on the paper. The woman's instant jerk of motion stopped Sarah in her tracks; she seemed to jitter with constant nerves—all of her motions more in jerks than smooth movements. Deciding not to enter into what was clearly this woman's territory, Sarah stood at the door to speak to her about the proposed change. Skipping any kind of small talk or formalities, Naomi immediately pointed out that it was a good thing there was someone else to waste time on the newsletter since she had so many more important tasks that demanded her attention, nodding to the mess around the room. Sarah expressed her enthusiasm to do so, and Naomi instructed her to return after lunch to get full instructions on preparing and printing the newsletter. She was so anxious to get started that she didn't know what to do with herself until then. Borrowing a pen and some paper from the front desk, Sarah decided to sit in the gardens and begin the story portion right away.

> *... standing in admiration of the girl in pink, wishing herself back to a different time; a time of ribbons, bonnets, and whimsical love ... the girl turned, her soft, flowing white dress spinning slightly to wrap around her slender stature, the hem of the dress flared slightly with the movement as if a magical wind had suddenly blown ... as her eyes reached up towards the door, that moment in time became frozen; her eyes immediately captured by the gaze of love ...*

Sarah became so caught up in the moment of writing and the beauty of the surrounding lily pond that when she finally decided to look down at her locket watch, she jumped up and ran back inside to find Naomi. It was later than she thought, and she hoped the nervous woman wouldn't be too cross with her. Luckily, she found her also engulfed in her own work back in the room, organizing and cataloging. Just as before, Sarah's knock seemed to startle her. Lost in apparent thought, she held her finger up for Sarah to wait a minute while she continued to mumble out loud to herself and scribble down information.

The next hour was spent learning how to handle the full operation of the newsletter. Sarah couldn't feel more proud to be taking over the task. She knew it would warrant a celebratory dinner when she arrived back at the vacation house to tell her parents. On the way home, she could think of nothing but writing. She spent the entire ride taking note of ideas for the general information in the columns so that she could get it out of the way and focus more on the real reason she wanted the newsletter: to publish her mini novella series. The compulsory feeling to write the story seemed so strong, as if it was just bursting to come out of her. Of course, she was writing it as a fiction piece, but to her it was an embellished recollection of that day—when she was just an 11-year-old visiting California for the first time—locking eyes with the boy who she was sure was her soul mate. The memory had not diminished in her mind from that day, and she remained convinced that they would meet again. She was sure it was just her hopeless romantic side clinging to the dream of a great love story. But dreams do sometimes come true. Perhaps he still came to the library on occasion, where their paths would meet once again in the very spot where she was smitten the first time. She had to admit to herself that deep down there was also another reason for wanting to publish her story. Secretly, if she was honest about it, she hoped that maybe he was still connected with the library. Maybe he would read the newsletter, and their story could resume.

CHAPTER 9

"To Adventure"

One giant teenage sleepover: that's how David felt about the college experience so far. He didn't fade easily into the crowd of hundreds of new students. Rather, he was one of those who stood out. At least all the freshmen knew who he was: the attractive ladies' man whose actions and charisma got him noticed. It was not entirely uncommon for his medium-length hair to be combed under a top hat, a slight flip waving out from underneath.

To many on campus, he had become well-recognized as the door greeter to the cafeteria. He had taken this on from the first days—a great opportunity to observe his fellow mates, he felt. Most often appearing around lunch time to hold the door, sometimes he felt as though he wasn't only making observations about those coming and going from the cafeteria—the hefty football players and their group of ladies that followed behind, the guy with a dreadlock trailing all the way down his back, and the girl who always wore a bow that was half the size of her head—but that he was looking for someone. It wasn't that he knew who he was looking for, but a feeling that someone specific might walk through those doors one day. Then, he would know.

More than one reputation followed his illustrious character. Apart from becoming known as the doorman, he was also known for being the founder of a group of self-proclaimed "adventurers."

Every week, he and his comrades gathered over a beer at the same table and time.

The Founders Pub was known for being a place where the fringe crowd spent time. Most were regulars—the kind to eye a newcomer in a suspicious way. The offbeat décor attracted those who appreciated something a little different. The deep blue and red painted walls, wooden stools and chairs, revolutionary-style guns, and odds and ends—including a Paul Revere statue—were perhaps not a part of the environment that every university student was seeking for their weekend binges. For David, Michael, James, William, and Brian—the "adventurers"—it was perfect. The corner booth, under the shelf of metal toy soldiers, was theirs every Sunday night.

They had all sworn that their college experience was going to be more than studying. Although they considered themselves to be intellectuals, enjoying stimulating conversations surrounding the wave of hippie movements and government involvement in international affairs, David was the ringleader who pushed the rest to feel the rush of life. Based on the contributions they had made to discussions in various classes, David had recognized the slight, daring characteristic in each of them.

Brian was the last to join, having only participated in one stunt thus far. He was the most vocal, often coming up with ideas that were too extreme to execute. Michael usually sat quietly, absorbing and listening, contributing his engineering genius when the time came to draw up plans. William and James had been best friends since childhood. David had picked up on their tandem affinity for the extreme in his Intro to Psychology class. The two acted more like twins than friends. Brian's tall stature had served them more than once on their adventures, and William's humor always kept things light. Together, the five were a well-balanced and dynamic team.

Their goal was to do one stunt per month. September had involved stealing animal legs and feet from Brian's biology lab and placing them strategically around campus in various positions: legs dangling out of the grand piano in the music hall, arms outstretched under the door to the girls' dorm, and some feet creeping out from underneath the salad bar in the cafeteria. The prank had made the school newspaper and caused a lot of buzz around the lunch tables. Of course, the administration and dean of biology were outraged. Though as weeks and months went on and the boys gained their reputations, no one could ever prove that they were behind any scandals.

Just before Thanksgiving break, it was time to start masterminding one more stunt to pull off before the long Christmas holiday. They had thought of pranks involving elf costumes or late night caroling at professors' houses, but they finally settled on a gift to the students. Brian had been sent to boarding schools and summer camps since the age he was able to enroll. His parents were too busy with work, both independently wealthy in their own right, to spend much time with him. The choice, therefore, had been a slew of nannies, boarding schools, and summer-long camps. To make up for their lack of presence, they had granted him access to unlimited funds since he was fifteen. This method of parenting had given him a hard emotional edge, but he didn't hesitate to use the funds available as compensation. For this particular project, they were going on a shopping spree with this money.

Part one of the plan: acquire exceedingly large quantities of wrapping paper, ribbons, yard figures, and packing tape. This was to be done together before they all dispersed for Thanksgiving break. Jumping into William's station wagon, they headed out to hardware stores and home shops all around the area, buying up stocks of Christmas supplies. On the way back, sufficiently squished into the car surrounded by rolls of paper and other various bags of decorations, they lit up a traditional roll to celebrate the commencement of another plan. After six stores, they had enough wrapping paper and packing tape; the yard decorations were yet to come. Brian declared that he would bring back plenty of outdoor decorations from Thanksgiving break. No one questioned how or where he was going to get them—they just knew that he would.

After subsequent planning for dates, cover of night security, costume, and strategy of execution, the guys had decided to wrap up campus in the middle of finals week. They always chose costumes and masks for their endeavors; for this particular excursion, they chose to paint their faces white with red circles on their noses and cheeks, top their heads with green elf hats, and complete their look with green elf costumes. Brian had indeed mysteriously supplied close to fifty lawn ornaments: a variety of Santas, Frosty the Snowmen, toy soldiers, and reindeer. They had been stored in an abandoned warehouse room until needed.

On the Tuesday night of finals week, at eleven o'clock at night, the boys began to get ready, putting on their costumes, painting faces, and transporting their supplies to the edge of campus. A few hours later, they sat down to smoke a rich bowl of weed before beginning their runaround. As they finished the bowl, they grinned in satisfied mischief and gave the nod of action.

Off they went like little elves in all directions, working in two teams to get their job done with urgency. They dashed about on trips back and forth for supplies, visiting building by building until the decorations ran out. No words came out of their mouths, and only the bright white glows of their painted faces were easily seen. Their dark green tights, jackets, and hats blended perfectly into the night, and they enjoyed the challenge of being as stealthy as possible—perhaps living out their childhood dreams of being double agents and spies.

Meeting in their designated location, they stood for only half a minute to enjoy their work before scurrying off to dispose of their costumes. They had done what they could—covering four buildings in total; the most central on campus. Standing in between them, all the students and staff would walk to their classes to find the buildings wrapped like giant presents. The boys had put as much wrapping paper as possible around each of the four buildings, secured it well with packing tape, added a huge bow, and an army of lawn décor across the front. Michael had created wooden boards to look like gift tags, lit up with lights that covered each set of main doors. The tags read, "Merry Christmas UCLA Students."

Though they knew their Christmas prank wouldn't stop exams or cancel any last reports due, they knew it would at least postpone things in the morning. Perhaps some students would get a little extra time that was needed, but all would surely smile with appreciation. As the campus woke up the next morning, it was exactly like that. Of course, the maintenance crew began taking everything down as soon as possible after the first staff members arrived and began making phone calls, so only those with the first classes got to enjoy any part of the decorations. Exams were indeed delayed as the students expressed their amusement. A few early risers were able to capture some photos to share with the school paper, and once again, the suspected gang's notoriety grew. As with the November prank, they were called into the Dean's office one by one to be questioned.

When David entered the Dean's office, he found Professor Ralston engaged in a whispered conversation with the Dean. They had opposing opinions on some matter but broke off their conversation when they noticed him standing in the doorway. David gave Professor Ralston a cold glance and focused his gaze on the Dean, obviously trying to pretend that the object of his anger was not there at all.

"Sit down, please," said the Dean pointing to a side chair, and David obliged. "You probably know why you were asked to report to me, I dare say."

"No, sir," said David, well-practiced at denial.

"I have it on good authority that certain students close to you were involved in the latest practical joke involving inappropriate decorations requiring classes to be delayed, not to mention associated expenses to clean up the mess."

"Well, Sir, I know a number of students, but I'm certain that if any of them were involved, they did it solely out of the spirit of the season and only wanted to share their spirit with the other students," replied David with a look of bewilderment. He looked accusingly at Professor Ralston for a moment.

"Yes, I'm sure your estimation of your friends is very good, but this type of behavior will not go unnoticed. Those responsible will be found out eventually and their records will reflect the conduct demonstrated as being less than acceptable for any student wishing to remain at this institution."

"Surely you wouldn't expel someone for that. It was all in good fun, I'm sure," David stuttered as he realized that a threat was being made; a threat that could cost him his education and cause his family great embarrassment, especially his mother who—for any faults she may have—only ever wanted the best in life for him.

"In your case, although you were identified as a possible participant, Professor Ralston has assured me that you were with him discussing your desire to perform some extra-curricular activities to enhance your resume when you graduate … assuming you do."

David shot Professor Ralston a look of disbelief. The only other time they had met was the day he visited the campus with his mother, and he was pretty sure he had made an enemy of him, especially when his mother decided to stop seeing him for David's sake. Why was this man lying for him?

"I will expect to see some real effort out of you to ensure that you avoid any association with those who might damage your future. I will also expect feedback on your progress concerning the extra-curricular activities you decide to pursue. Good day, David."

David left the office, closely followed by Professor

Ralston. When they exited the building, David confronted his assumed enemy.

"Why would you do that? Why would you risk yourself for me?"

Professor Ralston gave David a look so similar to the looks his father used to give him when he tried to explain what should have been obvious.

"Your father and I were very close. I couldn't let you throw away an opportunity to make him proud of you."

"But what about my mother and what she did? She quit seeing you to try to appease me; doesn't that upset you in the least?"

"Your mother wasn't trying to appease you, David. She stopped seeing me because she loves you and realized that it hurt you to think she could replace your father. Neither of us wanted that. Look, David, I really care about your mother. I understand that you think I only supported you at the acceptance board meetings to gain her affection, but that is not why I did it. You were dealt a bad hand causing you to strike out and do stupid things in high school, and I just thought you needed a bit of help and understanding to overcome that and hopefully get on the right track. I'm sorry we didn't manage to become friends."

David felt confused and embarrassed again.

"Now, I'm sure your friends will be expecting a full replay of your meeting with the Dean. Emphasize the seriousness of their pranks, because this is the last straw. I won't lie for you again, so take this as a second chance to finish your education."

Professor Ralston placed his hand on David's shoulder, smiled at him, then turned and walked away.

"Professor Ralston," David called out as he ran after him. The professor turned as David put out his hand, saying simply, "Thanks."

CHAPTER 10

"Go Big U"

The last days had been filled with the anticipation of waiting for her college acceptance letters. One by one, they had arrived like little presents waiting to be opened. Sarah had applied to universities internationally, around ten in all. While most of her classmates had only applied to a few, Sarah didn't want to feel restricted in her options. Though California beckoned, she didn't want to limit herself.

As Sarah waited for the last of her letters to come in, she created an organizational system for her decision-making. Thus far, she had only been rejected from one university. Using her pragmatic side, Sarah separated the letters and corresponding information packets into "U.S.," "home," and "international," keeping a running list of the pros and cons for each in front of the stack. The topic of conversation was the same every night—always somehow revolving around the different universities people had applied to, who had gotten accepted and rejected from where, and who had already made up their minds and sent in their letters.

The final letter had arrived, and instead of pure excitement, Sarah found a range of thoughts and emotions surging through her body. Now, there was a certain tension that immediately stiffened her body. She *had* to make a decision.

Even though it was just after midnight in Sweden, Sarah phoned the two most sensible and reliable people in her life. Even though her mom longed to have her closer, she knew it was most important to see her daughter doing what she wanted with her life. The mumbled "halla" on the other end let Sarah know she had disturbed their sleep.

"Mama, Papa …"

"Sarah, dear! Is everything okay?"

"It's great! Sorry, but I just got my last college acceptance letter."

She could hear her dad groggily moaning and asking questions in the background. "It's Sarah," her mom whispered. "Your father is going to pick up the other phone."

"So?" asked her father.

"I've been waiting for them all to come in, and now that they have, I feel overwhelmed."

"Honestly, Sarah, you'll do great wherever you are." Her dad always gave her a vote of confidence. Sarah could still remember learning to swim with her dad. She was terrified, lacking faith in her muscles and movements, sure that she would drown the second he let her go. He told her she had everything she needed and gently took away one hand at a time. This lesson in swimming early on had been a reflection of their parenting in all the years that followed. They pushed her to be an independent thinker. Sarah could have guessed what their advice would be about college choices, but she still sought the comfort of her parents' words.

"You're a smart young lady, Sarah. We'll be proud of you no matter what you choose."

The conversation didn't last long, consisting of encouragement rather than any practical decision-making advice. After a few days of going over the options, both in her head and on paper, Sarah made another phone call to her parents. This time it was to inform them that she would be staying in California. Over the years, the L.A. area had become a second home. Her formative years were spent vacationing on the beach and creating memories with friends at the boarding school. The Golden State just felt like the right place to stay. Her final decision had been made: Cal State, Los Angeles. Having been told that she should turn the mini-series she did for The Huntington Library into a novel, Sarah felt as though writing could be her future. When she allowed herself to daydream about it, she imagined her photo on the back of a book, propped up on a stand in all the popular bookstores. She would look distinguished: writing behind an antique wooden desk, glasses in hand, cup by her side, posed behind a beautiful typewriter.

It was great to finally feel the relief. She could now participate in all the discussions about college choices instead of constantly replying, "I don't know." Instead, she joined the conversations to share her plans with enthusiasm. Instead of mailing in her letter of acceptance, however, Sarah decided she wanted to hand-deliver it. A great idea was forming for a celebratory day.

Staying in the area was a popular choice for most of the students at Southwestern Academy, but as students made their various choices, new cliques formed. Detachment began as a subconscious effort to make things easier in the end. Sarah did the same—beginning to surround herself with a few who were also going to Cal State. It created a certain cushion of comfort as they faced the unknown. Their small crew had begun to familiarize themselves with the university already, celebrating their new fall beginnings by attending a spring baseball game.

Arriving to the stadium, they could hardly believe the size of what lay in front of them. The group of six soon-to-be Cal State students was basking in the excitement of the noise, smells, and spirit. The sea of blue, black, and gold swarmed around them. They stood wide-eyed and frozen for a minute, taking in the surrounding action. Looking back at each other, they excitedly moved forward to join the swarm of students in the stadium, buying some hot dogs and peanuts before taking their seats just in time for the starting announcements that elicited cheers and shouts from the crowd.

UCLA was winning by seven runs by the seventh inning stretch, but the group of students didn't mind. They were enjoying the overall experience of pretending they were college students, even though their clothing colors didn't particularly attach them to either side. With the score looking so dismal, many fans were already heading out. Sarah's concentration was less on the game and more on conversing with Julia, who was sitting next to her. The girls had lost interest in the game after the first few innings, distracted by the ambiance and their pending status as students. As the girls broke open more peanuts, letting the shells fall to their feet, their attention piqued as a loud commotion erupted from the crowd. Both cheers and shouts of disapproval grew with a wild crescendo. There hadn't been such noise throughout the game— even when there was a home run.

The girls' mouths were glued in momentary silence as their eyes grew wide with surprise, observing five students running across the field. It wasn't necessarily the running that had created such an uproar, but rather what they were lacking.

"Are they naked under those capes?" she asked Julie without turning to look.

"I think so …" Julie's voice trailed off.

The five were running in a line, each with a letter on their gold capes that caught the wind as they dashed quickly across. "UCLA!" Though their stunt was over in a few seconds, the noise continued. Bursts of laughter exploded from everyone as security attempted to reach the culprits. They were much too late to do anything about it.

Sarah began to let her imagination run with all the adventures to come. And if she got to meet men daring enough to carry out such acts … she was sure she would find some interesting young lads. She was profoundly curious about someone who would put a stunt like that together but highly doubted that she would find him running around in his cape after the game. They were long gone by that point, hopefully avoiding all security.

The ride back was full of excited chatter. All were more excited than ever to begin the next phase of their lives in the fall. The running of the caped men had added excitement to the usual discussion of program plans, turning their minds instead to the fun they anticipated and Sarah's voiced admiration for whoever the ringleader of the group was. This elicited a certain poking response from one such gentleman in the car who had his eye on Sarah. She paid no mind. Instead, she was saving her interests for daring, wild, yet highly intelligent men that she was sure she would meet in college.

CHAPTER 11

"Ulterior Motives"

David felt a great deal of success upon exiting his freshman year. The memories created would last a lifetime —stories to tell his children … or not, due to the slightly scandalous nature of most of them.

His close call with the Dean concerning the unauthorized Christmas decorations had a lasting impact on him, and he had suggested to his comrades that they change their ways to avoid expulsion. At first, the other guys thought he was being sarcastic, but he finally convinced them —through a barrage of jeers and uncomplimentary name calling—that college was better than being drafted and shipped off to Vietnam, and that their reign had come to an end with the passing of freshman year.

After dabbling in a few anthropologic and psychology courses his final semester, David had decided to move on to engineering and financing the second year.

Dreams of creating inventions and patents spurred his desire to advance in engineering, and his mother's practical voice urged him to pursue finance. "It's sure success," she told him. "And you can play with your inventions on the side."

Psychology 101 had profoundly piqued David's curiosity. He found the discussions stimulating, creating a driving thirst for decoding the human psyche. What he didn't like, however, was the challenge he received from his social psychology professor. In a debate about the need to break social boundaries as attention-seeking behavior, she had suggested that he look inward to question why he defended the defiance of rules so strongly. In a private discussion following that class, she had told him that he had a deep need to participate in extravagant behaviors in order to draw the attention of people—or at least someone. Denying that he had anyone to impress, the debate shortly escalated as he vehemently insisted that any draw to extreme actions could be performed solely out of one's own desire.

After walking away from that class, he found himself questioning the motives of his actions the rest of the day. Could it be subconscious? He thought of the feeling he often had when greeting people at the cafeteria during the previous year—that feeling that he was looking for someone. Could his desire for daredevil actions actually be a subconscious maneuver to gain someone's attention? He left the question unanswered in his mind, long after making the decision to drop the class.

**

Sarah made one more trip to the Huntington library after graduating high school. She had one more newsletter to finish before departing to Sweden for the summer. She had saved the final chapter of her story of Sarah and Danny for this occasion.

Instead of placing it at the end of the newsletter as she usually did, she decided to make it the front page headline, a tribute to the influence on her life by the paintings in the Thornton Gallery. The title read, "Pinkie and Blue Boy – A Love Unrealized."

Sarah printed out copies, placed those for mailing in envelopes, and applied the printed mailing labels before dropping them in the outgoing mail bin.

***

David's mother opened the weekly newsletter as usual, scanned it briefly, then placed it in an envelope and mailed it to David, just as she had done every week since he had gone away to college.

***

David and his freshman buddies seldom hung out during his sophomore year, but he had found a new group. Janice, a green-eyed witty girl he had met in the library, introduced him to her liberal circle. Having a strong pull for all things anti-societal and against the grain, David immediately felt camaraderie with this new clique. The hippie movement had been largely subdued by this point, but he found himself sympathetic to the continued cause of those who kept the movement alive.

His greatest interest was in their movement to legalize marijuana. Though David had significantly cut down his consumption of the drug, he still backed its legalization due to the health benefits it offered. The group often discussed studies coming out that supported the role of raw cannabis as an aid for symptoms of Tourette's, seizures, multiple sclerosis, and most importantly, as an inhibitor to tumor growth. Their small group joined many others in the area to express their disapproval of the government's choice to keep it from those who could benefit. They claimed a conspiracy between the drug companies and the government— that the two did nothing but feed each others' wallets—and the pro-marijuana movement would be one that David would continue to fight for in the years to come.

His sophomore year had also brought about another scandalous interest of his. Fulfilling one of his general education requirements during the second semester, he found a surprising interest in his art appreciation.

He had not returned to the Huntington Library since entering college, but summer after summer of returning during high school had already fostered his appreciation for art for many summers. What caught his attention, however, was a slightly different topic—the art of forgery. Breezing through all of the other information about different art styles and periods, he often skipped class while he aced the tests with a little book-reading brush-up before each exam. Feeling compelled to attend one art history class, he was always pleased when he chose an interesting day to attend.

The discussion began with comparisons of the *David* replicas, taking a turn towards forgery in ancient times: the Roman sculptors copying Greek sculptures. As they debated through the centuries, the question students volleyed back and forth over was whether forgery was a crime or flattery to the artist. After all, even Michelangelo himself made a forgery of *Cupid*, which ended up in the hands of the Cardinal Riario of San Giorgio.

Though the discussion closed at the end of class, David had discovered a new interest. In the days that followed, he spent many hours scouring the library for books with accounts of famous forgery cases throughout history: Han van Meegeren, Abraham Wolfgang Küfner, and the recently revealed scandals of Elmyr de Hory. David was mesmerized by the careful attention to every detail that had to go into forgery. He saw it as its own art form. It was no job for an average criminal, but a challenge to one's talent.

The wheels began to slowly turn in his head. He certainly didn't have the talent to duplicate any classical art of his own free hand. Deciding to see what he had, though, he headed down to the student supply shop to pick up some oil paints, canvas, and a brush. His objective would be to make a Renaissance era replica of a fruit bowl. It was the most basic, after all: the one that all apprentices would attempt in an effort to hone their skills.

After toting his supplies back to his room, David turned the dial on the radio to classical inspiration and eyed the room carefully for the perfect set-up. Turning to the page in his art book with the picture of a fruit bowl, David propped it up in front of him and began dabbing the brush in some paints. After forty minutes of squinting, applying strokes, and sitting back to examine the canvas, David let out a good, hearty laugh. His replica was a virtually distorted interpretation of the picture that lay in front of him. Maybe painting replicas wasn't in his near future, but he was sure there would be another way. Professional forgers had to know a painting backwards, forwards, and sideways: brush strokes, hairline cracks, signatures, medium, materials, and format. How could it be done without having the talent of a professional artist? The most painting he had done was paint by numbers when he was a kid. But ... what if that was it? What if he created a sort of paint by numbers?! He could get a print on canvas, study the brush strokes, and paint over the print. He would start small and simple, moving his way up to an ultimate goal.

It didn't take him long to decide what that would be. What greater challenge—and therefore greater reward—than successfully replicating a painting at The Huntington Library? His constant trips as a boy had made him more familiar with those than any others. And what painting would be more symbolic than *Pinkie*? After all these years, he still thought about that girl—Sarah—whose violet eyes still mesmerized him in his dreams. He knew that if he ever saw a girl with those eyes again, there would be no denying it was her, as no one could duplicate such perfection.

Determined to accomplish a monumental goal, he managed to obtain several prints of "Pinkie" and applied most of his time and energy into replicating that one painting.

*   *   *

The final days of his sophomore year arrived. As David lay on his dorm bed that late afternoon, staring at his latest iteration of his painting, a young student appeared in the open doorway.

"Mail. Just the one item, the Huntington Library," said the boy as he tossed the envelope to David without entering and disappeared.

David opened the envelope without averting his eyes from the girl in the painting. It was good, he thought, although he had not completed it. He found he had adequate skills to paint background and clothing but had difficulty in detailing facial expressions. So there stood Pinkie, faceless.

He had long ago lost interest in the goings on of the Huntington Library, finding that college demanded all of his time now that he was focused on actually accomplishing something during his education. He had informed his mother that he seldom ever read the newsletters she forwarded to him, but she insisted it made her feel good to send them anyway. As he extracted the newsletter from the envelope, he mechanically scanned the front page expecting to find the same listing of events and other mundane information. He did a double-take as his brain registered the headline.

His immediate reaction was a flashback to that day when he and Sarah stood before the paintings of Pinkie and Blue Boy. As the more rational side of his brain kicked in, he laughed at the impulsive response he felt at reading the caption. Then he began to read what he decided was probably a story of the paintings, which he already knew too well. As the words of Sarah's story filled his mind he was jolted by the reality of the situation. He looked quickly at the heading again and there it was … "by Sarah Lillienburg." There was no doubt, Sarah had not only remembered him, but she was within a few minutes of him.

David flew from his room with one thought in mind … get to the Huntington Library as fast as possible.

***

As David rushed through the front doors of the Gallery, an unfamiliar face greeted him at the receptionist desk.

"My, but you're in a bit of a hurry, aren't you. We don't close for some time so, please, slow down."

"Sorry," replied David trying to catch his breath. "I'm looking for Sarah."

"Sarah? I'm sorry, but she's not here."

"When will she be back, it's very important that I find her!"

"I'm afraid she's no longer volunteering here. Her last day was last week."

"Can you tell me where she's gone?"

The receptionist gave him a sorrowful look. "Sweden, I think. Then she is off to college. A lovely girl, I'm sorry you missed her."

David said nothing, but walked slowly to the spot Pinkie and Blue Boy still occupied, their unspoken love still alive in the facial expressions. He stared at Pinkie until her face was etched in his mind. He somehow knew he would be able to capture that look in his own painting, but with one exception … it would contain features of Sarah, especially those violet eyes.

CHAPTER 12

"Search for Excitement"

College signifies the gradual passage of teenagers into the adult world. Characters change, interests are recognized, and maturity develops as young adults prepare for the approaching adult world—the intermittent stage of exploring new ideas and dabbling in possible career paths. Others focus on match-making, while others sow their wild oats, exploring many avenues of danger and mischief before settling into adulthood. This last group believes that college will be their last chance to be crazy, spontaneous, and adventurous—that it's all downhill after graduation.

For Sarah, college was the time to lay some bricks on the path to her future. Some of the other girls joked about earning their "M.R.S." degree, and Sarah couldn't deny that she hoped to meet a dashing, adventurous, and brilliant man. However, her first priority was to study and develop the skills she needed to pursue her desired career, and that meant an ambitious double major in theatre arts and creative writing. Her parents had always encouraged her in education—emphasizing the importance of a well-rounded intellect, and their example had motivated her ambition. Even holidays had held some sort of educational value in her family throughout the years.

That summer of writing her non-fiction inspired story

amongst the other reporting that she barely found to be mildly entertaining had inspired her to delve more into writing. With this newfound passion, her dreams began to take shape, and she visualized the years that lay ahead. She could picture her books on display in a bookstore. She heard the phone calls from her agent informing her of the upcoming schedule for a book-signing tour. She pondered the answers to questions that reporters would ask about her childhood and upbringing during their interviews. In between all this, she would dabble in acting, only appearing in minor roles to ensure she could devote adequate time to writing. This was the path she set for herself, and was sure that she could make it.

All she knew was that she wanted to be noticed and recognized. What she couldn't decipher was whether she wanted to be recognized by someone in particular or more expansively by the general public. She was never an attention seeker, as her parents showed their great affection for her. However, it was clear to her that she wasn't the center of the universe, nor did she show any desire to be. She didn't act out to gain attention, try out for star roles in plays, or raise debates in class. This desire had come more recently, though she was unsure as to why.

Though Sarah was doing very well in her classes, by the end of her junior year she hadn't felt that the social piece of the experience met her expectations. She realized that she had been so focused on her theatre and writing courses that she had skipped any of the extracurricular electives or student clubs she was eligible to join. Lamenting the fact that she lacked great adventures and stories to share aside from writing her novel, she resolved to join a group with a purpose or pursue an extreme elective for the next year.

Sarah looked over the list of courses offered in athletics, but nothing there seemed to stand out. She didn't want to learn basketball, and she already knew how to dance, swim, and do anything else she found remotely interesting on the list. Languages? Maybe. Senior year seemed a little late to start a language, though her Spanish needed improvement. Maybe a neuroscience class? It would be interesting, but not quite the socialization and adventure she was looking for. She put down the book and looked at the poster-covered wall in front of her. Since both she and her roommate, Eliza, participated in the theatre program, their walls were decorated with programs, posters, and record sleeves. It was almost time to take it all down, and Sarah heaved a sigh at the thought. She paced across the room to sit down at her typewriter, just as she did most evenings when she wasn't involved in a program or working on another creative writing assignment.

The novel had been a work in progress over the last year and a half. It was more or less the same story she had written for The Huntington Library—her own dream of a love story that evolved after those two young children locked eyes in front of

Pinkie and *Blue Boy* that day. There had been a lot of torn up pages and scratched out lines, but she hoped this book would be the start of something great—a lifelong affair with the written word.

Sarah sat in the student center working on an assignment to pass time until her next class. Bored with the reading material, she found herself doing more daydreaming than studying. Her feet curled up under her long floral skirt, comfortably relaxed on one of the plump orange sofas against a brick wall in the main area, she focused her attention on the bulletin board of flyers and programs on the side wall. There was an international group dinner coming up, a push to be in the honours program, a request for tickets to an upcoming concert, and one particularly interesting advertisement with a thumbtack straight through the middle:

"Fight for Sensible Cannabis Use.

Join the Marijuana March downtown on Saturday morning, May 3rd. Fight back against the Controlled Substances Act. Legalize cannabis.

Contact the Students for Sensible Drug Use if you want to join or find out more information about why marijuana is harmless ..."

Sarah recalled that the government was running anti-marijuana commercials in an effort to fight the movement for legalizing marijuana. Warning about the dependency of marijuana, the educational film commercial claimed that the kinds of users were "burned-out Bohemians" and "crazy-eyed custodians." Although its effects were rather ill on the crowd it targeted, the commercial gave most young people a good laugh.

Despite her support of the drug's decriminalization, Sarah had never considered joining the fight. Though she had never smoked weed herself, Sarah felt there was no need for the government to spend money in an effort to fight this particular issue. Many people wanted the drug for medical purposes, while others smoked in the privacy of their own homes. Moreover, even though this government was not hers, she strongly disagreed with its control over an individual choice. Sarah decided to stroll around the campus to wait out the remaining time before her next class. As she crossed the area between the student center and her next classroom, she noticed Larry the Hippie, as he was referred to by most students. As she passed closer to him, she smelled the unmistakable aroma of marijuana. *What better way to research her possible involvement in the pro-cannabis movement,* she considered, *than by going to someone who must certainly know much more about the subject than she?* She paused as she came up to Larry where he sat leaning against a tree trying to hide the source of the smell that had got her attention.

"Don't worry," she whispered to Larry, a wry smile showed her assurance of discretion. "I've been considering joining the support movement and thought you might provide some insight as to what to expect from both sides of the argument. Mind if I sit down for a minute?"

Larry silently motioned to a patch of grass beside him. As she sat, he offered her the small remainder of his roach.

"Thanks, but I'm not much of a user. I am really looking to provide research and time to volunteer based on the wider need for the legalization of cannabis."

"Well," said Larry with his gaze toward the sky, "it's gonna take all kinds to help the movement. Maybe your approach will add more credibility to the cause."

"What do you mean by my approach?"

Larry turned to look at Sarah. As their eyes met he leaned his head back as though trying to focus better. "Maybe it's the weed, but your eyes seem to grab a man by the soul," he said.

Slightly blushing Sarah replied, "Thank you, but what did you mean by my approach?"

Larry looked around at the students moving to and

from classes. "Most of the supporters I've met are heavy recreational users and their position is stereotyped the way an alcoholic fighting prohibition in the thirties would have been. The movement needs informed, non-users to speak out for those who find relief from pain and mental stress they can only get from a little marijuana."

The melodic bells rang a short tune across campus, signalling to everyone that it was ten minutes until the hour. Sarah closed the book that she had only read a few paragraphs from and tucked it into her antique leather satchel.

"Thanks for the input," said Sarah rising and smoothing the hem of her dress. She stuck out her hand. Larry took it without rising as he again looked into those violet eyes.

"Any time," he said.

"Thanks," she replied.

As she moved on to her next class, she continued to think about the Marijuana March. "It sounds fun and adventurous, and it's certainly a cause I support," she thought. "Maybe I could even be arrested. *That* could be a good story to tell—but not if it affects my scholarships. Dad would surely make me cover the cost if that happened."

She continued to weigh the pros and cons the rest of the day, and her interest was fuelled by some articles she picked up that night in the library. Oregon had already decriminalized cannabis, and in that state, possession of less than an ounce was merely a "violation." Many other states, including conservative Midwest territories like Nebraska, Ohio, and Southern Mississippi, looked like they would soon follow suit. Having made up her mind before bed, Sarah decided to find the Students for Sensible Drug Use desk the next day to get more information about joining their group and participating in the march. Now, senior year would surely make headlines.

CHAPTER 13

"March for Marijuana"

Large-scale marches around the country had been making headlines in the last few years, and the July 4, 1970 Washington D.C. invasion was one that inspired many more. That day, thousands of hippies, yippies, and social fringers gathered at the Washington Monument in a giant smoke-out as a counter-statement to the "Honour America Day" featuring conservatives like Billy Graham and Bob Hope as hosts. Skinny dipping in the Reflecting Pool, gas grenades, fist fights, and an invasion of the stage led to widespread chaos, arrests, and widespread excitement in the alternative media.

The students of L.A. universities were ready to organize their own smoke-in downtown. Each university had its own chapter, the heads of whom had started meeting earlier that year to plan their march: rallying people and creating catchy statements, flyers, and logistics.

"Hey, I heard they did a 'guess how many joints are in the jar' game in NYC last year," David said as the black fringe of his doobie slowly reached his fingertips. The "head council," as they called themselves, took turns providing the hash for their monthly meeting. The goal was to share a different form each time: bongs, water pipe, joints, hash brownies, and cookies, to name a few examples. Their mantra was that they did not advocate addictive behavior, but rather responsible recreational consumption. "We're not potheads, just people who enjoy the occasional use of the herb for its relaxation properties." They did, however, want to plan one great parade with plenty of marijuana supporters: a day to raise awareness about the plant's special effects.

"That seems like a waste of a lot of weed," David piped up.

"It wouldn't go to waste, man. The winner would get to keep the jar of joints. Brilliant."

"I don't think I like that. That means we wouldn't be allowed to win."

"Well let's think about it. Let's talk about the bands. We have to get on this stuff. We're only a few weeks away from D-day."

"Yeah, but it's not hard. Who doesn't want to play at the event? We've already half-secured a few people."

They all began to chime in with their ideas. Various thoughts whirled around the room as they passed the joint, sinking into the worn couches of the basement meeting room. David often passed up his turn in the rotation to maintain clarity. He had done his share of extreme enjoyment from the plant's dried leaves, but now was not the time. Though he believed strongly in the decriminalization and legalization movement, it wasn't because he himself wanted the right to possess a large quantity. He wasn't the kid with a plastic bag stashed under his mattress or tucked in a sock. He didn't judge those who did so, though. After all, he hadn't seen anyone addicted to it like some were to heroin or cocaine.

Needing an outlet for his adventurous, attention-seeking soul, David had joined the pro-hash group earlier that year, even though it was his senior year. A sophomore, Jerry Meisenheimer, had decided to get a group going after transferring from New York, where his university group there was already a well-established chapter in the Yippie community. When he saw the poster tacked up in the lobby of the dorm, David grabbed it and set out to find Jerry. He had a feeling this would be a good start to his senior year. At least this would be for a worthy cause, rather than for the pursuit of adrenaline or recognition for boisterous activities.

He had taken the cause by storm that year, and his intensity brought him to the front of the group as a leader. He enjoyed being a part of the controversial issue, though his mother didn't seem to show much appreciation for his latest endeavours. She worried about how it would affect the level of respect that their family name held at the university, respect earned by his late father. A fun-loving, free-spirited man, David's father surely would have backed the movement, and this intuitive observation of his father's character recalled to mind the famous phrase, "Like father, like son."

Breezing through his senior business classes, David devoted a much larger percentage of his time to his art forgery and UCLA Students for Responsible Use. He was disappointed about the approaching end of an era. In the last months of his student career, he felt his mind constantly spinning. He'd be damned to let his life slip into a boring tunnel of desk work. He may be on the path to a career in finance and business, but boredom was not an option.

Eliza secured a headband over her long hair with the help of a mirror.

"Well, I'm ready when you are. We'll probably be the first ones to show up."

"I'm calculating for the traffic," Sarah defended, "and I'm ready for some excitement!" She grabbed her keys and the roommates started on their way to Santa Monica Boulevard.

"See, we're not the first to arrive. We're going to drive around forever looking for a place to park."

Her anticipation grew as they drove past other marchers, parked the car, and carried their hand-painted signs to the main location. She felt that a free spirit was bursting forth from inside her—something she had felt before, but not to this extent—save, perhaps, a few impromptu skinny dipping endeavours her freshman year with one particularly mischievous lad she was seeing. The streets were buzzing with smiles, hugs, and an air of camaraderie. The actual march wasn't to take place until the afternoon, but there was plenty of action happening in Beverly Gardens Park before the crowd planned to get on the move. As Sarah looked around, she knew her style didn't fit with the others, but then again, she felt it was exactly the place to stand out. This was the realm of free love and acceptance, wasn't it?

Sarah felt it was impossible for anyone there to be serious, disgruntled, or harbouring anger in this environment of positive commotion. It was instead a sea of young people who were there to celebrate together and unite to represent a common belief. They stood first at the edge of the park, taking in the activity, and there was no denying the sweet aroma of marijuana. Meanwhile, the crowd occupied themselves at the food and information booths, or sitting in circles; some chattering, and others with their guitars and percussion instruments.

The girls began meandering around and through the circles, booths, and flow of fellow college students, admiring the music stage set up in front. Eliza was surprised by her free-spirited roommate. Sure, she knew Sarah had a love for freedom, the arts, and most things counter-culture, but she was used to seeing her roommate at her typewriter or running around the theatre department in costume. She could immediately see a light in Sarah's eyes that she rarely saw.

Sarah began to pay less attention to ensuring that Eliza was close by. Instead, she began to feel free to move about, stopping to dance along with the guitar in one circle, and even edging out the man on the bongos for a turn at some drumming. Instead of dragging Sarah along by one wrist, Eliza was now keeping an eye on her curious roommate, following behind her as she moved.

Directly in the middle of the park, under a mid-grown oak, a girl with long dreadlocks piled in a large bun sat cross-legged on her blanket. She had canvases, paints, brushes, and supplies spread out around her as if the whole park was her own personal studio. Sarah stood at a distance, watching her for a short time. Mesmerized by the movement of her arms as they threw brush strokes across a canvas, Sarah felt as though she was frozen inside a bubble, fixated on the woman's art while increasingly unaware of anything and anyone moving around her.

The girl, eventually noticing Sarah's unbroken stare and curious eyes, stopped her movements and stared back. Sarah smiled. "They're beautiful."

The girl's returned smile was equally warm and welcoming. She motioned with her head for her to come and join her. She moved aside a few paint receptacles, making room for Sarah to sit.

"Which one is your favorite?"

Sarah's hands gently revealed each painting stacked against the tree trunk, her eyes exploring the colors and strokes of each one. Trying to decipher the signature at the bottom of each one, she turned to the girl to ask, "Alexandra?"

"That's me."

She pulled out an ensemble of leaves and flowers that overlapped each other, covering an entire canvas with textures, layers, and colors.

"Your eyes are like a painting; a color I've never seen before. Would you like to sit for a while and allow me to paint them?"

Sarah blinked, always modestly flattered by the compliments she received about her unusual eye color.

Feeling a kindred connection with the girl, she sat down to oblige her request. Alexandra turned to light up the short water pipe sitting next to her, offering Sarah the hose after she nurtured the hot coal to begin burning the strawberry-flavored tobacco.

Eliza had eventually made her way over after spending some time flirting with a guy at the "information on medical benefits" booth.

"Wow, look at that!" she commented with raised eyebrows.

"Hey, where'd you run off to? This is Alexandra. Take a look at her stuff," she motioned over by the tree.

Eliza began to move that way, beginning to relate the story of her last hour spent chatting with the "witty and smart, though slightly lanky guy."

The three women spent the following time discussing paintings, boys, and other casual subjects of interest. Nearly finished with the replica of Sarah's violet eyes, two piercing images staring back from a black background, Alexandra paused to pull out some Polaroids of body paintings she had recently done. They spent a bit of time looking at Alexandra's collection of paintings and pictures before Eliza insisted that they see at least a few exhibits before the day's end. Sarah thanked Alexandra, and she and Eliza began to stroll the area while popping into each booth they passed.

As a band set up on a stage at the other end of the area, the usual "test, test" and instrument tuning could be heard above the murmur of the crowd. Sarah suggested they go back and listen for a while, but Eliza hinted that she had already made other plans with one of the boys she had met earlier. Upon agreement, Sarah and Eliza strolled slowly in the direction of their car.

**

"Man, where have you been?" Kevin, head of the University of Southern California's group, questioned.

"Sorry, I stayed up most of the night working on a late paper and had some beers."

"You missed most of the day, man."

"But I arrived just in time, and I'm ready to lead a march!" David's gestures, charm, and nonchalant yet polite attitude yielded him many friends and nearly no enemies over the years. "But first, I need a beer."

Kevin squinted his eyes for a half-serious look in return, slapping him in the shoulder before starting the lead through the park.

They happened to pass by an artist displaying her work. Leaning against a tree was a picture of two violet eyes, and David was captivated. He had painted those eyes so many times in his attempt to perfect the color, shape, and overall essence of the force that emitted from his long remembered encounter with the gaze of Sarah many years ago.

"Nice, don't you think?" said the girl noticing David's attraction to the painting.

"Yea," said David, "I actually knew a girl once with eyes that color."

"They certainly were unique. I just had to paint her for my collection."

"So that's a painting of a real person?" asked David.

"Yeah, it's still wet so be careful. I just finished it about half an hour ago."

"You mean she was here?" David asked as he suddenly began to look around in every direction. "Did you see where she went?" he pressed urgently.

"No, they just left to see some of the displays. She's with another girl. Is something wrong?" she asked as David's actions seemed a bit tense.

"No, no, nothing's wrong, I just thought for a minute …"

The band began to play an old rock and roll song … "my name should be sorrow, my name should be woe … "

***

As they neared their car, Sarah became aware of the music. She paused for a minute, smiled at the memory of the boy so long ago singing that very tune, and then began humming the tune as she got into the car.

***

The rest of the day was a big success in the view of the student leaders. They estimated the attendance at around one thousand students from various universities in the city. Before the start of the march, they had encouraged all pot usage to remain on the insides, as fringe smokers were usually the ones arrested. The crowd had headed south, down Santa Monica Boulevard, crossed over on Wilshire, and back up North Beverly; only about an hour for the total route. Ending back in the park, the crowd united to light up in a cloud of smoke, kicking off the post-march celebration to the tune of "Children of the Sun."

The group had conjured up three local bands of students who took turns setting the mood, and the crowd only dissipated minimally as the hours passed. Most were ready to continue their mass hangout well into the hours of the morning, but the police arrived to remind them that they were edging into the hours that were considered a "disturbance of the peace." The guys made the announcement that socializing must continue elsewhere, and before long, the park that had been so full of life became an empty lawn littered with debris.

The student leaders met together to enjoy a beer before beginning their clean-up plan. Sitting down in the middle of the park, a big pile of the materials and trash next to them, the men reviewed the day's successes. There had been no problematic run-ins with the police, they were satisfied by the park's cleanliness by the end of the night, and they were proud of their work as student advocates, confident that the same event could be pulled off again next year. It was bittersweet for David, knowing that next year he wouldn't be a student anymore. Nonetheless, the next phase of life awaited him, and that would also be an adventure.

CHAPTER 14

"Blue Boy, Cont'd"

"The passion in their eyes had never left after all those years. It was a love story to be recorded in history; a great among the greats. And on their gravestones would be engraved their nicknames: 'Pinkie' and 'Blue Boy,' 'Love at first sight; a twinkle turned to flame that will burn love for eternity.'"

And with that, Sarah slid her typewriter's round cylinder over with a great sense of satisfaction. She pushed the heavy wooden chair back from the desk, reaching to pull out the last page. This project had been her baby for years, giving up hours upon hours of her college social life to work on what she was sure would bring her fame.

Two years after graduation, this final chapter marked the completion of her fourth novel. The first three, written mainly while still in college, hadn't had any success and thus far no publisher. With this project, she had decided to do a different spin using the same character in a separate novel. She loved the original trilogy based on the life of a modern-day gentleman who looked and dressed just like the boy in the famous *Blue Boy* painting that she loved so much hanging in The Huntington Library. Of course, this was inspired by the memorable chance meeting during her first visit to the library.

Her imagination formed a background and future for the boy, whom she named Danny. The first book led up to their meeting in the room that day. The following two continued on with his teenage years in search for the young girl at the library, giving way to the sad tale of how love lost affected him for life. He would never marry, but instead followed a career path that wouldn't accommodate a love life—that of an international spy. She felt it had all the elements of an exciting story: love, tragedy, and adventure. Yet she had sent the manuscripts to six publishing companies so far, rejection letters returning every time.

In her frustration, Sarah concluded that the publishers might be more interested in a dramatic story of romance. For this novel, she let her mind play out what would have happened if the two young lovers had actually spoken that day. What if they had exchanged addresses? Visited each other in their countries? Declaring and devoting their undying love? Although trials came through the years and war separated them, they would live with a passion others only dreamed of until the end.

One year later, this idea was complete. Securing the last piece under the paperweight on the stack, she skipped over to her record player and danced about her tiny apartment in her underwear. While working steadily on a piece, Sarah would barely move from the chair. The scenery would change little, and the base of her outfits remained the same. Layers would come and go, and she would remain stripped down, sometimes in her robe, or other times with only a partial outfit. Sometimes, Sarah would sit on a pillow wrapped in a blanket, and other times, she found that the hard discomfort of the chair helped to keep her alert. Dishes piled up next to her as she survived on bowls of porridge.

As she moved about the room, she held her posture as though ballroom dancing with a handsome gentleman. Finally allowing her body to fall and sink into the dishevelled comforter atop her bed, she reached for the phone. It was time to return to her social life after she copied the manuscript and sent it off to the first publisher. All that to be done ... just after she slept awhile.

Approximately eighty percent of those Sarah spoke with about her career choice gave her the sympathetic eyes and well wishes. She knew that choosing acting and writing instead of something more generic (or marriage!) wouldn't be the easiest path right away. It could possibly be thousands of words written and interviews attended before she tasted success. Nonetheless, she was convinced that her eccentricity fit in perfectly with this crowd, and her efforts would not be in vain.

Until then, she adapted to the stereotypical starving artist's lifestyle. Her apartment was less than what one would call "modest." It closely resembled her college dormitory: small, one room, with white walls decorated by various posters of plays or movies. Her doorless cupboards usually contained only a few items at a time, unless her mom had just come to visit or she was just returning from their summer holiday house. They had urged her to move in with them after graduation, but Sarah was determined to support herself.

Hollywood and the writing world were proving to be tough critics of her work, though she got her few seconds of fame in a toothpaste commercial that aired for some months in the area. Seeing herself on the screen had actually proven to be less satisfying than she imagined, yet pride rose within her; pride that her face was being noticed by an audience. This would take some getting used to—the ongoing criticism and limited visibility before her big break.

Her latest manuscript wasn't proving to be a desirable piece for the publishers, either. The same saga continued despite her best efforts: manuscript sent and rejection letter received. She felt she was about to go mad with the constant cycle of attempt and denial, but tenacity was in her nature. It was only the beginning.

CHAPTER 15

"Café Rouge"

The flames flickered in a dance, turning the pile of white pages into black ash. Sarah watched, her body frozen as she stared down, keenly aware of her senses. The fire was small, yet a strong heat radiated from their combined efforts. Sarah wondered if some of the heat she felt was the passion being released from the pages. The tips of the orange flames seemed to be playing a game of tag as they moved closer and further from each other, sending little bits of paper jumping at their feet. She imagined a playful tune; one that said farewell to a dream. She should perhaps feel more mournful, but instead, she felt a joyful energy from the fire. The smell of the ash lingered sweetly in her nose as she closed her eyes and reflected on the stories now encompassed in those flames and disintegrated to nothing but black, chalky ash—black like the ink that once graced the pages.

The flames eventually died to tiny little specks of orange and red protesting their death in the black soot that was left behind. After all the time and emotion put into her manuscripts, Sarah felt like the publishers' rejections of her books was less a rejection of her work and more a rejection of her soul. After she received the last, "thank you, but …"

letter that morning, she flew into a rage, collecting every paper she had that contained creative content: all manuscript copies, cover letters to publishers, outline notes, and letters received back. They all went into her bath tub and without a second thought she lit a match and watched them all burn.

There were no tears. It was but a release; allowing her dream to die so a new one could begin. All that remained were black pieces and a charred bathtub.

Sarah felt that she was chasing the dreams of a young and foolish version of herself. It was time to move on. The Blue Boy that had been so enthralling to her was apparently not as such to the publishers. Her acting career hadn't gone past a few commercials. Figuring she should join the adult world of more serious work, the idea of producing a journalistic documentary piece seemed a good compromise for her; it would allow her to utilize her creative talents while pursuing a lucrative career.

Many long walks over the last weeks had been her time for contemplation. In the middle of the night, she would sometimes wake up, throw her jacket on, and head out on the town; sometimes for twenty minutes and other times for two hours. Reflecting back on years past, Sarah began thinking more about her time with the Students for Sensible Drug Use. Why not do a journalistic piece on the underground world of marijuana? That night, she didn't even realize how long she had walked until the sun began to peer over the horizon. Suddenly noticing the exhaustion in her legs, she lay down on a bus stop bench to take a nap.

Sarah realized this would be her greatest challenge. To really get into the underground world, she needed to start making connections. She had been to many natural medicine shops that were rumored to sell for healing purposes, however, none of them would give her any information. She realized then that she had to go with safer options first. The leader of their student group, Jack, was still living in L.A. and had agreed to meet her for lunch.

He was working an eight to five desk job now, so he requested that Sarah meet him at Café Rouge downtown near his office. It was a beautiful day for sitting outside, typical of California weather. The cafes that lined the sidewalks always reminded her of Europe. Her parents financed her trips back to Sweden at Christmas, but other than that, she hadn't done much traveling on the continent in the last few years. Moments like this made her miss it, but s still held onto the assumption that she would someday have the means to travel.

Sarah wore her pink, wide-brimmed floppy hat and puffed-sleeve dress to the lunch meeting. Pulling her stopwatch out of her satchel, she realized that he would be arriving at any moment. Now she folded her hands on top of her notebook, pencil in hand, glancing around to see if she noticed him anywhere.

"Hey, Sarah!" He had come up from behind her.

"Hi there, Jack. Thanks for meeting me."

Jack grabbed the menu in an attempt to conceal his discomfort. After all, he wasn't entirely sure what Sarah wanted. Was it supposed to be a date? All she said on the phone was that she had some questions that maybe he could answer.

Very few words of idle chat were exchanged until their meals and drinks were ordered. Sarah decided to cut all of the catch-up chat and get to the point.

"So, I called you because I have a project that I need help getting off the ground. I'm hoping you'll be able to contribute. I want to do a journalistic piece on drugs— ninety percent focused on marijuana—but I want it to be about the roots level. I'd like to illustrate the invisible underground."

"And you want …" he ended with a question in his voice.

"I was wondering if you had any contacts; anyone who sold, grew, or distributed—for whatever reason, whether recreational or medicinal."

Jack stabbed at his potato wedges. "You're asking a tall order."

"I know. But I can't get my project started if I can't access any of these people." After a long pause she added, "You know you can trust me. You know I'm pro-marijuana."

"What if you went DEA?" he smiled, scarfing down the last of the sandwich on his plate.

"Can you give me an anonymous tip?"

"Look, I'll give you a place and a code word. They sell for medical purposes there. It'll be up to you to convince them you need it. From there, maybe you can work your way behind the scenes some more. I happen to know that they grow their green on site."

Sarah had hardly even touched her tuna quiche, almost

forgetting she had food in front of her. She watched with elbows propped on the table as Jack scribbled a few words on a napkin. It was a start at least! Passing the napkin over at her, he glanced down at his watch.

"Oh! 12:53—sorry, but I need to rush back to work. Here," he pulled some money out of his wallet. "For our lunch. It was great seeing you. Don't be a stranger," he added as he stood up from the table.

Sarah decided to leave the whole amount for the waitress, even though it was a large tip. She wanted to get out and find this place right away.

"Damn it!" David looked down at his watch. 12:53. He was late. He was supposed to meet his potential dealer at 12:45; a private financier he found through his old college buddy, Danny, who had been lucky enough not to get killed in Vietnam. Danny had made it clear that this money man might not always work within the boundaries of the law, but he had money. David had no doubts that his inventions would easily sell and that he would be able to pay back the investment in no time.

The most excitement on the job with Crocker was when an attractive woman or off-the-wall character came into the picture. The rest of the time, he felt as though the creative side of his brain was dying. At the end of one ordinary Wednesday, he coolly walked into his boss's office and declared that he would not be returning to work anymore, certain that his fortune was about to be made with the help of Danny's acquaintance.

In the six months since that day, he had been exercising his brain to come up with as many ideas for inventions as he could: a single-wheeled vehicle, a hands-free cigarette head strap, a tingling face mask, a phone-answering robot, and phones shaped like various animals that made their respective noises when ringing, to name a few examples. He had submitted applications for all, along with a small fortune, and hoped that at least one would be wildly successful. While waiting for news regarding the patents, he took it upon himself to search for buyers.

David called around California, Nevada, and Arizona to contact the head buyers of any large distributing company, setting up as many appointments as he could. For everyone else, he sent off a packet of information about products he thought might interest them, and this day would be his first meeting. Though he was excited about his new entrepreneurial activities, he dared not tell friends and family. As far as his mom knew, she was still proud of her son, the banker. "What a boring place," David thought to himself as he pedaled quickly downtown, thinking back on the months he spent sitting behind a counter.

Trusting in the luck of the day, David didn't even chain up his bike in front of the restaurant. Café Rouge was a fairly small place, so he figured he could keep an eye on it. It was already five past two—twenty minutes after he was supposed to be meeting Mr. West—and David was hoping he could chalk up his late arrival to being a frazzled inventor. He found Mr. West sitting in the two-seater by the left window, just as he had said—or at least, he hoped it was him and not someone else who had taken the spot. David straightened himself upright and walked confidently to the table.

"Mr. West?" he held out his hand, ready for a firmly-gripped handshake.

"David, I presume?" He, contrarily, did not extend his hand for a welcome.

"I apologize for my delay and the inconvenience of keeping you waiting. I got carried away with a project." David tried very hard to maintain his cool, confident demeanor.

"All right, well, please call me Fred to start, and your forty-five minutes has now dwindled down to twenty-five."

David didn't even look around for a menu. He couldn't worry about food or drink now. Instead, he pulled his papers out of his leather satchel and began his spiel. The words spilled out of his mouth quickly and enthusiastically as he placed paper after paper onto the metal table space in between them.

Fred sat quietly for the duration of his pitch, which made David question his motives. At the end of his speech, David took a deep breath and mustered the most charming smile he had.

"There you have it, Mr. West—Fred. I believe we could have a wonderful partnership. You'll find some of these products to be great sellers for your company, no doubt."

"No doubt, huh? To be honest, son, I have my doubts."

David nearly visibly cringed with the patronizing reference.

"Your confidence intrigues me though. So, I have a proposition for you. One year. For one year, we put up the cost of production, marketing, and selling any of these products you choose. For that year, you get to keep forty percent of the profits you've made. If you can show an increase in sales, we'll buy the patent and rights from you. If it hasn't made any money, then you will incur all costs that were lost in production. I should warn you: this is no small sum."

David looked back at him with a glowing thrill in his eyes. "Yes, si—"

"And unfortunately, our time is up." Standing up to leave, Fred left the money for his lunch and a business card. "Call me to finish discussing the details if you want to accept the offer."

David nodded his hand in gratitude, remaining frozen, unsure of whether to sit and have lunch or go for a joyride. His bike was still in front, thank God. He looked down at the table. Fred had left a large enough amount that he could order some eggs and the waitress would still get a tip. His conscience won, however, and he decided to grab the corner of the sandwich left on Fred's plate before heading out the door and around town in his car.

David felt as though his confidence lifted him ten feet off the ground. He caught a few stares as he rode like a schoolboy down the streets, waving with one hand or sticking both feet straight out to the side as he coasted down a hill. His lucky suit had made its way out of the closet that morning: a blue suit with ruffled cuffs and a rounded hat. He was a spectacle on the streets, but then again, it was L.A. Telling himself that he shouldn't count his chickens before they hatch, he kept the ride short and headed back to the apartment to focus his efforts on securing other offers. Nonetheless, he couldn't keep from humming the fa-la-la's of the "Merry Month of May" until the sun went down.

CHAPTER 16

"In the Making"

Sarah visited the Sunshine Herbs shop and curiously presented the code word that Jack had given her. She had expected to find a dread-locked headband-wearing hippie standing by a Bob Marley poster. Instead, the shop was white and tidy; a young woman in a cardigan and short braid was waiting behind a counter ready to help. Unsure as to how to go about it, Sarah first meandered her way around the shop, touching various bottles on the shelves while glancing at the lady behind the counter, who was busy reading her book most of the time. Finally she worked up her courage to head to the counter.

"Hi, there," the woman offered a friendly smile.

"Hi, ummm … I'm here for sunflower dances?" Sarah clumsily recited what she had been told.

The woman simply nodded and motioned for her to come behind the counter. "Just leave your ID and doctor's report on the counter, and I'll take you back."

I don't have a medical report, but a mutual friend thought I might be able to get a short interview with the owner.

"Wait here and I'll see if he can spare a minute," the woman replied with a look of derision.

Sarah looked around the small store taking in everything she could in hopes she would be able to use the memories in her article. As she stared at the labels on various items she was interrupted by a man's voice.

"You want an interview with me?"

"Yes, I ..."

Sarah turned and her train of thought was broken when she stared into a very familiar face.

"Aren't you Larry, from UCLA?" she asked.

One look into her eyes and Larry recognized the girl who sat with him years before discussing the movement to legalize cannabis.

"So, you still fighting the battle or have you switched to using? I think I remember you saying you didn't use back in college?"

"Actually I'm trying to do some research into the 'behind-the-scene' activities to get a grasp on just what it takes to provide medicinal marijuana to those who need it to lead a reasonably good life and I'm really hoping you can help me. Nothing too detailed or incriminating. I think I remember you offering to help me in any way you could that day we met."

"Believe it or not, I do remember even though I think I was pretty wasted at the time."

That was the beginning of an eye-opening lecture on the varietals of the marijuana plant. Not wanting to bombard him right away with her journalistic questions, she instead purchased a few samples (which she had little intent for using) and guaranteed she would return. The plan was to be sure he trusted her first instead of causing any reason for skepticism.

Sarah used the weed she purchased to offer "sunshine brownies" at parties, and some people offered to pay her by the pan to make them. After nearly two months, Sunshine Herbs and Larry behind the desk had become her "in." She had eventually revealed to him her intentions, and he surprisingly complied with answering questions, though he wouldn't give names for any other growers or distributors. For that, he suggested that she go undercover and join the underground.

Sarah politely declined the suggestion, remaining convinced that among the millions of users, growers, and dealers out there she could find some willing to share their voice with a journalist. She did a lot of her general research at parties, spending time and talking with marijuana users. It was the growers and dealers that were difficult to come by. Any time she got a lead and introduced herself, she was immediately shut out. Understandably, it was apparent that a foundation of trust was needed first.

Her "rainy day" cash fund had disappeared towards the end of the year. Nearly all of her time was devoted to her piece, only working the weekends as a waitress—not nearly enough money to cover her monthly costs. She knew that she would have to find a way to make more money by the end of the Christmas holiday, balancing her time between earning a living and continuing her project.

Walking across *Kungsträdgården* Park one night while visiting friends in Stockholm, she smelled that familiar, earthy smell. She looked around but saw no smokers. "That would really give my piece a boost … international perspective," she thought to herself. The crunch of her boots in the snow provided a melodic rhythm as her brain turned over more ideas. Rumored to have been a relatively tolerant place for mild drugs in the 1960s—illegal still, but tolerantly illegal —Sarah noticed a distinct change in the decade. It became a largely political game fostered by the *Riksförbundet Narkotikafritt Samhälle*, Sweden's national union for a narcotics-free society. Media, police, and politicians suddenly seemed to be cohorts in a nationwide drug scare. Even just passing a joint was now considered trafficking.

Talking to anyone besides her friends about marijuana during her short visit proved nearly impossible, as it would take a lot more than a few days. Still, it gave her a great idea to expand her research into other cultures. From California, she could easily reach both Mexico and Canada, and it would surely make for an award-winning piece. She was well aware that controversy made a good story, and if done well, this piece could throw her into the literary spotlight.

The winters of her two homes, Sweden and California, were as different as night and day. She was happy to look out over palm trees as the plane landed and stuff her coat into her luggage when she picked it up from baggage claim. Arriving back in L.A. had its disadvantages, however, as the reality of Sarah's stuffed apartment and drained savings account confronted her all at once.

For the rest of the week, Sarah stayed inside except to shop for groceries, eat a sushi lunch, and visit the library to check out some VHS documentaries for inspiration. She reviewed the information she had collected so far and began the opening paragraphs of her article. The first few paragraphs were written and thrown away day after day. What she had was okay; she still needed more dirt to stand out among the rest. Maybe going undercover wasn't a bad idea. Though she needed some money, it would give her the perspective she was looking for—the means by which to extract more real field material.

Sarah didn't really pin herself as the drug dealing type, but maybe that was all the better to steer clear of the police. "Certainly a new adventure," she thought to herself. "It's what a serious journalist would do, after all." She finally convinced herself it wasn't a bad idea, and a surge of motivation held her confidence in place. She crumpled yet another start of the article, threw the ball of paper across the room towards the trash can, and laced up her boots for a ride down to Sunshine Herbs. It was time to learn how to really get involved in the business.

"You think you can pull it off?" "Larry" smiled at her.

"I'm ready to do it. I wanna sell. How do I start?" Sarah was surprised at how confident she both sounded and felt.

"First, you need to buy in; get a stash from a grower you like, then establish your clientele—hard and easy all at the same time. You have a lot of smokers in L.A., but a lot of dealers are already established ... and very territorial. I might suggest you brush up on your Spanish and, as a favor to me, find a location outside my area."."

"I was thinking of paying a visit to Mexico soon ..."

"I wouldn't go trying to smuggle any across the border on your own, but then again that's me, and then again you don't exactly look like the drug dealing type."

"So, can I buy from you?"

"You know my product. Tell me what you want. And I'll tell you what—I think I can trust you after all this time. I'll give you the name of another small grower. Tell him I sent you, and you shouldn't have any problem. That is, only if you purchase from me first."

"All right, I'm in! Why don't you give me a mix—a bag of each."

Larry did the calculations for each bag and turned the calculator around for the total. "Holy shit." Sarah slumped in her chair. Do you take instalments?

"No way, no how. It's cash up front only."

The total would wipe out the rest of what Sarah had. It meant she would have to sell quickly if she wanted to eat by the end of the month. She gave her word in a handshake, promising to be back that evening with the cash and a backpack for pick-up.

CHAPTER 17

"Shadows"

David had placed the "Madame Butterfly" record in his player and now sat with his eyes closed, listening to the melodies and crackle of the flames. He was mourning the loss of a dream with each burning page, but just as the phoenix is born again from the ashes, he was confident that another adventure lay ahead. The smell of the ash lingered bitterly in his nose as he closed his eyes and reflected on the piece of himself now encompassed in those flames and disintegrated to nothing but dust—black like the ink that once graced the pages.

After eighteen months of many meetings and phone calls, none of the patents had provided any promise of production. Nearly every day had been devoted to securing a deal, and he just needed one. He wanted his name on something and didn't want to give up, but he had taken the quest as far as he could go. Mr. Fred West had called him several times to remind him of the dismal sum that David owed. Luckily, some of the telephones he had put into production sold, but not enough for his financial channel to feel that it was a good investment. There was still money lost, and now David was being pressed to come up with the difference. He had no money to spare, which meant that he would soon commit to the drudgery of well-paid, steady work.

The original patents and blue prints for each invention were still in David's closet, locked in a filing cabinet. Burning the rest of the pamphlets, copies, and letters was a symbolic gesture to let this chapter rest in peace; a release of the frustration from temporary failure. The flames eventually died to tiny specks of orange and red, protesting their death in the soot that was left behind. Nonetheless, he wouldn't let it get him down.

The most sensible option seemed to be a return to banking. It paid well, at least. "I'll just work long enough to save up a sum and get on with something more interesting. I'm not getting any younger. Maybe I should do something like Everest ... who am I kidding? I'm in no shape for that." David talked to himself out loud, now sitting on his couch smoking a long, hand-carved pipe that had been given to him by one of his pothead buddies—the real wake-and-bake kind. He chose to use it for tobacco instead. "Thinking of the devil, we need to get together."

As he sat there feeling dejected, on the opposite wall of his apartment his painting of Pinkie seemed to float in the blue haze emitting from the pipe, her always alluring violet eyes reanimating a childish memory that always put a smile on his face and just a touch of regret in his heart. Destiny had brought them close so many times but he had never managed to actually find her again. So he had lived with his memory of Sarah in the form of his version of Pinkie.

"Maybe I could sell some quick copies of old masterpieces or market my by-the-number painting technique," he thought. But then the reality of his situation hit him and he realized he had no time to take on either of those far-fetched plans.

A throaty barking disturbed his thoughts. David made his way across the dated brown-tiled floor to answer the summoning of his seal-shaped telephone; one he had invented. He hesitated to answer at first, afraid it would be Mr. West giving him a miserable ultimatum. Deciding that hiding wasn't going to help him any, he answered the phone with a quivering "Hello."

David set the classifieds section of the newspaper on his coffee table as a reminder to check into any job opportunities that were even slightly less boring than banking. For now, though, he needed to apply for some

guaranteed income before meeting Danny for drinks. He
pulled out a blue suit from his closet—one that the general
public found as acceptable work attire—and added his own
usual twist with a bow tie and buckle loafers. To the banks
he went, pushing off on one foot and effortlessly swinging
the other over his penny farthing bike. Though the thought
of being behind a bank counter again was dismal, he was
hoping for a job by the end of the week to pay off his debt.

"Look at you, fancy man. Am I worthy of your
presence?" Danny teased. He had already been waiting for
David at Founders. They looked a world apart: David with
his slick-combed medium-length hair topping his only
slightly-quirky outfit, and Danny in his crocheted bill cap
that matched his orange suede jacket draping over his bony
shoulders.

"I was trying to pick up a new job at a bank this
afternoon. Have to conform somewhat to society, eh?" He
waived for the waitress to bring a beer.

"But you hate doing that. It drags you down, man."

"Yeah, well, I have a pretty steep bill to pay off. Your
buddy, Mr. West, has been suggesting that I might have an
unfavorable future if I don't make good on my debt. I'm

not sure how long I can put him off, but I figured if I can start making payments to him, he might back off a little. Do you think you could, maybe, talk to him?"

"Well, hey man, you know, I warned you about his financing requirements. I hope you don't blame me for your problem."

"No, it's just that I was sure at least one of my ideas would sell big. I guess I over-estimated the public's need for whimsical gadgets."

"Look, I don't need to see the guy any more than is absolutely necessary but, if you want some extra cash, there are people who can use your financial skills but can't advertise in the traditional way. Know what I mean?

Leaning in he added, "You know, the money has to go somewhere."

That sounded a lot more interesting than helping people deposit and withdraw money from their regular accounts every day. He looked around the bar to wager how safe it was to have such a discussion there. The tables immediately next to them were vacant, but the place was busy enough to be buzzing with noise. David scooted his chair in a little closer as he said, "So, what exactly do you need?"

"Well first of all, it would be helpful if you were still working at a bank. I've already got my system set up, but for example, I know a woman who needs to start doing something with some of her stash."

"A woman?"

"Yeah, man. Seems surprising, but she's a force."

"More power to her. Not that I've really met any dealers besides you, but I've always just pictured men."

"Yep. She's quite the deal, though—up and coming at quite a pace."

"What exactly are people's needs? How do you clean out your money?"

Danny wore a half grin on his face. "Let's say that my money is very international. Pesos, Columbia, and imported goods all have something to do with it. I don't like to share too much with people because it's a pretty brilliant scheme we have going on. If it grows too much in popularity, it runs a higher risk of being exposed. What I would recommend is either some offshore accounts …

we're talking Hong Kong, Panama, the Bahamas … or shell companies."

"You remember my mom works for the IRS?"

"Yeah man, doesn't that make it wild? Classic! It sounds like the kind of thing you'd do, though—a little bit of adventurous problem-solving, a hint of danger …"

"Maybe a little more than a hint," David laughed, raising his hand to order another beer. "This is perfect! Man, earlier today I was so down about going back to work at a bank. By the way, a few of my stops seemed promising. I'd be willing to bet that I'll be back at a bank by the end of next week."

"You're the perfect candidate for a money laundering operator."

"Tell me more about these shell companies you mentioned."

They allowed the conversation to cease a moment as the waitress approached the table. The waitress delivered David's beer order causing a momentary lull in the conversation. "Keep the change, honey," Danny gave her a smile and lengthy once-over as she left with their money.

As she disappeared Danny regained his thoughts. "Cheers to making trouble in an all new way." The clinking of their glasses seemed to be like the starting bell for David's new business.

"Speaking of, do you know where 'cheers' comes from?"

"No, but …"

"No, really, this could be important for you. They used to clash their glasses in such a way that the liquid would exchange cups. That way, if anyone was trying to poison the other, they would also get some of the poison into their own glass. It created trust. If you get too far into this business, you may want to be sure you're clanking your tequila shots hard enough."

"I'll keep that in mind."

"So anyway, the shell companies …" Danny waived on. "I think this would be good for you. You're smart and inventive. What you need to do is create a real, live business that seems to sell something but actually doesn't. It actually just takes in the dirty money and makes it look like it's coming from a real source. Laundromats, car washes …"

David nodded slowly as his head began to turn with ideas. His excitement continued to mount as he began hashing out business strategies. As the plans continued to evolve, they grabbed napkin after napkin to note important details. Four beers each and a large basket of fish and chips later, David felt more than ready to dig in his heels.

"So, you're going to help me gain some clientele?"

"I'll set you up with one, and I'm sure you'll be able to take it from there."

"This girl, right? Is she a looker?"

It doesn't matter because you'll probably never meet her. It's safer for both of you that way. I'm not guaranteeing anything. I'm just betting that she'll need someone to help her with her inflow, and I bet you can start up quite a laundering business."

Danny grabbed one of David's napkins and wrote down a name and number. "This is her right-hand man. I'll give him a call. He'll check with her and then get back to you."

"Right-hand man? Wow, I'm impressed by this lady."

"You should be."

David happily pedaled home, feeling lighter from the certainty that his debt wouldn't be a problem, certain that better times were coming, and not giving a second thought about the type of people he was about to meet.

CHAPTER 18

"Growing"

Sarah drove through the Mainstream Car Wash; her shiny black Chevy not exactly looking like it needed much of a wash. To an observant eye, it may have looked strangely unnecessary for her to be there; however, there was no one around to witness. Only two other cars graced the presence of the remote parking lot. Sarah usually had Joey do her drop-offs, but she wanted to check out this "business" in which she had been investing.

"Inside detail, boys." Sarah swung her legs out of the car, her long pink dress wrapping around them with grace as her gloved hands handed the keys over. She did not to get too friendly or personal with anyone, keeping her sunglasses on and her large hat atop her head. As the young gentlemen took her car keys, clearly understanding the orders, she nonchalantly began to wander around the premise, arriving back to the front desk.

"Things look good," she seriously stated to the other young man behind the counter wearing a shiny silver-colored name pin read "Benjamin."

"Yes."

"Ma'am," she demanded.

"Yes, ma'am," he repeated, widening his eyes.

"Anything I need to be aware of?"

"No, ma'am. We've had a few extra customers, but no need to be concerned about them. We have them all on video if you'd like to see them."

"Well, it'll be your head if anything happens, so I assume you're alert about everything."

He gave a nervous nod.

"It's not a bad gig for you, kid. Lighten up, and just focus on keeping a tight ship." Sarah still felt too out of her comfort zone to be a hard, cold drug lord. It was a face she had learned to wear, though. At home, she was so happy to put it away and relax with old movies and ice cream when she had the time. It was then that she would smile in the mirror, just to feel more like herself.

The other young man had come back with her car only a few minutes later. After doing her own inspection of the trunk, she sped off to check in on her supply man. When Sarah began dealing, she never dreamed it would get this far. Initially, it had been for project advancement. Each move was just to get more backstage information. It was all paving the way to a Pulitzer Prize-winning article that would give her national recognition and lead to other journaling opportunities; perhaps for the newly-established CNN or *The New York Times*. She was sure that this piece would showcase her raw talents and dedication. Dreams of the future once again teased her mind. She would submit her article to all the famous journals. A few days later, she would receive multiple calls to discuss her brilliant writing and how she had gotten all of the insider information. After it was published, Ted Turner himself would call her up. He would tell her how he had read it that morning and had to call right away. He wanted her on his research team—digging to get the real and raw information. Maybe she would even do a special performance with David Walker.

That was how it was supposed to go. She had figured six months in the business would be long enough to dig up the real information behind-the-scenes and make the right connections. Everything just kept snowballing, though. She had surprised herself by selling out of her first stash in just a few days. Her father's advice rang through her head: "Acting is most of the game. If you act the part, people will believe you." Of course, he probably never intended that advice to be used for selling drugs.

As far as her parents were concerned, she was making most of her money as a waitress. As money started coming in, she had to give some excuse for her apartment upgrade and extra cash, so she offered the explanation of continuous promotions and finally moving on to a prestigious restaurant in town. Of course, they insisted on trying the restaurant during their next visit. Unsure of how to dodge the bullet, Sarah told them that she would be too embarrassed to have them there. Family vacations had indeed become a sticky part of the operation. With American vacation time being significantly less than any of its European counterparts, she had fallen back lately on the excuse that in order to have the longer Christmas vacations, she could only spend weekends with them during the summer holiday. Still, with weekends as prime selling time, she had needed help clearing her stash, so she had hired one of her regulars. Coming back from the first weekend with her parents, Sarah found herself pleasantly surprised with this order of business. While her profits were smaller, she skipped the leg work and still made money.

After returning from the weekend and catching up on that August Monday, she sat at her old typewriter to make some more notes that evening:

Note: first time using a lackey gave me

small insight about how the tiers of dealing work. I can purchase more, disperse, give small profits to my sellers, and keep a decent portion myself. Less work on my part, but larger risk.

Requirements: a frequent enough mass purchase, lackeys to sell, a large market or target audience, the best quality cannabis (without getting killed for infringing on someone's territory; small parties won't be enough to sustain).

Questions: What are the essential qualities for a leader? Is it possible to 'take over' other territories?"

Sarah had been doing well enough on her own at that point to acquire a second, larger apartment closer to her business sources, maintaining her little studio apartment to satisfy her need for a place to retreat; some place not tied to her activities. Her studio was where she could be just Sarah. Money wasn't exactly in abundance, but at least she wasn't cooking meals in her bedroom anymore. Hot dogs were still on the menu too often, and the penny-farthing her parents bought her as a graduation present was still the main mode of transport. She had only ever seen one other like it in all of L.A., once curiously parked outside a bank. The saving grace of her sacrifices was that one day she would be a renowned journalist. Though she had to be honest with herself that it wasn't so bad: she was essentially only working part-time hours — certainly not at a grueling job—with plenty of time to take notes and write portions of her article. Her routine was not bad at all, once she got over the initial discomfort she felt in the business.

From that weekend, Sarah began slowly collecting other dealers and buying larger stashes at a time, which set her into the "discount" bracket of purchasing. At the end of the day, it never quite seemed a reality to her. A limit had been reached, though. She had taken over small weekend parties, university advocacy groups, and students here and there. There was no more room to expand on the streets without overtaking someone else's territory.

"Miss, unless you're ready to back me up with whatever artillery you've got out there, I don't get paid enough for that shit," one of her girls had told her after Sarah suggested that she sell in one of the parks. "All I did was meet someone there once for a deal and boom —out of nowhere, someone's there threatening to slice my ear off if

I ever try to sell there again. Uh-uh, I'm not doin' that shit."

Sarah wasn't so sure she was ready to take on well-established drug lords—failing to acknowledge that she was becoming a drug lord herself. Her team wanted more, though. They complained about wanting more than just enough to sell at a weekend party, and Sarah certainly didn't mind that they wanted more. After some individual discussions with her girls, she decided it was time for a team meeting. Maybe it was a little unorthodox in this line of work, but hey, she was an unorthodox kind of lady.

Some wine glasses and two tall red wine bottles sat in the middle of a large, cold concrete floor. These sat on top of a stripped blanket along with Sarah, sitting with her feet gracefully swept to the side, waiting for her staff to arrive. Candles encircled the blanket, providing the only light other than that which peeked in through several windows. Arriving nearly all together to the half-constructed business complex, Sarah poured each a glass of wine, raising hers to clink glasses with them all.

"Do you know where the tradition of toasting glasses comes from?" She went on to explain the story from centuries past. "We didn't exchange wine between our glasses, but I can assure you none of you will be poisoned tonight. We're here to discuss an expansion of territory, as you have expressed your individual desires to expand your own sales opportunities. Angela, you've already experienced a run-in at Holmby Park with one of the Lone Wolf crew. My business model is to use my head first, not my guns, so we'll go about expansion without resorting to violence. We'll do it with wits and class, and the first places to look are gaps we can fill. Next, we'll look for ways to slowly edge out the competition. Any thoughts?"

"Well, we just target college kids and young adults right now. Let's be real, though, everyone smokes grass. What about more working people? Middle-aged white collar? Or even old people? You know they need it for 'medical purposes.'"

"Great. I feel the medical field is already taken care of. I don't yet see a void there. Most suppliers either grow themselves or buy directly from the grower."

"But what if we made special brownies and took them to retirement communities? I'll bet those oldies would love that stuff."

Sarah held in a laugh, trying to maintain her presence

as the dominating boss.

"Are you willing to take that on, Erica?"

"Yeah, sure."

"Yes, ma'am," Sarah corrected her with stern eyes.

"Yes, ma'am," she repeated.

"All right, next we're talking about white-collar business workers. This week, I'll take some samples out with some doughnuts and start the talk. We'll start with that and see where it goes. I'll appoint you accordingly as opportunities open."

Sarah couldn't believe how her confidence was soaring. She felt cool and level-headed, in-charge, and ready to organize an entire caravan of street-level dealers. The business model seemed to flow out of her as she continued speaking with her group. She may not have felt like a drug boss, but she sure felt like she knew how to run the business. Details seemed to just flow out of her mouth, even without the permission of her brain.

"I'm only willing to buy top notch, okay, so this is how you sell ... we're providing a superior service —

above and beyond the cheap street-level. We're going to hone in on a line of products which people will know comes specifically from us. Let's call this 'Acapulco Gold.' At first, while we're building clientele, I'll make small sample bags for you to hand out to potentially high-paying clients."

"Wow, high-class weed dealers," Erica pitched in.

"That's right. This is not a drug gang; this is a cannabis business. You've all asked for more to distribute, and this is how my business will be developed. Let me know if you are or aren't interested. The more you sell, the larger your cut will be."

Sarah envisioned an office, business cards, and a growing employee base. She needed space, a right-hand man, and to establish herself as a serious buyer. Up to that point, she had only been buying from the lot behind Sunshine Herbs. That week, initially unbeknownst to her, she had shifted her focus.

The typewriter received zero attention in the weeks to come. Instead of seeking out information and contacts for the purpose of typing notes and article paragraphs, she was charging ahead on the business front. The notes changed from thoughts about what the inside trade was like to scribbles on paper about business ideas, to-do lists, and potential clientele.

Happy Acres, Healing Gardens, and no-name back-of-the-house gardens were on the list of visits. Sarah enjoyed herself more than she would have imagined, visiting the likes of people who gave themselves names such as "Old Man Fishy" and "Bangi" (Swahili for marijuana). She felt a connection with these quirky characters who enjoyed the feel of the earth on their hands. This was the target grower—not some string-bean post-college kid growing sub-par plants along the fence in his backyard so that he could make some cash handing it off. Sarah was picky. The ultimate goal was to have someone growing exclusively organic, high-quality heirloom strains just for her. First, she had to show them she was worth that investment.

Sarah's footprints had traipsed through all kinds of terrain on her search. She had followed growers as they pushed their way through tall bushes, dodged around bamboo shoots, ducked through hidden entrances inside nondescript sheds, and trampled with large rubber boots over hoards of sticker bushes. Farmer Bud had greeted her with a shotgun by his side and a beekeeper hat adorning his head; her favorite first impression. Bud claimed to have been in the business for twenty years and was sure to make the point several times that he didn't just sell to anyone— or even just meet with anyone for that matter. It was only with the right connections that he had agreed to meet Sarah, who had already chosen a business code name of Belladonna. Her code name was a flower also known as Deadly Nightshade because of its potentially lethal effects if ingested.

Bud handed her a beekeeper suit to zip up and led her past hundreds of hives before arriving to his plants. Though he maintained his stoic appearance throughout her visit, it was clear that her search for the ideal grower had come to a close. The pride in Bud's plants was evident in his lengthy explanations of plant care and varieties. Sarah managed to keep her excited comments to herself and instead worked on her straight-forward, serious demeanor that demanded respect.

Bud's product proved to have the desired quality that Sarah was looking for, based on the popular demand it immediately created. Her plan had been spot on—playing the business game with business people. She had wagered on the professional business potential of Larry's brother—a suggestion Larry had made, as he was unable to hire Ricky himself for anything at the shop. Sarah gave the conditions that he start with a one-month unpaid trial period, but in the first week of distributing samples and marketing to their new targets, Ricky showcased his skills as an operating manager and got hired soon after.

From there, they established an undercover office hidden by the facade of an antique costume shop. There was certainly nothing suspicious about Sarah running such a shop, and the number of truly interested customers would be substantially lower than, say, a bicycle shop. Among the stock of costumes in the back was a desk, a safe box, some extra chairs, and wrapping supplies. It was everything her ground runners needed to be organized and deliver their top quality product inconspicuously.

The few girls she had started the business with had now grown to be an employee base of eight street sellers, plus Ricky. She had only taken on anyone by recommendation, and they all started on a trial basis. Bud had agreed to farm a portion of his land only for her as long as she gave him an upfront compensation. Everything was falling into place, and though Sarah felt strange admitting it to herself, she was proud. She was proud that she was accomplishing something she would have thought was out of her realm. Also, she was quickly and naturally succeeding with the respect—and dare she say fear—of many.

Larry had become a close friend, confidant, and source of valuable advice for her. He was the only one who actually knew what her original intentions had been. On a number of occasions they got together, he would try to push her into a larger variety of product.

"You've got this down. You know, they say crack is going to be the next marijuana. Why not expand—stake an early claim on the market?"

"Because I believe in people being able to smoke pot. It's a mood lifter, a stress reducer, and a symptom reliever for many illnesses. Crack's not the same thing. I'm not advocating its use."

It all seemed a bit ironic to Sarah, nonetheless. She didn't smoke weed, but she very successfully sold it.

CHAPTER 19

"Territories"

Sarah played around with the brass key in the lock until it turned, mumbling a curse and a promise that she needed to get the locks on the store changed soon. As she stood there in the doorway, the thought crossed her mind that maybe she couldn't get the key to work properly because the door had been unlocked. She shook off the feeling, chalking it up to paranoia.

No one ever likes Mondays. It was her day to check in with all of her lackeys, place another order with Bud, and wrap up some nice samples for more potential high-class clientele. She sighed as she noticed one of her mannequins knocked over, dangling in the arms of another with her clothes disheveled. "Romantic," she half chuckled out loud to herself. Time to straighten up and make the business look like it was actually in operation.

As Sarah flipped on the light, she felt her body freeze in shock at the figure sitting behind the counter. The flash thought went through her mind that she was glad she didn't scream or jump. She reached her hand into her satchel to feel the gun she had recently purchased; a recommendation of Larry to carry as an extra precaution.

"No need, Belladonna. You can feel safe for now. This is only a warning visit."

Sarah was calm but firm, standing tall before her opponent. "I assume you're here with something to say. Get on with it." She put on the most piercing look that she could muster.

"You are selling in our territory."

"I haven't taken over anyone's territory. We opened up our own demand."

"No. One of your sellers was spotted making a deal in the Inglewoods. That's mine, and if you don't want a bloody battle, then you'd better stay out of it. Maybe you haven't been selling long enough in this area to know the rules of the game, but you just broke them." The bald, bulky man remained unmoved, hands folded atop the counter with an unwavering stare.

"You sell on the streets. That's not what we're doing. We have our own game, and we're playing fairly."

"If you want to sell in that area, you owe me a

twenty percent cut."

"I have clients you would never touch. They're mine, fair and square."

"If you want to invent a new game, perhaps we will play by new rules. Let's see if you like my rules." With that he didn't give her another look. He simply walked straight out the front door; Sarah herself staring straight ahead at the empty chair he had just occupied and reminding herself to breathe.

"Wow," she stated out loud to herself after she heard the door close behind her. "Okay." She turned back around to lock the door so she could re-group her thoughts. Not more than five minutes later, she felt her heart jump at the sound of a knock behind her. Turning calmly, she was relieved to see Ricky and opened the door for him.

"What's with hanging out inside the door with the shop locked?" he asked in a teasing manner.

"Who's over at the Inglewood territory?" she responded with a straight face.

"That's one of Quintaro's. He claims that and a few others like Westchester and Santa Monica. He's quite a force."

"Well he was just here. He's angry that one of ours was spotted selling in Inglewood. Who has a building down there?"

"I'm not sure. We'll have to check."

"We offer something to clientele he would never be able to reach, so he'll just have to move over."

Ricky looked back at her with raised eyebrows. "As the saying goes, sometimes discretion is the better part of valor."

"Look, I only plan on expanding, so ... speaking of which, I don't want to use this store for all my laundering anymore. I need something else, something more. I need to outsource to someone trustworthy who will handle my finances—a CFO. I think I'd rather keep this set-up with companies and cooked books than offshore accounts. Do you know anyone?"

"As a matter of fact, my buddy was just asking if we needed any financial help. A friend of his works for a bank and manages money. All you do is give it to him and he'll set up the clean filtering."

"A banker sounds both smart and risky. He should be well-equipped, but at the same time, he makes a good set-up for a rat."

"This guy likes life on the edge. He actually hates banking, and this makes it more interesting for him. You want me to contact him and have a chat?"

"Do that, and then let's talk about it again. I'll probably want to talk to him myself over the phone."

Ricky dialed the phone number that Danny had passed on to him and demanded a meeting with David the next afternoon. Ricky was skeptical about his lack of experience, but David talked a convincing game. He had brought with him a notebook to pencil down Ricky's requests and stipulations, then drew up a general plan by the end to take back to his boss. David thought Ricky's mention that Sarah owned a car wash to help launder her money was quite humorous and brilliant.

Sarah looked over the page that Ricky returned to her that afternoon, skipping any word usage and only using head gestures of approval instead.

"I'm impressed that he has an initial plan drawn up. So, you feel confident with him?"

"I did. His knowledge and aptitude for the job is certainly solid."

"Okay. Check into him more. Dig up any small and interesting details. I'll give him a call later when I decide to make the move.. I'm heading over to Bud's for a quality check right now." Sarah tucked the paper with a phone number into her bag and left Ricky manning the store.

On her way out to the farm, Sarah thought about all the unusable money sitting under the trap door of the store's backend. She could only cook the books of a small shop so much, and the pile was almost beginning to outgrow her little storage space. Not to mention, she had a few modest purchases in mind that she'd like to make. She trusted Ricky's business sense, and this David character seemed to have a good head on his shoulders. She wanted to be sure he'd be up for her up-and-coming plans for expansion, starting with Mexico. This had better be someone who was willing to handle large business across international borders. Instead, she decided to save her time and wait to speak with him after Ricky finished checking into his background and personal details. During the rest of her drive to the farm, Sarah contemplated what she would do once her hidden money was clean and usable. The key was modest usefulness, but she already had a few plans in mind.

CHAPTER 20

"Inspiration"

David put on his usual suit with a twist. It was another dull day at the bank: greeting customers with a cheesy smile, taking their deposit slips, handing out and receiving money ... But now David went in each day with a lighter skip to his step. He was mastering a new business day by day. Sure enough, he had passed through the interview and received a phone call from the elusive yet supposedly powerful Belladonna.

His imagination ran away with him during his phone conversation with the mysterious woman. In a foreign accent he could not place, she hammered him with questions about his family, particularly his mom's employment with the IRS. She had preceded such questions with serious threat of repercussion should he be lying or hiding any intentions. Through her firing inquisition, he was taking in the sound of her voice and creating a face to match it. As their conversation evolved, so did his vision of her. In his head, she started out as a short, stout, butch-like woman, but as the conversation evolved, she changed form into a tall, slender brunette with long hair who was holding the phone with gloved hands and puffing on a long, slim cigarette. Though her voice and questions rang serious and firm, he suspected a deep sensitivity about her.

By the end of the conversation, she offered him a fair cut for his work with expected stipulations. First, she let him know that she would be his sole customer. He had countered with an agreement to the stipulation, so long as his minimum cut didn't go below twelve hundred per month. She agreed. Next, she warned him that he would be involved in international business, as she was planning a trip to Mexico. He informed her that he would brush up on his Spanish. Lastly, he surprised her by placing another clause on their relationship.

"Should you sell anything but cannabis, I will drop my services."

"Interesting proposition. I'm curious to hear why," she inquired.

"I previously participated in the decriminalization of marijuana activities because I believe in its benefits. Even though a lot of people just use it recreationally, I believe in its purity as an herb. Thousands suffer from adverse effects of pharmaceutical drugs annually, yet this

natural medicine is illegal. I think it's all the work of the
pharmaceutical companies handing out money to the
government. There's multiple sclerosis, glaucoma, arthritis,
depression, and symptoms of many other serious diseases.
Why shouldn't people have access to this natural healer? I
personally don't smoke it, but I certainly don't see why
God put it on this earth otherwise. All natural. I'm sorry,
tangent over. Anyway, I'm not willing to aid in the sale and
use of any other drug, save peyote perhaps."

"We are on the same wavelength, and you have my
word that I do not plan to sell anything else—not even
peyote, sorry to say. I do, however, sell to anyone who
wants it. I don't limit my sales by questioning the
intentions of those who buy. I'm quite removed from the
clients by now, anyway, as I have an excellent team of
sellers. Ricky, whom you met, will be your contact. I need
at least one business up fast, as I've got a growing mound.
Then we'll expand from there. Ricky will get you an
upfront sum tomorrow to get things started."

David began his work that day, scoping out
businesses, properties, and setting up the accounts. He was
glad she wanted to stay local instead of dealing with
offshore accounts, layering, and re-integrating the money.
The pesos and international currencies would be another

ballgame once she had that up and running, though.

David cruised the L.A. outskirts with a Coke and hamburger in hand, thinking about what he would do with the extra money. He calculated in his head that the debt should be payable within twelve months, provided Mr. West was willing to wait that long. With the exception of this looming financial responsibility, David was pretty satisfied with life. After the debt was resolved, he would live as he preferred—making the most of each day with no ties, obligations, or dependencies—although a new car might help.

Having made his way within a two to three hour radius of the city, David congratulated himself for an entire day spent in the car. However, his drive was not all in vain. He had collected a long list of possible businesses, buildings, and lots to buy. One of them was listed as a "quick sale," which sent off the signals of perfection. The owner would likely be willing to do the transaction quickly under the table for cash. He turned out to be exactly right, reporting to Ricky the next day that they had a second rundown car wash to buy. He knew he was already on the path to being a successful launderer.

David maintained his front at the bank to keep up

appearances and closely monitor Belladonna's accounts himself. What he didn't count on was how much extra time it would take to manage and clean dirty money. He managed the employees at three locations now, plus all the money's inflow and outflow.

Sarah swung her leg over the middle and dropped her feet down off her bike to come to a smooth stop in the front of the costume shop. Immediate rage ran through her veins as she stood and stared at the picture in front of her. Large, jagged holes donned each window on either side of the door. She grabbed the gun from her satchel, stepping inside through one of the holes and onto the broken glass. A noise from the corner turned her aim quickly that direction, but only a cat moved from the behind the rack. The racks remained untouched, but all of the mannequins were lying face down in a symbolic, macabre fashion. Though no one was in the front, she proceeded cautiously towards the rear of the store.

She nudged the door with her foot, allowing it to swing open. Entering slowly into the racks of extra clothing, she was sure after some minutes that no one was on site any longer. She checked the trap door for her stash of money, but it remained undiscovered. The next place she went was to the desk. There, she sat down to observe the damage. A hand had been dislocated from one of her mannequins and was holding the note,

"You invade our space, and we invade yours."

Furious, she began frantically opening all of the desk drawers, but they were empty. Not a paper left. Pulling the desk towards her to look behind, she saw nothing but a hole where the safe used to be. All of her contact information, plans, and records were gone, but that wasn't the problem. She had copies of everything at her original apartment—the studio that she had kept. She quickly picked up the telephone to have Erica come in as quickly as possible to start damage control and sped off on her bike towards the old apartment.

Upon her arrival, everything looked safe and intact. Even if they had known to go to this apartment, they would have had to search hard for the copies. There was no drawer or safe to pull them from there. Still, she entered slowly, gun in hand and prepared to use it. A small amount of relief came over her as she entered and saw that the apartment untouched. She certainly wasn't in the mood to deal with two messes. She went down the short hallway, looking tentatively into the bathroom and finally her bedroom. Satisfied that no one was there, she allowed herself to evaluate the overall situation. She was ready for a fight. Irrational thoughts began running through her mind, fueled by anger and the desire to retaliate. It was time to hunt down Quintaro's headquarters and pay him a friendly visit. She was ready for a personal confrontation, though she needed a sting of reciprocation to match his. She needed something of his: either his weed supplier, his clients, or his staff. Her first thoughts were to contaminate his next supply, creating a load of unsatisfied customers, but ethics won her over and gently urged her to leave his clients alone. The day called for a little more research into his operation before deciding on a course of action. And after that little mess was settled, it was definitely time to expand south of the border.

As she stood there in deep and volatile thought, the sound of footsteps from the living room seized her attention. She raised her gun and stood just inside the bedroom door, where she would be able to see anyone coming down the hallway. The steps came closer, and she all but stopped breathing. Suddenly, Ricky appeared at the end of the hallway.

"What the hell?" she shouted louder than she had intended due to the sudden release of stress.

Ricky jumped back, throwing his hands up and away from body showing he had no weapon.

"Shit … you scared the living hell out of me!" he said, lowering his hands slowly.

"What are you doing here?" she asked pointedly.

"Erica told me about the break-in, and I thought you might need some backup in case you ran into trouble. You know, chasing after the bad guys is never a good idea. It's usually better to run."

"Yeah, today has not been full of good ideas," she replied.

"Did they get anything?"

"They got all the records from the store, but nothing from here. We'd better get back and help clean up before the whole town knows about it."

Sarah locked the door, visibly agitated. What was it that was bothering her? She shook off the thought and climbed back on her bike as Ricky drove away.

Ricky ran his hand over his newly shaven head and

pushed his sandwich aside. "You gonna take him on?" he asked with his mouth full.

"Not necessarily. He just needs to know I'm not moving. He can have his clients and I can have mine, fair and square."

"People don't usually think of this business as fair and square, especially people like Quintaro."

"Well, I run a different game than he does, and I think there's room for us to coexist. We have different clientele."

"So, what do you propose?"

"I thought about tainting his next bulk supply to sabotage his customer base. Then, I thought about stealing all of his employees to come work for us. I never intended to sell to any of his regulars. In the end, though, I think I'll just give him a little nudge."

"I don't know that Quintaro will care about a 'nudge.'"

Though her employee base had now expanded to nine sellers, plus Ricky, Sarah still held meetings in the same fashion as that first night at the third floor of the vacant building, adding a bar stool for her to sit higher than the others. Everyone arrived to the back of the store after hours, greeted by a glass of wine waiting for them in the middle of the candle-lit circle.

"All right everyone, just a few items to discuss tonight." I know I sound repetitive, but everyone parked on the street at least a block away, right?" Everyone nodded. Sarah went on to discuss with them the latest territorial dispute. "I don't back down. Just be aware. Quintaro shouldn't have anything to do with you, but if anything comes up, notify me quickly and I will take care of it right away. I'm trying to keep things civil for now, but any involvement with my staff is over the line. Has anyone had any problems thus far that I don't know about?"

Sarah was happy to hear silence. "Great. Then speaking of territories, I'll be exploring a new set-up in the upcoming weeks. We are moving down to Mexico. Everything stays the same here. Now we're just starting to move internationally, and Mexico will be the first step since it is closest. After that's established, I'll look at heading north, as well. I, myself, will be down there a lot, and here's what that means for you: Number one, when I'm away, Ricky will be running things here. Number two: I will need a new operating manager in Mexico. I can find someone new of course, but if any of you are fluent in Spanish and are interested, let me know. Third, also if you're fluent, you're welcome to change locations once things are established. As I said, Mexico is only the first step, so if you think you'd be interested in international relocation at any point, just let me know of your interest. Is there anything anyone wants to talk about as a group before you go?"

They all remained silent, which Sarah took as satisfaction. "All right, then. Here's a sample of a new breed that our grower has worked on. Take it. Try it yourself or let your friends try and give me your feedback. Remember, all of our products are always organically grown."

Everyone grabbed a baggie from the basket as it passed by and stood up to socialize briefly before heading out the door. Sarah wouldn't have minded to join some of the chatter, but she made a conscious effort to separate herself as the authority figure. It didn't matter what business it was—illegal or not—they could all be run with some of the same principles: mutual employer/employee respect, to start with. Thus, it was her principle to treat her employees well, yet maintain her distance to establish authority.

As the first of her team headed for the stairwell an alarmed voice spoke out.

"Um, Belladonna? I think something is going down outside. There are several police cars heading this way without lights or sirens and one is already parked out front."

Sarah ran to the window, then turned to the others.

"Quick!" she shouted as she bent to blow out the candles. "Everyone down the back stairs quickly. Scatter two at a time. When you get clear of the building, walk slowly to blend in with others on the street. Don't return to your cars until everything clears! Got it?"

As her team vacated, Sarah threw the bottles into opposite corners, where they smashed and kicked the stool over into an empty side room. She wrapped the glasses in the table cloth and carried it down the stairs with her, hoping to avoid an encounter with the police. As she cleared the building, she headed down one of the adjoining streets where the nightlife was thin but adequate enough for her to blend into. Two blocks from the meeting site she dropped the table cloth and its contents into a half-filled garbage can.

***

Sarah kicked off her shoes as she sank onto the couch in her apartment. The adrenaline was beginning to abate and her shaking hands were the only remaining effects of the close encounter. Her mind was busy sorting out how the police came to know about her team meeting. Her first suspicion was that Quintaro had informed them. But then how did he know of the meeting? Was someone in her organization feeding information to Quintaro? Either way, she felt he was involved in some way and she decided she had to take action to let him know she could not be intimidated. If she did nothing, the pressure from Quintaro would continue. The issue had to be resolved once and for all and she would have to handle it alone to prevent her plans being leaked.

She waited for the night when one of Quintaro's main men would be bringing by the next delivery batch. Hiding in the shadows, a ski mask hiding her identity, as if she had been trained in such things, Sarah caught him by surprise from behind as he came around to the back of his van to unload. Clicking the gun held against his temple, she hit play on a voice recording, warning him to back away slowly with her and sit quietly in the corner. She slipped a canvass laundry bag over his head, then-handcuffed him to a pole and played the next part of the recording to let him know that if all went well, he would be un-cuffed within a few hours. After playing the entire recording, Sarah transferred the bags from the truck to a van she had acquired, drove to another part of town, hid the bags of weed and went to have a less-than-friendly chat with Quintaro.

Sarah waited outside the rear French doors of the address she had finally acquired for Quintaro, watching him drinking beer and eating peanuts while he stared at a television. From a corner phone booth a few minutes earlier she called the number she had scratched down on a piece of tablet paper. Her final recording had been a male voice reporting that someone had asked him to call this number and let someone know that he needed help with his truck, which had broken down some miles away, stranding him on the side of the road. She watched until Quintaro's two goons pulled out of the driveway, having fallen for the false call for assistance.

She walked in boldly and shot within a half inch of his foot. Quintaro sat calmly, staring at the television and not even acknowledging her presence.. "You should work

on your aim, princess, if you want to be taken half
seriously. I could have done you a favor to burn down your
shop instead."

As he reached for his shot glass on the table in front
of him, she instantly sent a bullet that shattered it to pieces.
"You don't want to test my aim," she said. "We have
'Black Jack,' as he called himself, waiting for your release,
as well as the delivery you're expecting. How many
thousands are in there? Looked like quite a lot. We need to
have a little talk first, though."

She placed a pen and paper down on a nearby table.
"I'd like to try to fight fairly before I get nasty, so let's
negotiate."

"What makes you think I need to do any negotiating
with you?"

Sarah was determined to bluff her way through this
meeting. Her acting instructions had prepared her for the
role and she played it perfectly.

"You're small-time, Quintaro. You talk big but
you've got no backup if things get heated. And believe me,
things are about to get very heated if you don't cooperate."

Quintaro put his arm up on the back of the couch and turned to face her, a false laugh shading his feelings. Was he confident, or just trying to appear so?

"I don't need backup to handle a child like you. You think you can take me on? Hell, your entire organization consists of a few street sellers and you. I'll bet you're the only one who owns a gun and the others wouldn't know what to do with one if you gave it to them. So, don't make empty threats against me 'cause I don't scare easy."

"Well, I'll admit you've done some of your homework," Sarah replied as she walked over and stood in front of the television, blocking Quntaro's view, "but it seems you've only checked out the local team."

"Local team? You saying there's more?" Quintaro replied in a doubtful tone.

"My partners, or let's just call them friends with financial interests in my business, they think you are becoming a thorn in their sides and that thorn needs to be removed. Like I said, I like to play fair first if I can, so I'm offering you a chance to make an agreement with me or deal with my partners. It's your choice."

"So you expect me to just turn over my business to you?"

"We're not interested in your business. If we were, you would already be gone. As I said before, we only deal in select markets," she assured him. "We don't want your business and we don't want your interference in ours. We just want a nice understanding that you will stay out of our business and stop playing junior mobster. Getting rid of you does us no good. If you move out, someone else will just move in and we'll have to go through all this again. That's time-consuming and a bit irritating."

Quintaro sat there weighing every statement, obviously irritated by being reprimanded by a woman but not certain who she spoke for. Perhaps in an attempt to save face, he smiled at Sarah.

"You know, sister, you've got guts and I can appreciate that. We've felt each other out and I think we can put that behind us. I just have to protect what's mine, you understand."

"Completely," was all she said.

She assertively assured Quintaro that she wouldn't take any of his current clients, and that her crew would stay off the streets. They drew up respective boundaries, both agreeing not to cross them.

"I'm expanding outside of the L.A. area. You have my word that I'll only stick to the office buildings we agreed upon in your area. This was my nice move. If you pull any bullshit again, I won't be so nice the next visit. Shall we?" she asked, standing up and extending a hand to shake. Quintaro looked at her hand, then up to her face with his narrowed gaze. He responded with some warnings of his own before Sarah informed him where to re-claim his delivery, made deliberate eye contact with him one last time, and with grace, walked out the door. She then stormed out the door.

Sarah kicked off her shoes at her apartment, allowing herself to laugh out loud as she poured some wine and threw herself down on the couch. She realized then that she hadn't touched her typewriter in nearly two weeks; nor had she spoken to her parents. Was this life overtaking her? She had convinced herself that she enjoyed it for the sake of research and undercover reporting—the cause of uncovering the real story of the world of cannabis. She questioned if her game had changed. What was she doing? She believed in freedom of choice in the matter, and she put herself on a higher ground since she wasn't selling on the streets or at college parties anymore. Now, here she was holding delivery men at gunpoint and visiting drug lords under the cover of night, but there was something stimulating about it. Her new life was exhilarating … thrilling … whatever words she could think of to express the giddy feeling that passed through her as she arrived through the door of her home. Was she really still writing an article? Inspired by recent events, she sat down at her typewriter—convinced that the international expansion would allow her to grasp the true world of growing, buying, and selling.

CHAPTER 21

"South of the Border"

Sarah pulled down her sunglasses and took another sip of Coca-Cola. They had stopped in Tucson the night before to break up the trip and make sure everything was ready for the border. Erica's half-brother, Mateo, was also half-Mexican He had been recommended by Ricky and volunteered his services for a descent sum. Sarah agreed to use him for the initial few months of set-up with further employment dependent on performance. He didn't leave the most trustworthy first impression, as he mostly wanted to discuss finances, but Sarah trusted her wits, briefing him on their two-week plan. It would be a busy few weeks, but it wasn't time to party and make friends. It was time to search for a CEO and drum up some interest.

Eventually, the idea was to have an entire operation set up just as she had in L.A.: a personal grower, an operating manager, sellers, and regular buyers. She tried to be realistic with herself about the time it would take and was prepared to do all of the initial legwork herself. It meant a lot of trips across the border, complete trust in Ricky, and hopefully not too much smuggling. This trip was easy. They were only bringing samples to get a client base rolling and show product to potential sellers. The small stash was carefully tucked away in the back seat cushion, Mateo's dog in the back with a meaty bone for good measure.

The last few days, she had practiced calm breathing and heart rate control exercises in front of her mirror at home in case any questions from border patrol should arise. Nogales wasn't the most common crossing for a California license plate, but they said they were visiting family after their recent engagement—hers in Arizona and his down in Hermosillo—which was indeed their final destination for the trip. One quick look at the massive dog protecting his meat bone was as close as they came to an inspection.

The crossing went more smoothly than Sarah expected, but then her dad always quoted to her, "Prepare for the worst and hope for the best." She was doubly relieved that she would only be carrying one way and that the hard part was over. They played their part well with no suspicion from the officer, and now they were cruising down the MEX-15D with her sunglasses on and Mateo snoozing in the passenger's seat.

She glanced over at him with a smile. He wasn't bad looking at all, really—not a bad view to have next to her on the drive, she thought. His build was full without being too bulky; his skin color, a beautiful mix of his mother's and father's. Too bad she didn't find that his inner beauty and intrigue matched the outside. Only a few more hours of driving lay ahead, where a much nicer hotel than the previous night awaited them.

Hermosillo may not have seemed like the obvious choice on the map, but she was giving it a go. First, it was less monopolized than the other options already were, such as Tijuana and Cabo. Second, it was more reachable by car than somewhere like Guadalajara or Morelia. Third, it's manufacturing and economic status, as well as its population, were exactly what Sarah desired.

Should her staff prove trustworthy and capable, and if all went according to plan, Sarah would be prepared to expand outward. She kept her head level, however, as there was a lot to do in this two-week time; not to mention making sure that Mateo was going to be worth his pay.

Sarah was tired of driving around the city looking for their hotel destination. It was time to use the Spanish she had been perfecting and ask for some directions. At the next intersection, Sarah leaned out her window to get the attention of the person in the car next to them.

"Desculpeme, me puede decir dónde está la Plaza Zaragoza?"

The man in the car gave some rather unspecific directions for a few blocks ahead and a right turn, followed by a wink. Not being overly friendly, she gave a nod of gratitude and headed off in the pointed direction.

"Bold," Mateo mumbled, still slumped in the passenger's seat with his eyes shut.

"Why don't you open your eyes and help me look for the damn place? I expect total teamwork," she shot back at him.

He straightened himself up and set his sunglasses on top of his head, remaining silent the rest of the way.

"All right, here we are."

"A little better than last night," he commented with a sarcastic tone.

"Listen, I have no room for attitudes and superiority complexes on my staff. You must be tough, yes, but you have twenty-four hours to show me your enthusiastic, hard-working, no-nonsense team player before I tell this hotel staff and the police that you're not supposed to be here, you've forced yourself on me, and I leave you to figure out the mess and your way back over the border. Clear?"

He broke his stare with a few blinks. "Yeah."

"Yes, ma'am."

"Yes, ma'am," he repeated, feeling a bit awkward about using the response for someone who was nearly the same age.

"Good. I'm parking the car here; it's discreet. While I go check-in, you transfer the stash in the seat to our bags."

Sarah went ahead into the large, open lobby, requesting one suite and one regular room. Mateo joined with their bags just as the woman was handing two brass keys across the counter. She nodded politely at the woman then motioned with her head for Mateo to follow.

Sarah could feel the awkward tension as Mateo followed her through the doors of the suite. "No need to think anything. Your room is down the hall. I just want to get all the sample bags out and stored in here. I gave specific instructions for room cleaning services only as requested, but we still need a safe keeping place. It'll be top priority to get them out first."

They searched the room, finally deciding to store the small bags behind an air vent. They stepped back to examine the scene, and Sarah was satisfied with the lack of evidence. She gave a nod of approval and went to retrieve Mateo's room key.

"Do as you wish for the next few hours, but meet me in the lobby at half past six for dinner. Tonight, we'll set out to check the already established scene. We need to know who's already here and how they run."

Once the door was closed behind him, Sarah eyed

the Spanish colonial décor. She went to run her hand across the long dresser, flopped her body backwards onto the four-post bed, and finally decided a long bath was in order. Her body melted into the small sea of warm water and soap, her eyelids drifting shut. Just as her mind had drifted off into shallow relaxation, the knock at the door jolted her back to reality. She sat for another minute to be sure the knock had been at her door. Another firm knock proceeded. Sarah let out a huff and shouted to let them know she was coming. She had contemplated pretending as if she wasn't there. Instead, she mumbled grumpily to herself and slipped the hotel-provided robe over her damp body.

It was Mateo standing at the door. His smile was not reciprocated on the other side of the door. Seeing him there, Sarah turned to look at the clock behind her.

"It's still forty-five minutes until I said to meet." Her gaze turned back to him with a slightly annoyed edge.

"I know, I know, but I've been out the last few hours and already have some headway on our research."

Sarah gave the nod for him to come inside. As soon as the door shut, he reached into his blazer pocket and pulled out two joints.

"Well, what have you been up to?" Sarah dried off the wet ends of her hair.

"I thought I'd get a head start, and it didn't take long to find a few sellers. That means the street scene, at least here in the center, is well covered. I bought the two joints to compare our product with what they're dealing."

Sarah grabbed her clothes and headed to the bathroom to change. "Well done," she shouted back into the main room. Returning mostly clothed, she headed to the room's minibar. Mateo sat on the sofa, smelling the contents of each of his purchases, watching her move across the room. She flipped over the glasses, deposited two ice cubes in each, and poured a half glass of the rum as if it were something she did every day.

Bringing her brush and glasses over to the sitting area, she joined Mateo on the couch. "So, brief me on your first few hours."

"It's not hard to ask around and find the street dealers. There's no fear in asking, which means we're in a location where it's common. Both guys I bought from looked pretty rough. I wouldn't want to scuffle with them. My hunch is that it's rare to sell only weed here, but I didn't ask for anything else. Just from smell and appearance, I can tell you that ours far exceeds theirs in terms of quality. This is a fairly low grade, half-heartedly grown bud." He gave another sniff.

"Well, it's good to know what's happening at the street level. We'll spend some time in high-end places tonight to see what people are getting there and how they're getting it. When the time is right, we'll say we're looking to buy a very large amount and demand to be taken to their supplier. We need to know the kings in town."

That night hadn't led them much further than discovering where the high rollers spent their time. They spent the next few days becoming more familiar with their future clientele and dealing locations. After pinning down a few key neighbourhoods, Sarah decided it was distribution time. They took out sample joints, each with a small piece of paper wrapped around it that said, "Disfruta, Belladonna." The point was to pique their interest and start a buzz before bringing down a load to sell a few weeks later.

For two days, they used the "divide and conquer" method, meeting back at a small, low-key restaurant for dinner to compare experiences and mark the maps. All the highlighted areas indicated where they had distributed. The green dots represented promising locations; the red were either heavily trafficked locations or areas where they had run-ins with other distributors. By the end of day, all of the samples were gone and they had made their way around the major financial and manufacturing sections.

"I think we'll go ahead and cut the trip short. Don't worry; I'll still give you your bonus pay for the whole two weeks. I still want to meet a few big bosses in town, which we can do over the next few days; but after that, we'll have accomplished everything I wanted to on this trip."

"Meeting a boss isn't necessarily the easiest thing. How many random people have made their way to you?"

"No one random, of course, but plenty of other business players have, and I've made my way to them. Just come along for the ride."

Three days later, Sarah checked them back out of the hotel and Mateo was in the passenger's seat, commenting on all the sights he had missed on the way down. He had befriended a small, furry companion that morning and was unwilling to give him up. All of the joints were gone, there was a bag of liquor and souvenirs on the floor to make their vacation story look more legitimate, and a half-eaten rat lay between the dog's paws. This time, they were driving straight up to L.A. without an overnight stop. Mateo sat with a notepad and paper, jotting down their plans for the next trip and a to-do list for the time in between.

CHAPTER 22

"Phone Calls"

David was now making a decent sum each month—
enough to almost double his income. He had been making
sporadic payments to Mr. West, each meeting making him
feel worse about his association with him than the last. At
the conclusion of their last meeting, almost two months
earlier, he was shocked to see how little principle he had
paid; most of his payments being applied to a substantial
interest rate being tacked on to cover the "convenience of
making payments". He was laundering his own money
through offshore accounts but hadn't done much by way of
purchases. Most of it was accumulating in savings, for a
rainy day, he figured. He no longer hesitated to spend
money on nice meals or an article of clothing he really
wanted, but the only large upgrades he had made were his
car and apartment: even those were nothing extravagant,
just a little more comfortable and dependable than the last.
He had decided he deserved a little less stress in his life and
had been avoiding Mr. West, acknowledging that he wasn't
so much the big mobster Danny had made him out to be,
but rather, a sleazy loan shark who would prefer another

week or two of interest to build up.

David was dressing for work, standing in front of the mirror to adjust his collar and cuffs, when the phone rang. He thought of not answering it since it was an unusual time to call, but figured it concerned one of the shell companies. They were all run smoothly by now. David hardly even had to put any effort into them, except to continue checking in to make sure the staff was doing as they were supposed to. He put his cufflink on the dresser and headed to the kitchen to answer the phone.

"Hello?"

"David, my friend, this is Frank; I hope I didn't catch you at a bad time, but you have been a little difficult to reach lately to the point I'm beginning to think you are avoiding me."

"No, no … I've just been real busy at work and a little tight for money."

"Not so tight that you couldn't afford a new car and apartment."

David suddenly realized how foolish he had been to assume Frank would wait on his money without any repercussion. He had apparently been under the watchful eye of Mr. West and his associates.

"Well, I uh ..." stammered David not sure how to get out of this dogma.

"I'm sure you would like to take the time to catch up on your debt, so I took the liberty of scheduling a little time this morning to discuss with you a new payment plan. I'll expect you in thirty minutes."

There was no time for an answer. The phone went dead for a second and then went to dial tone.

David's heart skipped a beat, and he swore he could taste his stomach in his throat.

David arrived at the office where his earlier meetings with Mr. West had been held. As he entered the office, he noticed two men, obviously hired for their brawn rather than their brains. Mr. West sat behind his desk but did not look up when David entered. David wasn't sure whether he should be presumptuous enough to sit or just stand until Mr. West acknowledged him.

"Sit," said Mr. West, still without looking up from the document David noticed for the first time. It apparently held some interest for the financier, as he continued to review it as he spoke. "I find your activities of late very interesting," he said in a very accusatory tone. "A young man with wild ideas for crazy inventions and no money is suddenly buying new cars and moving into better living accommodations, yet still making minimal payments to the only one who would help him. I would think you'd appreciate the help I provided you and be anxious to repay your debt to show that appreciation."

"Well, believe me …" David started.

"I also see that you have found some new associates who might or might not be involved in business matters that could result in some real money."

David's mind was racing while he tried to remain calm. What did they know? How did they know? The only people aware of his other business dealings were Danny and whoever Belladonna had entrusted. He decided to see how much they knew before admitting to anything.

"I'm not sure what you are referring to. Maybe you got some bad information or misunderstood something."

"A mutual friend of ours let slip that you were working on something big enough to allow you to pay your debt and that I shouldn't worry. Unfortunately, he has recently skipped town. But my associates here have been observing you, and I have the feeling there is more to you than you are divulging."

Danny! That had to be who he was referring to. David had not heard from him in over two months, maybe three, but apparently, he hadn't told them much before skipping out. His throat was tight but he managed to contain his nervousness.

"I think someone has turned a simple brag made over a couple of beers into something bigger," said David doing his best to keep his breathing even and slow.

"Then, why would he suddenly disappear right after our friendly little conversation? He was only into me a couple grand."

"Well, knowing Danny it probably has something to do with a girl. He tends to get into trouble when it comes to the opposite sex."

"Maybe so," said Frank with a casual move demonstrating he didn't really buy David's story. "But I think you're into something, and I feel you owe me for my investment in you. So, here is our new arrangement. You still owe me twenty grand on our last business venture. I'll give you three days to either come up with the money or divulge some information regarding this non-existent business you're not involved in that will allow me to recover my investment. Otherwise, I don't see a happy future for you."

Mr. West nodded his head, indicating to his associates that it was time to escort David from the office. They walked on either side of him until they reached the curb.

David tried to walk as calmly as he could to his car. "Shit. Shit, shit, shit, shit, shit!!" he finally let out. His mind began to race on the way to work. He had three days to get himself out of the country. Even if he paid off the loan, he was sure West was not going to give up until he discovered what David was involved in and that would be the end of his association with Belladonna and his newfound financial status. It was time to retrieve the rainy day fund. He started a mental checklist: "acquire cash in small enough sums to remain under the radar, call Mom and tell her I'm going on a holiday, pack some stuff, make sure things are set at the companies, call Ricky and hope Belladonna doesn't want to kill me ..."

That was it. Belladonna had mentioned she would be expanding to Mexico, and everything was coming together south of the border. He could appoint someone to keep it going and then skip town to set up the same operation there. Perfect.

He decided it was best to come to work as usual, just in case West's goons were tailing him. The morning hours seemed to crawl by as he waited to contact Ricky.

CHAPTER 23

"Operation: Go"

Sarah's new satellite company was slowly collecting its arsenal of employees. On their second trip, she and Mateo had reeled in a few white-collar workers who were game for an income boost. Once again, they brought a relatively small stash with them—enough to test the sellers and the market.

She met with her three potential employees in a dead café with cervezas and a Grand Centenario Leyenda tequila shot awaiting them instead of the usual wine that she had made her tradition in California. The main agenda was to establish her authority and due respect while briefing them on her operation. They were not to sell on the street. This was high-end, organically-grown special strains of marijuana, so the preference was that it be used for medicinal purposes or de-stressing.

She tried to feel out any cultural differences. Would it be harder for them to take her seriously? Would they respect the quality of the product and her request for its clientele? She came to the meeting with full vivaciousness and authority, but this masked the timid uncertainty that she was trying to push away. She left them each with a small quantity to sell within the following two days, reporting back to her with the "who's and where's" at the end. If she was satisfied with their performance, they would earn her trust and get more to sell. She also encouraged them to bring along anyone else interested in selling, especially women, to promote gender balance within the team.

Sarah had no reason to believe that things wouldn't take off there just as they did in Los Angeles as long as she had the right crew and all the right components. Her financial agent had already called with the request to transfer down, and she approved the proposition with time to spare due to the needful plea in his voice. They made an agreement that he could start researching and setting things up around Hermosillo so long as there wasn't even a hint of a hiccup with the money operations in L.A. David asked if he would be meeting her in Hermosillo to talk over some details, but she told him that Mateo would address any questions and concerns. Her initial doubts about him weren't holding up, as he had proven himself by paving a lot of headway on their trips.

Their second trip culminated in another successful border crossing, though Sarah wanted to find a grower and build clientele immediately. The three men had come back empty-handed the first day, reporting that they easily sold their small stash at the locations where samples had been distributed the last trip. They needed to bring back a much larger stash the next week, but better yet, they needed to establish a grower to lower the risk of getting caught and transport some of the plants to ensure the same product they were already importing. She would have to talk to Bud about it and develop a different transportation scheme. That's when things would really get serious.

David furiously ran from room to room, trying to decide what was essential to pack. He could only guess how long it would be before West's men would be calling but remained thankful for a stash of money and a continued flow of income. Many questions lingered: His mom thought he was going on vacation now, but what would he tell her when he didn't come back? What would he do with his apartment and the rest of his stuff? Was his Spanish definitely good enough to cut it in the business world down there—let alone the business world of laundering? Would West track him down in Mexico? He questioned his level of paranoia. Maybe West was making empty threats, but he decided it was best to at least lay low until he was sure the coast was clear.

David didn't want to alert West's watchdogs in any

way if they were keeping tabs on him, so he didn't intend to inform the bank that he would be leaving the country. He decided just to call them a few days later with some excuse that he accepted a job at another bank.

Clothes began to fill the trunk of his car as David made one trip after another down the stairs of his downtown apartment. He grumbled to himself about how much he hated moving as he stuffed his trunk to maximum capacity and made two attempts to get it to close properly.

"Are you heading out somewhere?" the voice from behind him asked.

David felt his body involuntarily jump. Putting on a cool face he turned to look. It was only his landlord standing there, hands in his pockets, wearing a tacky Hawaiian shirt that was one size too small and one too many buttons unbuttoned as he always did.

"Oh, all this? No, no. I'm just doing a clean-out of the apartment—taking a bunch of stuff to Goodwill, you know? Got a new promotion at work, and it's time to get a new wardrobe!"

"Ah, well, congratulations there then," he said in a genuinely jovial manner as he gave David a good slap on the back.

"Say, Mr. Davis, speaking of promotions—could I go to paying quarterly for my rent instead? I'm just always afraid I'm going to forget to pay rent when it comes around and that would just be one less thing to worry about." David thought this would help throw off any suspicion on the part of his landlord.

"Don't worry, son, I'd never let you forget to pay," he laughed. "But if you want to that's no problem. Doesn't matter a wink to me."

"Great, thank you, sir. I'll get a check for the next three months' rent into your mailbox soon."

David let out an unexpectedly long breath as Mr. Davis walked away. That was exactly what he hoped wouldn't happen. Back in his apartment, he started to create another pile for the backseat. He planned on purchasing most items when he got there but tried to evaluate belongings in each room for what might not be replaceable, like his dad's chess set. He grabbed a few pictures, his stereo, antique clock, toiletries, medicine, bedding, and towels for good measure. He then stood in the center of each room to do one turn-around for certainty that he was comfortable leaving behind everything he saw.

He was meeting his mom for dinner the next night, having made the Saturday night reservations for her favourite seafood restaurant downtown. One last box of memorabilia remained in David's apartment, and it wasn't something he could stand to leave, yet not something he felt secure bringing with him. He was going to ask his mom to keep it with her; the excuse being that it made sense to keep it with his other childhood memorabilia that was at her house. One other item would be left behind, this one for safe keeping. David had decided to leave his painting of Pinkie with his mother. As he placed it in the back seat of his car, he couldn't help but think that he was leaving the closest thing to Sarah behind, and any possibility of accidently finding her again. He was more likely to run into her again in Los Angeles than in Mexico.

His mom was the most difficult part of leaving. Dealing with rent, packing, working, and making sure all affairs were in order made for a hectic few days, but not knowing how many weeks or months it would be before seeing his mom again tugged at his heartstrings. Polly loved her children dearly and depended on the occasional company of David. She had invited him to move back home with her on many occasions after college, but he had insisted on maintaining his independence.

Polly met her son with trademark enthusiasm, dressed in red pumps and a fur shawl. She expressed her shining pride in him as always, got him caught up on the latest news with his sister and brother, and asked him to bring some good tequila back from Mexico. David smiled and agreed, wondering what he would tell her when he didn't return the next week. He had a good drive the next day with plenty of time to think it over.

As he closed his apartment door behind him for the final time the next day, turning the lock, a mix of feelings swirled around in his gut. What if West had his goons watching him? What if his Spanish wasn't good enough? His adventurous side, on the other hand, remained giddy with excitement over unknown prospects. He had a map, a planned route, and a phone number to speak with this new guy, Mateo, who Belladonna told him to contact. The next days were sure to be full of new, exciting, and challenging events.

David placed the final bag of belongings into the already cramped front seat, climbed in, and with one last look around, started the car and pulled out of the parking lot. He felt a great sense of relief knowing that he would soon be free of everything and everybody in L.A., setting out with a clean slate full of opportunity.

As he sat at the corner waiting for the light to change, a big black sedan turned right in front of him onto his street. He hadn't seen the occupant, but a sudden fear gripped him, and he sat frozen with his eyes fixed on his rear-view mirror. The car had pulled up in front of his apartment building, and he watched as West's two henchmen got out. They apparently had not spotted him as they drove right by his car at the corner.

He was suddenly startled when the driver in the car behind him laid on his horn and yelled at him that the light had changed. He looked once more in his rear-view mirror to see that the two goons were looking to see what the noise was all about. At this point, they recognized David's car and rushed back into their black sedan.

David pinned the pedal, producing a shrill sound of spinning tires. Through the smoke that rose from the asphalt, he saw the sedan turning around in the street behind him and took immediate action, turning right at the next intersection as the light was turning red to avoid stopping. He raced on through traffic, hoping to lose the sedan behind him through a series of frequent turns. When he finally felt confident he had lost them, he headed his car toward the freeway and the promise of escape.

Though it wasn't the shortest route to his final destination, David had decided it was best to get across the border as quickly as possible, heading straight south from L.A., crossing into Tijuana, and then cutting east.

A few hours after his harrowing start, David parked his car just across the border. He stepped out to stretch his legs and heave a big sigh of relief. All things seemed fresh and new now. He leaned against his car, taking in his surroundings: shops, street vendors, and people from the north crossing the border just to buy medicine and alcohol. A big black sedan headed south on the road behind him.

A fresh mango stand and cold beer seemed to be calling David's name, so he grabbed a fifty out of his wallet to exchange. With new pesos in hand, he approached the grandmotherly lady with the fruit cart covered by the yellow umbrella. "Con chili?" she asked. He nodded, marking his first lesson in what *not* to order. As it turned out, he did not prefer his fruit with a spicy kick. He sadly tossed away the last half of his mango and moved on to acquire a beer to accompany his people-watching on the bench.

The sun seemed to be shining down in such a way as to say, "all is new and well." David looked over at his car and then down at his pocket watch. It seemed safe enough. Why not take a little cat nap under the tree?

The fly on his nose itched enough to wake him from his slumber. He slipped out his pocket watch again. Nearly two o'clock. It was still almost nine hours to Hermosillo, but speed was not his prime motivation. Granted, an earlier arrival would give him more time to acclimate to the lay of the land, but it was Saturday and it was his first trip to Mexico. Why not play tourist for a day instead of rushing off to a large industrial city? Having made up his mind, David moseyed back over to his car to start the search for a safe place to park and sleep.

He took in the surrounding signs. Direccion "el centro" or "la playa?" David nodded his head in self-approval at the decision to head to the beach. 'Welcome to Mexico!' he said to himself aloud as the ignition turned over. Nerves had subsided and he felt full-on ready for what lay ahead. He eased the car towards the arrow pointing to "la playa," and felt an excitement in his stomach over a night on the beach in Mexico.

CHAPTER 24

"New Buds"

Though business was off to a promising start, Sarah was beginning to question her decision about Hermosillo. The second small batch they brought with them also sold out in a matter of days. The drive was long, and they had made it every week to bring small deliveries and develop more plans. It wasn't the most business savvy plan; spending money on gas and hotels. She decided the next trip needed to include a real estate transaction and the hiring of a farmer. They couldn't keep making these small trips, she lamented, a by-product of exhaustion.

She gave Bud an extra bonus for a boost in production and harvest. What she had really wanted was for Bud to come with her on the next trip. She wanted him to bring some seeds and train a local farmer in Hermosillo. Bud replied with the excuse that he was just a small town farmer who had no place leaving California. "But you live just outside L.A.," Sarah had retorted. He responded by insisting that he wasn't the "travelling type" but that he could help her anyway.

Mateo was sitting at the wheel this time, but Sarah

didn't feel like snoozing. Instead, she munched away on some nuts and insisted on stopping every few hours to check on their cargo. Apparently, Bud was worth even more than just his contributions as a dedicated farmer. When Sarah mentioned their need to transport a much larger load, he mentioned that he knew one of the border patrol guards. For a small sum to Bud and a small sum to his friend at the border, they could acquire a business license to export machine parts. All they needed was a truck, some boxes, and the license, and Bud's friend would ensure they were waived through.

She sent one of her employees with cash to buy a delivery truck, writing it off as a business expense for the costume shop. Mateo arranged the licensing and boxes while Sarah got to work helping Bud harvest their delivery. They had agreed that since he wasn't willing to go down there himself, Sarah would instead pay a premium to bring a dozen plants with her on this trip. That way, the same strands and quality could be replicated.

Five days later, they were back on the road again. Sarah wasn't quite ready to be heading back over again, but they had to cross when Harold, Bud's patrol friend, was working. Once they were within a half hour of the border, Sarah hopped in the back with the boxes. She sat waiting with the envelope of money, bouncing along on top of one of the boxes. It seemed that the minute hand had only moved a few minutes every time she checked her pocket watch. She watered the plants in the back for good measure and for something else to do besides bounce up and down.

The car jerked to a stop, nearly throwing her off the box. She gave the wall between Mateo and herself a good smack in response. Once certain that the van was stopped for inspection, she tiptoed her way to the front to wait for Harold. She could hear Mateo exchanging conversation with some other voices; it didn't sound comforting as she heard Mateo repeat the name Harold several times.

Something had gone wrong with the plan. Sarah could feel the tension in Mateo's voice as he was apparently being asked to exit the vehicle and open the back doors. Mateo was speaking louder than normal, repeating Harold's name as he slowly walked to the rear of the vehicle. She sensed he was trying to delay opening the truck doors as he fumbled with the keys, dropping them and apologizing for his clumsiness. Sarah was desperately hoping the license and bill of lading Mateo possessed would satisfy the border inspector and he would not question why she was riding in the back of the truck, but that didn't seem likely. Not knowing what else to do, she crouched down behind some of the crates. Then, the latch of the back door was unlocked. The door slowly lifted, revealing first brown trousers, a belt, and a bulging midsection. The door stopped only partially open and a new conversation began, this time between the chubby inspector and a second uniformed official.

"I'll get this, Ronnie. Sorry I took so long on break; bad stomach this morning. I was in the bathroom. It could be the flu or maybe just food poisoning from that breakfast burrito."

"Oh hell, don't stand so close if you got the flu!" said the chubby guard as he hurried away from the truck.

The short, muscular man hopped on and walked straight towards her, holding out his hand and lifting his badge to reveal the name "Officer Harold Newbold." Sarah quietly handed him the envelope, not breaking her serious stare while he counted it.

"Well missy, Bud was sure right about you. You look more like a debutante than a criminal. I'm sure it will be a pleasure working with you in the future."

He gave her an appraising once over and then jumped out of the truck.

"All good here, boys!" he shouted as he brought the door back down with force, giving Sarah one more disgusting glance.

"Yes, I bet it will be," she said as she smiled to herself and leaned against the side of the truck as the motion began again.

Back down in what was becoming familiar territory, Sarah checked them into yet another hotel. Things had to move fast over the next few days to keep the clientele list rolling and get the goods in the back of their truck to a safe place. There would be no downtime at the hotel during this trip. It was nearly nine o'clock by the time they arrived, but they got to work right away, calling the crew to meet at a remote construction site in two hours. In the meantime, they hopped back in the van to find an open Mercado and look for any property with a "se vende" sign.

They hopped back in their large white vehicle, Sarah tossing Mateo the keys so she could look while he drove. Should she hide in plain sight in town, or was it better to hang in the outskirts? She decided it would partially depend on what was available to purchase, in cash, over the next few days. She had brought quite a sum of clean money with them in one of the back boxes and would be picking up more from her crew that evening. Available cash shouldn't be an issue.

They parked momentarily across the street from a house in town.

"Not bad for a central house," she began, placing another chip in her mouth. "Decent size, yard, fairly central yet quiet ... we definitely need something with a yard. It lends itself to more privacy, and I want to keep a dog at the place. I'll hire someone to feed and walk it when the house is empty. You see, this is the kind of neighbourhood I would be looking for. Let's keep driving around this area."

She took note of the house's location: "blue house at the beginning of Calle del Rio—no house number." Perhaps a little overconfident with their knowledge of the area at this point, Mateo finally confessed that he was no longer sure of the construction site location. They had decided to drive around that area to kill the extra forty minutes they still had before meeting. But too many curves and right turns had them confused.

"Well it's not exactly like we can stop and ask

someone at nearly eleven o'clock at night where the abandoned construction site is." The edge in his voice was harsh and annoyed.

"Hey, calm yourself down. It doesn't help. Just keep making turns, and eventually, we'll see a sign for something that will help us orient ourselves. Right here."

He decided to just give up and follow whatever direction she offered. "Hey, wait a second. Right here."

"Where?" he asked, not seeing a right turn or anything that looked familiar.

"There. You see that ranch?"

"Yeah ..."

"That's it. It's perfect."

"There's no 'for sale' sign."

"You know money speaks volumes. The location is perfect. The space is perfect. There's plenty of clutter, shrubbery, and forestry to mask what we need. This will work. We'll visit them tomorrow to start negotiations. Keep driving, and I'm going to make a map so we know how to get back."

After a few more turns, they could see the main road in the distance well enough to be able to make their way back there. By the time they arrived to the site, each carrying a box from the van, their three men, plus one, were waiting.

"Buenas noches. Mucho gusto." She nodded at the woman standing amongst them, looking around for an explanation.

"Belladonna, this is mi hermana. She works at the car manufacturing plant, and she thinks she can sell well there."

Sarah was happy to see a woman. She picked up her box, handed it to one of the men, and nodded for them to all go inside. Thinking more about sleep than money and buds, she did a quick exchange with everyone, collecting money and distributing a much larger supply than usual. A small sample set went to Enrico's sister to see how she would do. The men were all happy to see their supply grow almost tenfold this trip, but Sarah laid down high expectations to go along with it.

Without wasting any extra minutes, Sarah took the car keys from Mateo, and he followed behind her back to the truck. Back at the hotel, she checked on the plants in the back one last time, then pulled down the extra security door. She was stressed about getting the plants into the ground as soon as possible. Mateo assured her they were fine for the night and asked to be excused to his room. She agreed, with orders to meet and be ready to go at nine o'clock.

Sarah was almost grateful for her alarm the next morning. The night seemed to never end, as she woke several times to the darkness of the night. Each time her eyes opened, she wandered to the window to check on their truck, only to find nothing each time. The sun seemed to take longer than usual to rise, and the passing hour hand of her clock was the only assurance that time was indeed passing.

The minute the alarm rang, her eyes were open wide and she was thankful to see the sun had finally risen. She brushed her hair, slipped on the first dress she found, and grabbed her hat in a record fifteen minutes. There were forty-five minutes until she was supposed to meet Mateo. Sarah checked inside the truck first, then headed off to get them both a coffee and some breakfast sweets from the paneria.

Mateo stretched his bulky arms above his head and drew the curtains aside. He stared ahead to the empty parking spaces in front of them. Empty. Empty! He flew in a panic out the door to go knock at Sarah's room. He danced anxiously from foot to foot waiting for her to answer. "Belladonna!" he finally shouted.

"Hey," she came up from behind him coolly.

"Mi dio, I thought the truck was gone."

"I'm parked around front now. Come on, let's go if you're ready. Coffee's in the truck." She handed him a pan dulce on a napkin and turned to head back to the truck.

Instead of driving around to look for more "se vende" signs, Sarah grabbed the attempt at a map that she made the night before and started that way; one hand on the steering wheel, one holding the paper, and her eyes dodging back and forth between the map and the road. Mateo sat stiffly in the passengers' seat, gripping the side door handle as she made a hasty left turn.

"Oh, you're just fine over there. Don't be so dramatic," she laughed out loud.

"Yeah, just maybe ..."

"Oh, get over it. I drive better than anyone else around here."

He sat quietly the rest of the trip, quietly reciting a Hail Mary or two the rest of the way, and a prayer of thanks when he saw the house.

"All right, here's the deal: these people have a few options. I'm prepared to be more than fair, but this is definitely the house that I want. Just follow along."

A woman answered the door in a flowered gown and an apron. She had a curious expression on her face and looked to be about 50. Sarah offered a smile, some extra pastries that she had picked up, and the explanation that they were there to discuss some business. She introduced Mateo and herself, asking permission to enter. The woman instead called for her husband, a short, round man who approached the door with a serious face behind his beard and moustache, his coffee still in hand. Mateo gently touched Sarah's elbow in a signal to let him take over. He explained the same to her husband, who was willing to let them inside.

Sarah looked around the rooms, peering out each

window to survey the surroundings. It was indeed perfect: plenty large enough, yet modest, a long driveway, a good division of rooms, a lot of foliage ... yes, this was exactly what they needed. The woman began boiling water at the stove, and the man motioned for them to have a seat at the table. He sat in silence, which made Sarah nervously unsure as to whether to speak or wait. She decided she first needed to talk herself out of any nervousness; there was no room for that in this negotiation.

The woman brought some small white mugs, spoons, the boiling water, and a jar of instant coffee to the table. With all the items placed in the middle, the man began to serve himself, finally offering some words. He introduced them: Juan and Carla, and passed the coffee jar on to Mateo.

"You said you have business to discuss? If this is about my son, Carlos, I have not spoken to him; and if you are here for some drug negotiations, we don't want a part."

"Actually, we're here looking for a house. We urgently need to find one, and I understand that you have no sign, but we would very much like to discuss the sale of your house."

"Do you see a for sale sign?" Juan retorted, fingering his rough beard.

Mateo once again shot Sarah a look that signalled for him to speak instead. She kept her face calm, but inside she was a ball of instant frustration.

"We will give you exceptionally more than what your house is worth, sir. You could buy a bigger house if you wish, or buy a smaller one in the center and live off of the difference."

The conversation went on, and Sarah did her best to sit quietly. She knew in her heart she wouldn't be unfair or unjust in any way, but they needed to win the couple's trust. She finally asked what it was they could want. "What could I offer you?"

She could see that the man's original facade had already softened. "You can offer us nothing. We don't want to leave our home." It was the first time Carla had spoken in the conversation.

Sarah looked out the window onto their property; a large variety of shrubbery, trees, aloe, and what looked like a small garden in the distance. "Do you farm?" she finally decided to ask. It didn't seem that it would be possible to take the original path, so it was time to create a new one. If he wouldn't move, why not pay him to farm?

The minute she mentioned cannabis, his defenses went back up again, refusing to have anything to do with the substance that was driving his country to corruption, as he put it. Sarah stayed calm and allowed herself to think more. This was actually not a bad thing. It would be better to pay him than to pay someone who was looking for it— someone who just wanted money and cared less about the product. "Carla, I noticed you seem to have some problems with your hands. Is it arthritis?"

Carla nodded and the conversation took a turn. Sarah began to explain that she was only interested in selling marijuana; that she believed people should have it for its mood-lifting and medicinal uses; that she didn't just send her sellers to hang out in parks and sell to youth. She explained that she needed a grower to take good care of the plants and the land; someone to grow organically for the best quality.

She excused herself for a moment, left the house, and came back in with a small bud. Handing it to Carla, she urged her to use it, as many claim its healthful benefits for the symptoms of arthritis. Carla and Jose now sat quietly.

They exchanged a look that Sarah knew meant they were contemplating, rather than rejecting the words she said. "I'm prepared to pay you the same amount for the marijuana you produce, if it's top quality, as my grower in the U.S." Jose nodded slowly, not even raising his eyebrows to what Sarah knew was a generous offer for them. "This, however, wouldn't fix the problem of us needing a place to stay. I would like to pay you rent. We could build a house on the edge of your property and pay you rent monthly for the land."

She could tell that perhaps a little space would push them over the line to saying yes. She stood up and put a hand on Mateo's shoulder, signalling for them to head out. It was a much more friendly departure than arrival. Mateo handed them a paper with his name and a phone number to reach him. Sarah felt confident, though, that the final proposition would work. The thoughtful contemplation on their faces seemed to be a sign of acceptance. It was two birds with one stone: a house and a farmer all in one.

CHAPTER 25

"A Clean Slate"

David couldn't have felt freer at the time. No one was looking for him—or at least, there was no door for them to go knocking on. No one could get ahold of him. There was no great urgency to anything. Of course, he did need to get down to Hermosillo sometime soon, and he needed to check in with things in L.A. But L.A. was just one phone call, and he was sure everything was fine. Hermosillo just needed to be reached sometime within the week.

It took that first night on the beach for his mind to slow down and stop racing. A good night's sleep seemed to transform his mind set. He had sat on the beach for hours that morning; waves of relaxation washing up on shore. That's when he realized he could slow down; be at ease. Life was on a new path, and it was exciting. He could stay there for the moment. He could go. He had access to money and income without having to resort to banking. He had to think outside the box; dig underground; use some problem-solving skills instead of just book knowledge. It was always about being a little out of the ordinary, and that morning, David really felt that his life was pretty damn good.

He had debated whether or not to stay at the hotel or check out. Once the police realized he wasn't at work or in his apartment, they would most likely start their search in Tijuana. His backpack slung over his shoulder, he headed with his map to a café to decide over a coffee where he should be off to next. Cutting over east or staying along the coast, he followed his finger down to ... Puerto Peñasco. There! That would do. He gulped down his last swig of coffee, dug out some coins to throw on the table, and headed back to his car. He figured he should get on the road so there would be plenty of time to find some lodging.

He discovered along the way that (a) he should have gotten snacks before he left. There were no giant gas stations or supermercados off any "exits"—not that there were even any exits. He had settled for a lunch of rice, tamales, beans, and instant coffee at a restaurant along the way. And (b) there was nothing for him to sing along to on Mexican radio. Nonetheless, he danced along in his car; sure that all passers-by were probably laughing at the gringo. And (c) the holes in the roads were extremely dangerous.

After two more nights in Puerto Peñasco, he figured it was time to move on and get things started in Hermosillo. The plan was to ask around for a one-month rental for starters. That would buy him some time to get his feet on the ground and figure out if he needed to stay or return to California.

Arriving in Hermosillo, he did a drive around the town before stopping anywhere. "Hmm," he said to himself aloud as he put the car in park, sitting somewhere in the outskirts. "Largely industrial. A combination of desert and mountains. I wonder how far it is to the water." He sat for a minute taking in the scenery before heading back into the center. "What the?!?!" He quickly leaned forward across the steering wheel as if he could get a better view at what had just run past his car and into the distance. "Now that's exciting," he stated to himself upon realizing that it was a little roadrunner that had just sped past him. "Welcome to Mexico!" he shouted out his car window into the empty space of nature, turning the ignition and merging back onto the road in the direction of the city.

Arriving back in the center, he settled down at a restaurant for another hot meal. Parking his car in front of a large, grey office building, he opted to sit at a small restaurant down one of the side streets. While enjoying his carne asada and coffee, he asked the young waiter if he had any advice on a place to stay in town. The shy young man returned from the kitchen with a woman who appeared to be his mother. She asked David some basic questions about what he needed and how long he wanted to stay, then told him to wait a minute while she made a phone call.

Her black bun with slight grey streaks bounced as she scurried back over to his table a few minutes later. She was happy to report that her cousin had a small, semi-furnished, 3-room house that he could take for the month. "Perfecto!" he smiled at her. She pulled out the chair next to him and sat down to scribble a map to the house, supposedly just a few minutes away, along with her cousin's name in caps along the top: ALEJANDRO.

"Dos horas!" she shouted after him as he thanked her and left a tip for the help. He decided to spend the extra time orienting himself with the city center. Walking along the sidewalk, hands in pockets and turning more than a few heads, the payphone booth on the busy street corner caught his attention. At that point, it seemed like a great opportunity to try to get in contact with Mateo and let him know what was going on.

They had spoken briefly the morning that David left California. Mateo had phoned his apartment to introduce himself and brief him on the status of the operation there. David propped his foot up against the side of the booth and balanced his knapsack on his knee to dig out the small paper with Mateo's phone number and some coins.

"Hola," the voice came on the other end after a few rings.

Their conversation was a fluid mixture of Spanish and English. Mateo gave him the go-ahead to start getting things aligned, as they would have some money to take care of in a few weeks. Mateo didn't seem to particularly care that he was in the area. Instead, he was surprised to hear Mateo mention that he didn't really care if David was in Hermosillo or not, as long as he took care of things there. He told him to check out Guadalajara or Chihuahua if he wanted—so long as he was there to handle business when money had to be picked up.

David decided to stick with his plan to stay in Hermosillo for the month. During that time, he would test the waters of money laundering. If this proved lucrative, he would have one house there and another in Mexico City or somewhere on the coast. Maybe he could buy his mom a vacation house in Rosa Rita. He tried not to let his imagination run away with him, as there was still much to be done. Looking down at his watch, he figured it wouldn't hurt to head to Alejandro's place early. Maybe he would already be there and he could get settled.

He sat down on a nearby bench to study the haphazardly drawn map that was given to him at the restaurant. Looking up at the street corners, he tried to orient himself before hopping to his feet to get started. He started light on his feet, but thirty minutes later, a new uncertainty clouded his head. David wished he would have brought his car with him since his feet were beginning to tire.

After many stops for directions, many fingers pointing one way or another and promising "just that way," David was relieved to finally be standing in front of the little house. It was in good proximity to necessities, in decent enough condition, and all the space he needed. Its plain white exterior wasn't the most appealing, but he didn't care at the moment. He looked down at his pocket watch; so much for being early. At least he was on time. He looked around, but there was no evidence of anyone who seemed to be looking for him, so he sat down on the front doorstep to wait. His eyes just seemed to close naturally on their own in the hot sun, as if it was their duty to rest in such a scenario.

He jerked awake as a motorbike sped past him with

smoke and an even greater noise pollution. He blinked a few times, taking a moment to realize that he had fallen asleep. Taking another look at his pocket watch, he wondered if he should worry that it was now almost forty minutes later. He figured in another twenty minutes he would go knocking on one of the doors.

Finally, just when he was wondering about whether or not he was really in the right place, a broad-shouldered gentleman pulled up in a small motorbike, hopping off and propping the kickstand all in one swift motion. "David?" he asked with his southern accent. Alejandro approached with a smile and a handshake as if he weren't almost an hour late.

David paid upfront for a month in the house after Alejandro did a quick run-through. As soon as he was back alone with a key in hand, he plopped himself down on the brown checkered couch that looked and felt like it had a good twenty years on it. He was relieved that he had packed some sheets and towels, and all that lingered in front of him was a trip to the supermercado after he walked the half hour maze back to his car. In the morning, he could start his new financial endeavours south of the border.

CHAPTER 26

"Trouble in Paradise"

The road hadn't been without its bumps so far.

Sarah had been working way too many hours every day since the farm had been established. Little things kept happening to disrupt what should have been a fairly basic operation. Poachers appeared to be raiding the gardens, only to have the plants located in nearby ravines and other out of the way places. A herd of goats inexplicably appeared in the garden one night, and yet, none of the locals had reported any losses in their livestock. Sarah and a few of the others were taking turns staying up all night to keep an eye on the crops, but the strange occurrences stopped as suddenly as they had started.

The morning following Sarah's last night shift, she received a call. She was barely aware of the ringing phone but somehow managed to garner enough energy to pick up the receiver.

"Hello …," she half-whispered, stifling a yawn.

"Belladonna?" asked the faintly familiar voice at the other end.

251

"Yes, who is this?" she replied.

"It's Ricky."

"I hope this isn't something needing any immediate attention," she said. "I've been up for sixteen hours, and I need some sleep."

"Well," came the hesitant reply, "I just wanted to let you know that I'm leaving. I have an offer that I can't refuse. I'm sorry to drop this on you, but I just wanted to let you know that you've been really good to me, and I appreciate it."

"When will you be leaving?" asked Sarah, now much more awake than she would have thought possible.

"Today. I have to leave today."

Sarah wasn't sure what to say. She had come to depend on Ricky up north while she focused on Mexico. "I guess there's not much I can say except good luck wherever you're going."

"Thanks," said Ricky. "I really hope everything goes well for you," and he hung up the phone.

Sarah wasn't sure if she was feeling paranoid because of Ricky's sudden departure or because of her lack of sleep, but she acknowledged that there was something suspicious about his quick decision to leave.

***

Half a week in one country and a half week in the other eventually ran her so tired that it landed her a trip to the Casa Grande hospital after falling asleep at the wheel. A trucker had called in after seeing her car crash into position against a guard rail. Sarah awoke to hovering paramedics, plastic hospital machinery, and lights.

As she regained consciousness during her ride to the hospital, she tried to demand that they stop the vehicle and let her out. Of course, the paramedics paid no attention to her, which got her worked into an exhausted frenzy by the time they reached the ER. She tried so hard to protest; business wouldn't leave her mind. Her body told her to give up, though. It needed rest. She ended up thankful for those twenty-four hours in the hospital to clear her mind and regain the energy she needed to move ahead.

And she definitely needed the energy. In addition to the distraction of obtaining repairs to her car, those following months were busy finishing up the house they were building on the edge of the Rodriguez property, training Erica to take over Ricky's duties in L.A., and establishing her authority in Hermosillo. There weren't as many problems there as she had feared, and she had decided this time to seek out any other bosses before they sought her out. Since most of them were multi-drug lords, they didn't care much about her operation, and Sarah was beginning to think she wasn't being taken very seriously. One particular boss had even scoffed and tried to berate her. Sarah found it ironic, as he was barely her size. A quick thought of physical violence to teach him a lesson had crossed her mind, but she withheld and fought back with intelligence.

The summer had not proven easy on their plants, either. There had been many "translate" phone calls with Bud discussing concerns. Juan and Carla's property was perfect, and she really liked them, but she wondered if it had been a bad decision to hire people who had no previous experience with marijuana. Now that the unusually hot season had passed and a storm raged its way across the territory, they were down about twenty percent of their crop. The supply-demand ratio was tight, so Sarah was on her way back from California in the van with more plants to try a quick rescue.

Her parents had left to head back to Sweden after their annual summer holiday at the beach house. As with the last few summers, Sarah had only joined them on the weekends. They expressed their concern about her inability or unwillingness to take some holiday time with them. This time, she told them a partial truth. She told them that she was working on a journalistic piece—doing undercover research in her spare time, which made her schedule all the more compact. She said she'd rather not tell them all about it until it was done, so as not to jinx her success, and the answer satisfied them. It was that which made Sarah realize she hadn't contributed to her "article" in quite some time. Had she given up on it? She convinced herself she hadn't— simply that she got diverted. It was the beginning of this larger path she was now walking—and enjoying.

Sarah and Mateo used the same procedure as before, but this time, she made sure Harold was going to be waiting when they pulled up. Mateo had the paperwork in the cab with him while Sarah again rode in the back to keep the plants moist and pay Harold when he climbed in for his phony inspection.

Harold was waiting, but this time, he directed Mateo to pull over to an area used for detailed inspections. Mateo knocked on the wall separating him and Sarah, hoping she would understand that something was up. He pulled over and got out of the cab with papers in hand. Harold took the papers and ordered Mateo back into the cab of the truck. He took the keys from Mateo, telling him to remain in the truck and proceeded to the rear. He unlocked the latch and raised it just high enough for him to enter on his hands and knees. Sarah didn't like the implications but stood her ground, payment envelope in her hand and a steely stare in her eyes.

"Hello. Missy," said Harold wiping the dirt from the front of his uniform. "It's sure nice to see you again."

"I'm sure it is, Officer … Newbold, isn't it? What is this? demanded Sarah staring him down.

"Well," continued Harold, "I just thought you might want to renegotiate our agreement since this is twice I've covered for you."

"And just what, exactly, did you have in mind?"

"You know, there's only two things that mean shit to me; money and sex. Now, since you seem to have access to each of those I'll leave it up to you which you think you might be willing to part with. But I must admit, I'm kinda hoping you can't come up with the amount of cash I'm talking about."

Sarah had never wanted to hurt a man any more than she did at that moment. She could only hope that she would meet him again when she wasn't sitting on top of a load of illegal drugs being smuggled into Mexico.

"Is this how you work?" she said, "You take bribes to let people break the law and then use extortion and blackmail to supplement your government salary?"

"This job has its perks, and I know how to use them," he replied with a smile.

"I'm sure we can make some sort of arrangement to meet where we could have a little more privacy," she said, trying to sound as if she would like nothing more, and hoping he would agree to meet her at a later time in a more remote location where she would completely remove sex as an option for him in the future.

"You've got a point. Maybe the money might be more appropriate at the moment. We can talk about future arrangements when you plan your next trip."

"And exactly how much are we talking?" she asked, trying not to sound the way she felt.

"Well, about twice what that envelope contains would help me cope with the thought of missing out on what I'm sure would be a real nice experience." He reached out and ran his finger along the front of her blouse.

"Well, how about this," she said slapping his hand away from her. "How about we keep the original deal and I don't play back the tape recording you just provided as evidence of your criminal activity?"

He stepped back and looked at her silently debating how serious she was.

"I don't believe you have a tape recorder," he finally said sneering at her.

Sarah reached into her satchel and pulled out a portable recorder, the tape still running.

***

Sarah worked with Juan to re-plant the crop she had brought down, staying a few more days to be sure they rooted. A month later, all the storms seemed to have calmed. David, her financial operator, had the pesos flowing into her American bank account, and Erica was running the daily tasks well in L.A. She had gained much more confidence in Mateo, as he continued to prove himself over the last few months.

Ready to let her adventurous spirit take over, she let everyone know that she'd check in by phone in a day or two and then hopped in the van to take off. Unplanned destinations were her favorite. As she got behind the wheel and began heading south, she recalled a few similar college weekend drives—just getting in the car to drive nowhere ... just somewhere away.

Stopping at small beach towns along the way to enjoy a beer in the sun, she finally decided to stop in Los Mochis. It was late enough in the day that she wanted to find a hotel, get some proper dinner, and crash in the hotel room with some churros from the street Ordering three bags, she wondered if she should even try to make up an excuse that her husband and kids were waiting in the hotel.

Before allowing herself to get too relaxed (although after taking a good look at the bathtub, she had already decided to forego that method of relaxation for the night) she put in a phone call to Erica and Mateo just to check everything. All transactions were smooth, and there were no new alarms of suspicious activity. Now, she could crack open a book and submit to peace.

Anxiously biting into the deliciously fried, cinnamon-and-sugar coated dough, she closed her eyes and let herself melt into the single pillow on the bed. She picked up the remote in one hand and another churro in the other, deciding to watch a half hour of the news before digging her book out of her bag.

Mexico City was celebrating as "El Tricolor" won another match, and President Portillo made a statement about further plans to increase economic stability. A new and unknown pest had begun to show itself on the map. The areas of Sonora and Sinaloa were especially affected by this unknown pest who was damaging acres of important crops in the area. Local authorities suspected that this pest was brought in with some produce or other live plants crossing the border recently. They were searching the area for all evidence of the pest, which seemed to multiply at an incredible rate.

Sarah sat up straight as they showed the close-up of the bug and its effect on the crops. She didn't know much about agriculture, but she recognized the tell-tale silk webs of spider mites. The recent warm temperature was the perfect breeding conditions for these destructive mites that punctured the leaves and caused death to the area's crops.

She looked at the clock and debated whether or not to call Juan about it, ultimately deciding to continue her day of relaxation. There wasn't much she could do about it at that moment if Juan did have any concerns. Her thumb hit the red button on the remote. Not more than twenty minutes after turning the first page of her book, Sarah's head was hanging, eyes closed.

The sun shone brightly through the wide window. She had forgotten to close the curtains. Now, at six a.m. Sarah found herself staring, wide awake, at the white wall in front of her. Deciding that any attempt of going back to sleep would be useless, she slipped on her shoes and headed to the beach. She still had time before anyone serving coffee would be open. No matter how many previous walks she had enjoyed on a beach, she never tired of the feeling of sand melting between her toes. It was perfection for her. By the time she finished relishing in the morning's walk and packed her things back up, she figured Juan should be awake and eating breakfast.

After a few rings, Juan finally picked up the phone. "Hola," he answered in his serious tone of voice.

"Hola, Juan. I just have a quick question for you. Have you taken a good look at the newest set of plants we put in a few weeks ago? How are they doing?"

"Uh ..." he stuttered a bit with his words. "They are green."

"Have you seen any spider web-like threads on them?"

"No ma'am, but I didn't look closely."

"Yeah, I need you to do that first thing today, and I'll call you back later."

"Damn it," she said to herself after putting the phone back on the hook. She didn't want to be too far away should she need to come up quickly for any help, so she decided to drive back up to Guaymas. Lunch at the harbor town the day before had piqued her interest, so she figured it wasn't a bad place to revisit.

After arriving in Guaymas, Sarah was trying to enjoy the harbor view with her tamale and coffee. She closed her eyes, leaned back against the concrete wall behind her, and tried to focus on the warmth she felt as her skin soaked in the sun. It seemed useless, though. Beautiful boats and a blue span of water lay in front of her, and yet her mind was back in Hermosillo. She was worried both about losing more of their crop as well as the possibility of people snooping around.

There was no question that Juan was a good farmer. He already practiced organic pest control on his own garden, and Sarah loved watching the tender way he handled the plants. But marijuana was a new crop for him and Carla. No doubt he would be an accomplished grower in a year or two, but for now, Sarah was still holding his hand, via Bud.

Finally opening her eyes and surrendering to the anxiety within, Sarah decided it wasn't worth it to stay. She let out a long sigh and eased herself up. "Another weekend," she reassured herself before jumping up into the large, white van. She stopped for an ice cream on the way out and started the short trip back.

The hour and a half return after a short, one-night getaway left Sarah evaluating life at the moment. Life was exciting—twists, turns, and problem-solving kept her from being bored any day. There was always something new, and the moment there wasn't, she would begin plans to expand once again. It wasn't what she had dreamed of doing five years ago. In fact, if anyone had told her five years ago that this would be her life, she probably would have gotten a good laugh out of it. The overall assessment: she felt challenged and accomplished. Oddly enough, she was proud of all she had done thus far.

However, she realized she was less than satisfied with her social life. Most of her friendships had fallen by the wayside. Selling something illegal isn't exactly the best platform for finding new friends, either. There had been no hint of a romantic relationship in nearly two years, and she never calculated how difficult it could be to make personal connections be when you can't tell people what you do. "Entrepreneur?" "Enterpriser?" Sure. But then people start asking questions about what exactly that means. What really bothered her, though, was not being able to tell her parents. Even though they had been physically separated from her for years, their moral support never dwindled. She hated not sharing everything with them, but she didn't see how she could—not until marijuana became either decriminalized or legalized across the board.

Sarah recalled something she heard once: "You can have it all; just not all at one time." A significant other and social life would be for another season. For now, she would continue to draw satisfaction from the mountains she was tackling and people coming into her life along the way— like Juan and Carla, for example. Sarah helped Juan in the garden on occasion because she truly enjoyed his company. A tough exterior was only his protective facade, but he cherished all living things; from grasshoppers to anyone who proved worthy of his trust. She also kept on her tough armor around him so as to maintain her tough boss demeanor. But she always treated him more than fair, and she had a hunch that Juan knew she really liked him.

Upon reaching Hermosillo, Sarah felt like she had arrived home, but home didn't seem to be one place with a single definition anymore. Home was L.A. Home was San Marino, Newport, and Huntington Beach. Home was most of Sweden. It was anywhere with a tie, and it just dawned on her that Hermosillo now made the list.

Driving down the long, empty road, Sarah's crop anxiety tormented her. If there were spider mites in the area, they would definitely affect her crops soon. Given how quickly they multiplied, they may already be there. She was just hoping to arrive before any plants were completely ruined and before any authorities came snooping around so she could help Juan divert them.

Before heading to the main house to check in with Juan, she decided to stop at her house. The arrangements had all worked out well. Juan and Carla ended up selling a few acres of their property on which Sarah could build a house and grow her plants. She still hired Juan—at an average American salary—to grow for her, but this way it wasn't on his property. The house went up quickly, seeing as she paid top dollar to have a large construction crew working on it. Unfortunately, it was still rather sparsely decorated, but all the essentials were there.

As she pulled up the stone and dirt driveway, she noticed a figure pass by the window. Mateo may have been around, but his car wasn't parked under the overhang. He could have driven the four-wheeler over from the farm, but she didn't see it either. It could very well have been parked behind the house. Sarah didn't want to bank on it, though, so she prepared to enter the house with caution.

If it was a stranger, they undoubtedly saw her pulling up. Nonetheless, after exiting the vehicle, she eased the van door closed, not allowing it to latch all the way shut. Standing with her back on the vehicle door, she reached in the satchel for her gun. Peering through the van window back to the house, there was no sign of anyone at a window, so she ran low up to the front door. "It had better be Mateo," she thought to herself, "because if anyone is going to try to come messing with me ..."

She turned the key in the lock, gun held up and ready. The door had not been locked. Cautiously, she pushed the door open, positioning herself to inspect the scene unnoticed. To her surprise, Juan and Carla were there sitting on the couch with three members of the Policía Federal surrounding them. She took one look at their 7-pointed star badges and lowered her gun.

The look on Juan's face sent her stomach into knots. She maintained control of her face, though, willing herself to maintain a calm disposition. "Officers," she addressed them politely and firmly.

"Why you holding gun?" the officer standing closest to the couch questioned her, grasping to speak English. All three of them looked as though they could be brothers. Shaven heads, medium height, and bulky statures gave them all a strangely similar look.

"Wouldn't you enter your home with a gun if you saw someone inside who shouldn't be there?" she answered, still calm and straight-forward.

"You need to give us the gun; then sit down for

more questions."

Sarah complied without hesitation and resistance. She knew that staying calm and maintaining an air of innocence could be beneficial to the situation, especially if they were there without any proof.

"May I ask now what this is about?"

"There has been an outbreak of a new pest in the area, which has affected a large portion of crops in the area in just a matter of weeks. It's a pest unfamiliar to us, so the country's experts have been tasked with doing a survey of all farming land of the surrounding states. You own this land here, do you not?"

"Yes, I purchased a section of plot from Mr. Rodriguez some months ago."

"And would you like to tell us the purpose of purchasing this lot?"

Sarah maintained eye contact with the officer, who still had not introduced himself or the others. She didn't want to include Juan and Carla in any way.

"I purchased the land for the purpose of building

this house."

"And the extra land?"

"I like space. It's why I didn't purchase a place in town. I've lived my life in enough big cities."

"And that?" the officer pointed to a part of a plant sitting on the table.

"What about it?"

"It was found on your property."

"I'd prefer not to answer any other questions without a lawyer."

"Then you need to come with us."

"Am I under arrest?"

"Yes. The three of you are under arrest for the possession of marijuana on your property."

"And Mr. and Mrs. Rodriguez?"

"Yes, stores of it were found in a shed just over

their property line. Congratulations. Not only did you grow something illegally, you damaged crops we need for food. They labelled this strand as an American variety, which we assume you smuggled in."

"You can assume all you want until we're in court with lawyers—if this even makes it as far as court."

It was the first time she looked into Juan's eyes. The desperation she saw broke her heart but not her spirit. She was glad she had the finances to hire the best of the best, but she wasn't confident about fighting the Mexican judicial system. It was very unfamiliar territory that she had no time to research, but she heard that bribery was rampant, which gave her hope. Otherwise, she might have to rely on the expertise of the best lawyer she could find and hope it would be good enough. What she did know is that she wouldn't let Juan and Carla stay in jail.

CHAPTER 27

"Expanding Horizons"

After the first month, he had given up the little house he was renting in Hermosillo. Sure, the retro decorations had character, but he had decided to try out a few other cities since it didn't seem so pertinent that he remain in Hermosillo. Aside from a few nights spent at some bars and meeting with potential business partners, David's social life had toned down. He spent most of his time researching the ins and outs of business and finance laws in Mexico, acquiring hidden gems of knowledge that would help him establish a good laundering system there. The trick was that Belladonna eventually wanted the pesos to be in U.S. dollars in her American bank accounts. He was secretly hoping she would change her mind and want another bank account locally instead. This would ensure diversification of liquid assets while removing any need for him to travel back to the States before things settled.

David was satisfied with what was accomplished after the first month. He had found a front company to get things started; a little bar in town to cook the books and push some of the money through. It was satisfactory for the moment to help keep the money pile from growing too large. He decided a "maquiladora" corporation was the best business vehicle, since it would allow foreign ownership and duty free exports. He still had more work to do because of restrictions of ownership imposed on foreigners; however, he wanted to explore some other towns to see if he really wanted Hermosillo as his home base.

David had been hesitant to broadcast his whereabouts and had told no one in L.A. where he was; no one except his mother. He had regretted mentioning Mexico to her and was always anxious about whether Frank West would go so far as to investigate his family in order to recover the money owed to him by David. The thought of not knowing had caused him untold moments of worry and despair; finally knowing only made matters worse.

David had decided to place a call to his mother. He felt the need to warn her but wasn't sure how to do that without worrying her. He had taken a pocket full of change and located a working pay phone in town.

"Hello?" his mother answered after the fifth ring.

"Hi, Mom, it's David," he said, trying to sound as if this were just another call from a son to his mother.

"Oh, Davey," she replied with a smile in her voice. "How are you, dear?"

So far, David detected nothing in her voice that expressed concern. That was good.

"I'm fine, Mom, just been really busy. My vacation was short-lived and I've been working almost every day on a project that happened to come along out of the blue," he lied as persuasively as he could.

"I hope it doesn't keep you tied up for much longer. It would be nice to hear from you a bit more often. You haven't called in so long I thought maybe you might be in trouble," she replied in the usual motherly way.

"No trouble, Mom, I promise; just a lot of work to get done before I can relax. I promise I'll try to call more often after things settle down here. I may be here for a bit longer than I had planned."

"Will you be coming home any time soon?"

"I'm not sure. I really have a lot to get done, but I'll do my best. Have you been okay?"

"Oh, just fine Davey. I've been pretty busy at work

as well. Since you've left, I've taken lots of extra overtime, and I don't get home until late most nights. I have been eating out after work and sometimes don't even get home before bedtime. One of the neighbors happened to catch me leaving one morning and said she thought I had moved."

David breathed a sigh of relief. If West did look for her, maybe he would give up if he could never find her at home. Or maybe he would think she had moved as well. He decided not to mention anything about his situation, not wanting to excite her without reason.

"Well," he said, "I'd better get back to my work here. I promise I'll try to call a bit more often. But if I can't, don't worry, okay?"

"I'll try not to worry, dear, as long as you promise to let me know you're okay once in a while."

"I promise, Mom," he said, feeling guilty because he knew he would be lying to her about what he was doing on every call. As an afterthought, he added, "Mom, I want you to go out and meet people. Maybe even date."

"Thank you, Davey, but aside from the two gentlemen who called a couple of weeks ago asking questions for some poll they were taking, I haven't had time to socialize; I barely have time for work and sleep."

David's stomach dropped. "What kind of poll?" he asked, trying to make it sound like small talk.

"You know, I don't think I remember them saying exactly. They just wanted to know how many people lived at this address. When I told them it was only me. They asked if I was married and when I said no they asked if my son had moved out. Now why would they assume I had a son if I didn't have a husband? I didn't say I was widowed, just not married."

"Did you tell them where I was?" asked David

"I might have mentioned you were in Mexico for a little while. Is something wrong, Davie?" she asked nervously.

"No, Mom," he said calmly trying to hide his anxiety. "It's just that you shouldn't let people know you live alone; it's not safe."

"I didn't think of that. I guess you're right; you can't be too careful."

"So, what did these gentlemen look like; did they

wear any uniforms or have name tags?"

"No, Davey, they wore suits. But even their fancy suits couldn't make up for their rudeness. When I told them I didn't know where in Mexico, they acted like I was some kind of terrible mother for not knowing where her adult son was."

David had a sudden feeling that someone was watching him. He jumped as the operator's voice broke in on their conversation. "Será noventa y cinco centavos para los tres minutos siguientes." (That will be ninety-five cents for the next three minutes.)" It was time to change locations.

Other towns around the country looked particularly alluring: Playa del Carmen, Puebla, Todos Santos, and of course, Mexico City. The problem was getting access to Hermosillo. Until the day he learned to fly a plane and could afford to purchase his own, he needed Hermosillo to be no more than a day's drive away. The following weeks had led him to Culiacan, Chihuahua, Guaymas, and even a border town—Ciudad Juárez. He thought it could be interesting to live in a border town, not to mention a wide door of business opportunities, but after one week of hanging around, he was tired of watching all the traffic going back and forth. Guaymas charmed him the most, and with its especially close proximity to Hermosillo, he had decided to give it a try for a month.

Unfortunately, finding a place there hadn't been as easy as it was for him in Hermosillo that first day. Three stops at stores led him nowhere, so the afternoon turned into a trek around town looking for any signs of places to rent. Ideally, he wanted to be close to the water. In the end, however, he settled on a three-room apartment about five minute drive from the harbor.

The smaller city seemed to be perfectly serene at first, but after some days, David wondered if he liked it only for its stark contrast to L.A. Would he get bored after some weeks? It was hard to tell, as he filled his days with researching, networking, and looking into potential shell companies.

It was there the dilemma arrived. A small coastal town—small enough to be discreet yet significant enough to have a decent harbor—had attracted another businessman. Ignacio was not a one-drug wonder. He used the west coast of Central America to transport a myriad of drugs to and from coastal ports. His operations were known along the coast—not for being large, but for being widespread. His claim was that he could get you whatever you wanted.

David was walking back at a good pace towards the apartment. His stomach was growling, but he didn't have enough pesos to get anything more than a beer, which he had indeed done to tide him over. As he drew closer to his apartment, the pace of his steps immediately slowed. Two men were leaned against the little gate opening up to his walkway. His first thought was that West's goons had found him, but these were not the same guys from L.A. For a split second, his mind told him to turn and go away, but reality spoke up. They were clearly waiting for him and had made eye contact. He could count on his fingers the number of gringos he had seen around town the last few days, so he wasn't exactly mistakable. He had to approach them, and he had to do so with cool confidence. Maybe they were there for a positive reason—they heard what he was looking for and had an offer … maybe. They were just very intimidating. David told himself to stand up straight as he approached.

"Are you sure it's this clown we were waiting for?" the taller one in the leather jacket turned to ask the bulkier, moustached one next to him.

"Hello. How I can help you?" David asked coolly, despite the curious nerves building inside.

"We need you to come inside and talk to us about something," the moustached man informed him.

"Unfortunately, you caught me unprepared to entertain guests. I'm afraid I'll be a terrible host. I don't have any beer, tequila, or coffee."

"We'll be fine." They practically ushered themselves into the apartment.

Not wanting to give them a grand sense of submission, David first poured himself a glass of water before inviting them to sit down.

"How can I help you?" He decided to start, sitting down in the chair opposite them.

"Ignacio would like to employ your services."

Well that was promising news, he thought. These guys had not tracked him down for West, and no one was there malicious intentions. He didn't suspect he had done anything to bring two hitmen to his house, but one could never be sure. He, however, had the hunch that he didn't really want to be working for this Ignacio.

"In what way would your Mr. Ignacio like me to work with him?"

"Doing what you do best."

"I'm sorry. I don't really know Mr. Ignacio."

"But he knows you. He has operations all up and down the coast, and he needs someone to take care of the finances in the North Mexico region."

"How very kind of him, but I'm already employed by someone."

"He knows. But Belladonna only runs a small, one-city operation. And Ignacio only wants you to take care of his finances in one region. From what we've heard of your business skills, you should be able to handle both."

Without further conversation, the two men stood, and David knew he had no option but to accompany them to see this Ignacio.

As the sedan pulled up to the pier, David was a bit impressed by the yacht anchored there. Ignacio had money, and with that came power, influence, and special consideration when it came to stepping outside the lines of justice.

He was escorted aboard the ship and into a very well-decorated cabin on the main deck. Behind a large desk sat a large man smoking a large cigar and holding a rather large handgun. He stood frozen to the spot, his mind suddenly picturing what was left of his short life as being painful and final.

"Come in, Mr. Name," said Ignacio in very good English. David could not get his legs to move. Ignacio stood, placed his cigar in an ashtray, and looked down at the gun in his hand. He smiled and looked up at David.

"Not to worry, Mr. Name. This is not for you. It was a sort of gift from an associate who had no further use for it, and so you might say, I acquired it from him."

One of Ignacio's men pushed David lightly on the back, and he stumbled forward to a chair towards which Ignacio was pointing. Ignacio nodded, and the two men left the cabin.

"I have heard good things about you, Mr. Name. That is so formal. If we are to work together we should call each other by first names, should we not, David?"

"We haven't actually agreed to work together," David said, wanting to invoke some respect from this man who dared to have him whisked away from his home and intimidated by his wealth and henchmen.

"I like a man with backbone," said Ignacio, "it means he can be trusted to keep secrets his friends might entrust him with." His look changed and became hardened. "But let us not waste time sparring like two bulls, trying to exert our fierceness while hoping the other will simply back away. I do not back away, as you will come to find out."

Just as quickly, Ignacio was smiling again as he came around the desk and motioned for David to accompany him. "Come," he said, "let us take in the sunset from the deck; it is most inspiring."

David realized it would be wise to make the best of the situation, but he held a deep resentment and distrust for this man.

They stood at the rear of the boat, Ignacio resting his hand on David's shoulder like long-time friends. "Life is very good," he said quietly to him. "There are rewards for those who recognize opportunity and grasp it. You appear to be one who knows how to grasp, are you not, David?"

David had questions, but he was very tentative on how to go about getting answers. He decided the best approach was to act as though he was being offered a job rather than being forced into service. "So, how is it you know about me?" he asked in what he hoped was an offhand remark.

"In our business, there are many people we might consider mutual acquaintances. Let's just say you have been recommended to me by one who is indebted to me for some services I provided to him."

"And you want me to handle some financial affairs for your businesses?"

"Just some local business; you will not be inconvenienced and there will be no need for you to travel far. But, let us not talk of business tonight. Just be assured your compensation will be well worth your time."

David had a suspicion he would not want to do anything to be inconvenienced by this man.

***

After spending additional time in the uncomfortable company of Ignacio, the two men were ordered to drive David home. As he sat in the back of the sedan, he accepted the fact that he now had two bosses; one who inspired him and one who scared him. He just had to make the best of what his chosen career had presented him.

As they came into town, David had the men drop him off. His stomach was reminding him that he had still not eaten. As the sedan pulled away, he sat down to stare out into the harbor, watching the soft ripples of the water slowly bob the boats up and down. There was always something so soothing and clarifying about the water. Opening his eyes, he wasn't entirely sure whether he had slept or not, save that the hour hand on his pocket watch had moved significantly. He had decided that a homemade steak was in order instead of yet another diner-prepared meal.

***

David swung around his grocery store sack of meat and potatoes on the walk home, realizing that he really wished for a dinner companion. One and a half weeks in

Guaymas hadn't yet been enough to find some company to invite over. There was the local café owner with whom he had enjoyed many great conversations, but he was running his place six days a week. The only time they had met outside the café was during siesta to occasionally enjoy a cigar down by the water.

David sat at his little two-person table organizing his thoughts and working on his second glass of red wine while the steak sizzled in the pan. He told himself bravely that he would consider working with Ignacio, but on his terms. He wanted to make it clear that he was willing to work *with* him to provide an independent service. Second, he wanted to be upfront and forthcoming with Belladonna about the matter to ensure the continuation of his steady pay. Maybe it was the wine talking, but he had the feeling that this lady would take care of Ignacio if she didn't like him seeking her employees for shared services.

***

As the last portion of potatoes went in his mouth, David made the mental note that he should cook for himself more often. It was a shame that he didn't have a lovely lady he could cook for, but it was a bit difficult to date when he was moving about all the time. He debated whether to call

Mateoor wait until later, hoping to get through to Belladonna. Ultimately, he decided to call, since it could sometimes take a few tries to get through.

The rings began ... once, twice, three times, and four. Just as he was about to hang the Army green phone back on its hook, Mateo picked up with his greeting, "Hola!" David began to explain part of the situation to him, asking to speak with Belladonna after a brief overview of the events and his thoughts.

"Belladonna isn't taking any phone calls right now. Erica and I are running everything."

David hesitated as to whether or not to ask any questions. "I see. Then I'll ask for your input."

"As long as you keep us top priority and everything is going flawlessly for operations here, then do as you wish with any extra time that you have."

Mateo seemed almost not to even care about the question at hand. David felt confident he could take on more than one operation, especially once one was smoothly rolling. He could simply copy the laundering methods elsewhere. The difficult part would be to ensure that he remained his own boss. His mind dwelled for a moment on the seemingly curious situation at hand. He was used to having most of his questions answered by Mateo or Erica, only being diverted to Belladonna when it was a larger matter at hand, such as his move to Mexico. It seemed curious that she wasn't taking any phone calls. Trying to keep in mind that it was really none of his business, David moved on to the dishes.

CHAPTER 28

"Southward Bound"

She had never been in an American or Swedish courtroom, but somehow, the Mexican courtroom was different than she imagined. The initial hearing had not led very far. Juan, Carla, Sarah, and a very drunk homeless man all spent the night together in the same cell. The judge seemed to be angry with Sarah the minute she walked into the room. As it turned out, he had grown up on a farm; agriculture was their family's business for generations, of which his brother was now running the family crops. He gave a long lecture about the detriment she had caused in the area if she had indeed imported the pest with her plants from the United States.

There was no official case to be had yet, as the file was still being put together. The Hermosillo court hearing was only to set bail and establish the opening of the case. Since there were multiple violations to be investigated— starting with smuggling, illegal property and selling illegal merchandise that crossed more than one municipal district, she was to appear in federal court in Mexico City.

She was doing well in Mexico with business

negotiations and orders, but the thought of using Spanish, her third language, in a federal court of law intimidated her. She needed a good lawyer, to get in touch with Mateo and Erica, and to get Juan and Carla off the hook. Since their alleged crimes didn't cross any territorial borders, she was able to plea with the judge, who allowed their case to stay there. She negotiated a meeting with the judge after the gavel came down.

Surprised and thankful that the judge allowed the meeting, Sarah tried to show her utmost respect in his office. She would accept that she needed to go through a trial in Mexico City, relying on the best lawyer she could find, but she pleaded for Mr. and Mrs. Rodriguez. "They are wonderful neighbours who would never do anything," she insisted.

"Any questionable activity found on their property must be a simple mistake of property miscalculation."

"Are you willing to take full responsibility for all charges?" the judge questioned.

"If the court of law finds me guilty of any questionable activity, I won't plead guilty, but I do claim the property as mine." She was trying to choose her words with a calm and clear mind.

"Here's my ruling," he finally declared after hearing her out. Sarah's pleasing demeanour had softened his initial edge of attitude towards her. He saw past the situation and to her as a human being. "If you pay their bail, I will drop all their charges.

"It's done," she agreed. The guards escorted her out of the bare room and to the van where Juan and Carla were waiting in handcuffs. "Don't worry," she assured them before sitting in silence for the rest of the ride back to the prison.

The money was arranged for them within hours, and she wrote them a note to leave at the house for Mateo. It contained instructions for him and Erica concerning business operations as well as instructions for arranging money and the best lawyer he could find. She wasn't sure what to expect as a timeline, but things needed to keep running. Erica and Mateo were to run the show until they received further information. She'd figure out how to communicate with them later, but until she got to Mexico City, there were too many unknowns.

The drunken man from the night before had already

been released by the time they had returned, and Carla and Juan were discharged by mid-evening. Sarah was left by herself in the cell. She wouldn't have minded the company, but the sleepless hours passed alone.

She was unsure what time it was—only sure that it was very early. The light was barely peering through any of the jail's windows. A new guard had arrived to relieve the gentleman who had been there all night. One exhausted from his night shift and the other exhausted from waking at an early hour, they hardly exchanged words as they switched. He watched the leaving guard point in her direction, receiving an affirmative nod from the oncoming guard. After disappearing for five or ten minutes, the new guard appeared at her cell with the breakfast tray—bread and coffee. She wondered if the food would be any better down in Mexico City.

The guard stood staring at her as he passed her food inside. She was unsure as to whether she should feel concerned or flattered. He seemed to be staring deep into her eyes.

"How could anyone with such eyes be dangerous?" he questioned. Not waiting for an answer, he let her know that she needed to eat quickly. "Your transportation leaves in twenty minutes."

The guard escorted her with her things into the van once it pulled up in front. Upon first stepping into the vehicle, she concluded it was going to be an interesting ride on the way down. They would be stopping at two different prisons on the way, breaking the trip into three days. Some prisoners were to be dropped off along the way, and some picked up on the way down. At least it should make for interesting company, she figured; plus, it would be a good time to learn more about the Mexican prison system and practice her Spanish.

CHAPTER 29

"Settling In"

For sitting in a prison vehicle and eating bland food, Sarah halfway enjoyed her ride to Mexico City. She and her parents had flown into Mexico City from L.A. during one of her summer college vacations. This was certainly a different way to visit the city! Some stretches of scenery along the way provided hours of entertainment as she stared out the window, observing the changing fauna, small creatures, and pop-up pueblos. "How many people can say they've toured a country this way?" she figured.

Her morale was high, confident that she could get herself out of the situation; however, her spirits reflected nearly the opposite of all the other prisoners who joined the ride along the way. Her mood wasn't the only thing that put her in the minority. Skin color, hair color, and gender made her the curious attraction along the way. "What's the gringa doing on the bus?" one man, Emiliano as it turned out, asked as he stepped his first foot onto the bus. "The woman is here to keep you in line," Sarah had shot back at him in a light manner. The mood of the bus was heavy enough that no one made even so much as a smirk.

The ride mostly included thieves which had crossed many territorial borders. One older man provided a great amount of intrigue and hours of imaginative play. Boarding at Sinaloa for the day's ride to Guadalajara, Sarah tried to make some small talk, as she did with most of the other riders. While most responded to her with a look in their eyes seeming to imply that not only was she a gringa, but a gringa *loca*, they at least answered her questions and usually responded with some curious questions of their own. "Serpiente" was the only kind of name the old man would give to her. Everyone else was younger or bulkier, some with tattoos and scars, and one other woman who seemed to have had a vicious altercation with an ex-husband while on vacation. The old man, however, was neither bulky nor scrawny—no tattoos. One single scar by his jaw line was the only outstanding feature. He would give no definitive answers to any of Sarah's inquiries. "What's your trouble?" was answered by, "Something you'd like to know about." "Your name?" only provided the answer, "You can call me 'Serpiente,' or any other animal you feel like." Only slightly frustrated by his lack of conversation and answers, Sarah was ultimately intrigued by his mystery. She spent a good few hours of the trip studying him and making up her own story about who he was and why he was travelling with them.

As it turned out, the disgruntled Emiliano became her favorite co-passenger not too long after he joined in Sinaloa with his snide remarks. She got the middle-aged man to let out a chuckle or two; and even though he maintained his straight face and squinty eyes most of the time, she figured he liked her as well, giving that he always sat somewhere in her close vicinity on the bus. His partial amicability also gave her opportunity to quiz Emiliano about the judicial system and prison life in Mexico. By the end of her trip and all their conversations, she was feeling less optimistic about her prospects concerning her possible stay in prison, yet more confident that if she got a sentence she wouldn't be staying for too long.

Her mind pondered how she had arrived at her current situation. She questioned why her remote, and still relatively small operation, had been targeted. Surely, the kings of the region presented bigger catches than her business. Was it a routine search that led the police to her doorstep, or was someone targeting her? Her mind began sorting and filtering facts as she sat silently, trying to eliminate possibilities and identify someone who might want her shut down. Who in Mexico might consider her a threat? Ignacio might see her as moving in on his territory, but they weren't selling the same products and her share of the marijuana business was far from the dominant player.

There were a few people who might have sold her out if the price were right; her street agents, Mateo, who else? Would David give up information if someone offered him more money?

She suddenly worried about the L.A. operation. Would she be able to maintain the business while in prison, or should she put Erica in charge and trust her to handle everything? Ricky … why did she suddenly fixate on Ricky? But how would he manage to put information into the hands of the police? He was aware of the L.A. operation but knew nothing of the Mexico end of the business. He knew Mateo, of course, and perhaps they shared information. Was that why Ricky left? Did he take the money and run? The thought of such a coordinated effort scared her.

She began to put hypothetical pieces together. Ricky was hired on Larry's recommendation, and Larry was certainly deeply involved in the drug network. Mateo was hired on Ricky's recommendation, and they would certainly be in contact with each other. Ricky knew of Sarah's private studio apartment, the place she kept to herself, but how? He was there when Sarah had gone to check it after Quintaro trashed her office. How did Quintaro know of her apartment? Or was it Quintaro who rummaged through the apartment? Was it Ricky who was searching for her business files, and would he sell information to anyone for the right price?

Her stomach turned. Was she just being paranoid? No, someone had to feed information to Quintaro, and that would be Ricky. Ricky had the most to gain and access to information valuable to certain people who might want her out of business. Her world now seemed like one big conspiracy, and she had to wonder how she didn't see it. If you play on the illegal side of the law, you were always going to be a target to someone. Her morale was suddenly not so high.

Sarah forced herself to clear all thoughts of what might be and focus on the present. As the bus pulled in through the large, sliding prison gate, Sarah gave a smile and a "hasta luego" to her new pseudo-buddy. In his cool, calm character he returned a nod. The largest prison in the country wasn't far from what Sarah had already imagined: the gray concrete, the fences, the dismal look of officers. Did it really differ much throughout the world? After all the check-in procedures, she found that the Mexico City prison differed in at least these two ways: she felt it overcrowded, yet glad she wasn't handed a hideous bright orange jumpsuit to wear.

She was uncertain whether to even ask about the clothing, afraid they might hand her just what she didn't want to wear. Keeping her mouth shut, assuming it might come later, she was pleasantly surprised to see all the others in their "street clothes" as she was walked down the gloomy hallway to her cell. It certainly made observation and people watching a lot more interesting.

It was early evening by the time all the processing finished, and Sarah was escorted to her cell, along with the only other female that had been on the bus. Sarah hadn't gathered much from her on the way, except her name—Lucia—and the fact that she had been involved in a brutal event with her ex-husband. She didn't share a lot of details. Sarah gathered that her quiet was a different kind of quiet than Serpiente's. She seemed nervous and afraid—not the tough type who had brushed up against authority or prison before. One of the others on the bus offered that she had killed her ex-husband in a fight over some possessions.

Lucia still hadn't offered any more information by the time they arrived at their cell together. Her nervous eyes hid somewhat behind her long, dark wavy hair and bangs. As they arrived at the cell, stuffed with eight other women, Sarah glanced over at Lucia. She was only looking straight ahead, though, in the reserved silence that she had maintained to that point. The guard pointed out two beds in the corner and let them know that breakfast was at seven. As the door closed behind them, Sarah let out a deep sigh and took a look around.

She started toward the beds, looking back at Lucia. "Do you have a preference of beds?"

An arm was suddenly shoved out in her path. She turned when she felt the obstacle; a large woman with bad teeth and a worse attitude was blocking her way. "I make the decisions in this cell, not some primped up little Americano," she said pushing her finger into Sarah's chest.

Sarah decided it was best to avoid any conflict in a hostile environment where she was the minority, and Americans were definitely an unwelcome minority in a Mexican prison.

"Sorry," Sarah replied, "I don't know the rules. I've never been in prison before."

"Don't worry," snarled the imposing woman, "I'll teach you the rules. Nice necklace," she said, reaching down and grasping the pendent hanging around Sarah's neck.

"Thanks," said Sarah, beginning to feel conflict was inevitable.

"First rule, I'm in charge in here. Second rule, anything of yours is now mine," and she let the pendent drop against Sarah's chest and held out her hand, palm side up which left no doubt in Sarah's mind that she was demanding the pendent.

Sarah bent her head down and reached behind her neck, unclasping the chain. She held it out and dropped it into the large woman's hand and in a single motion drove the butt of her palm into the woman's face. Several of the other cell mates let out surprised shouts as the large body slammed against the wall behind her and then slid to the floor. Sarah squatted down and took the pendent from the woman's hand. Instantly, a hand grabbed Sarah's shoulder from behind. She sprang up and turned, prepared to attack but her wrist was firmly grasped in the hand of one of the male guards.

"It didn't take you long to cause trouble, señorita," said the guard.

"No trouble," replied Sarah, glaring at the guard, "I was just showing this nice lady my necklace."

The guard lifted the wrist he held firmly to eye the chain hanging from Sarah's captured hand. He snatched the pendent from her and smiled. "I'll keep this to avoid any further problems. Maybe I'll give it back to you if you are really nice."

Sarah jerked her arm out of his grasp. He stood there for a moment, smiling at her. "I bet I could put a twinkle in those violet eyes of yours."

Sarah said nothing, just stared with contempt at the guard, fighting back the urge to hurt this buffoon and recover her property. He just nodded and left, dropping Sarah's locket into his shirt pocket.

There was no more trouble from the other girls, but Sarah decided it would be best not to sleep too soundly that night.

The night was long and mostly sleepless. Sarah was in disbelief at how soundly some of the other ladies in the cell could sleep—based on their unrelenting snores. From the first twelve hours there, she had gathered that prison life in Mexico could certainly be interesting. Of course, she had nothing to compare it to, but the ladies in her cell at least were full of color and stories. Lucia was still too frozen to share. Sarah was willing to say as much about herself as needed to claim a position of respect in the hall, but she was more interested in hearing about the others and their trials. If there was a silver lining, it was that she got to wear her normal clothes and keep some semblance of her identity. What she wasn't so keen on, however, especially after that first night, was the number of prisoners stuffed into one cell. A recent crackdown on drug possession and mafia minions had left Mexican prisons overcrowded. Sarah was hoping that a little money could get her somewhere.

She was already awake when the alarms sounded. Anxious to get some time to speak with a guard about her trial and sleeping arrangements, she was the first one waiting at the door. The unusually tall male guard, however, seemed uninterested in any questions that Sarah had to ask. Barely even looking at her, he maintained his orderly conduct of getting everyone out to breakfast. It was that magical word, "money," that did the trick, though. Continuing to move along with the routine still, he let her know that his ears were now open. By the end of the mostly one-sided conversation, she learned that she would have to wait on the overcrowded floor for two to three days until her trial date was set. However, five hundred pesos would at least get her into a less crowded cell. "Unfortunately, money speaks," she thought to herself. "I wonder if it could speak loudly enough to get me a decent breakfast." It seemed not.

An attorney arrived the morning after Sarah had been incarcerated. He had been hired by Mateo and informed her that they would appear before the judge the next day. Sarah beamed with optimism, but the attorney's demeanour didn't match hers. He scolded her first for complying to give her statement of what happened without an attorney present. He then informed her that she shouldn't be too thrilled about the court appearance. It was standard protocol within the first seventy-two hours, and it would be the first appearance of many.

Mateo had arranged for a few clothing items to be delivered by the lawyer, and he handed her a paper bag with a change of outfit. He also slipped her enough money to barter new sleeping quarters with the guard and a bit more for incidentals, warning her to keep it hidden from everyone until needed.

"You're not in the United States any more, my dear," he let her know. "Here, you are guilty until proven innocent. We operate under Napoleonic law. Your trial will take a long time—especially for drug charges. Settle in. Welcome to Mexico City's federal prison."

Heading back to the cell, it was the first time Sarah actually felt down about the situation. The other prisoners had all expressed their dismay about the lack of punctuality regarding the court system. She assumed it wouldn't be the case for her, though, and still held out hope that it wouldn't be.

The attorney warned her again the following day, "This will only be the first in a long line of court visits. Get used to seeing this place."

Sarah considered seeking a new attorney in the following days, as she found his pessimism draining. He was supposed to be one of the best in the country, though, and was famous for representing foreigners.

***

She had been surprised at how empty the room was. A line of people were waiting for their turn with the judge, and Sarah and Mr. Hernandez had spent almost two hours outside as well. Appearance with the judge went quickly. He seemed not only to have a disinterest in her case, but he wanted to move on with the line awaiting his appointments. Flipping through the file while listening to the statements, he swiftly made a motion that enough evidence was present to continue the trial. Her next appearance was in three weeks. Sarah felt the need to say something before they left, but her mind seemed only to be racing through her thoughts without putting forth anything coherent. Before she could speak, they were whisked out of the room.

"Three weeks?!" she turned to Hernandez when they reached the holding room where she would wait for the others to finish.

"I told you to settle in," he replied unsympathetically. "For serious charges, it can take up to one or more years to complete the trial."

Sarah stared back at him in disbelief and knew that she had some phone calls to make. How was she going to run things from prison? She needed to call Mateo and Erica, and it was finally time to call her parents. If she didn't contact the latter, she imagined this scenario of them putting out a missing persons report only to get a call that their daughter was actually behind bars in a Mexican prison. She wasn't going to let *that* happen. It was time to tell them partial truth—that she was doing underground research for a groundbreaking article. Then, she would include the lie that she was falsely accused of drug activity while researching in Mexico and only hoped they wouldn't try to intervene.

Back at the prison, those who had been to court were sorted through according to their results. Some had bail set, a lucky one was dismissed, and the rest of them were taken to switch floors up to a more permanent level. The move certainly didn't elicit excitement from anyone. Apparently, her accessibility to money had made its way around the guards, though. The gentleman overseeing the switch came in close to her, offering a spot in a superior cell with only two other cellmates in exchange for some money ... as well as some other special services if she wanted. She politely declined the second offer but took the first, settling in with her new cell mates and their back stories. Her next goal was to learn everything she could to make her stay as bearable and as short as possible.

CHAPTER 30

"Betrayal"

The sun had long set by the time his car pulled into Guaymas. Even though it was late, he did a quick walk around to sweep away the corner cob webs and open up the windows for a few minutes while he settled in. He sat down on the bed to peel off his shoes and socks, and one motion led to another. The next move he made with his body was a jerked awakening at the sound of a rooster under his window. His eyes fluttered open to the realization that he had fallen asleep with most of his clothes on and all the windows open. "I guess it saves time getting dressed," he figured.

David hadn't been up to Hermosillo in nearly seven weeks. It was time for a visit to Belladonna's front companies there, as well as a check-in with Mateo. It was one of his least favorite drives, so he made the trip as infrequently as possible—mostly just checking in on his main people there. The view certainly wasn't the problem, it was the length of the trip that bothered him; the drive didn't quite warrant breaking it into two days, but it was long enough to make his entire body ache with stiffness upon arrival. Packing a small suitcase and some snacks, he eased his way onto the highway to head up the 15, settling in for the long day's drive.

He drove until his eyes became blurred and realized he wasn't paying attention to the road. Road fatigue could be a dangerous thing. A person thinks they're driving just fine, and then suddenly, they wake up in a ditch … if they're lucky enough to wake up at all. He decided to stop when he came across a road stop with nothing more than a gas station that doubled as the local eatery, offering coffee, soda, and some local delicacies of questionable freshness.

A pastry and a coffee later, he was back on the road for the two-hour day trip to Hermosillo. He had called Mateo a few days before to make sure he would be available for a meeting. Often hard to reach, Mateo assured him he looked forward to catching up on financial affairs. Usually, they met at a discreet restaurant or cafe, but this time, he was given directions to a house.

He wasn't sure why, but he didn't trust Mateo; not that he ever really trusted him. Their last meeting left him with a feeling that Mateo was hiding something. His vagueness about Belladonna and his apparent lack of concern for David's involvement in the business had left him disliking the man.

David pulled up to a house in the middle of farmland.

"Not bad," he thought to himself, "but he could kill me out here if he really wanted to. Surely they wouldn't kill the money man." He felt that he trusted Belladonna but the nervous thoughts in the back of his head seemed to linger.

Mateo welcomed him in to the modestly-sized but now well-decorated house.

"You bought a house here?" David asked, nodding with approval as he looked around.

"It was built, actually. I just acquired it."

"Nice hideout. So you inherited it, did you say?"

"Well, there were some problems with authorities awhile back. We've since reorganized the operation."

David now knew that Mateo was hiding information about Belladonna's business, and he wasn't sure how to approach the situation. He also realized that he could no longer consider his situation simply a job and remain aloof and removed from Belladonna and her personal welfare. Maybe it was his dislike for Mateo, but he cared for the safety of this woman and did not like the idea that she was about to be personally harmed. Fearing that a direct confrontation might cause further harm to Belladonna or himself, David assumed an attitude of disinterest.

"Oh, I didn't hear anything. I guess it didn't affect the money flow," David let out a half-fake chuckle.

"Yeah, the business is still running fine. We just had to do some emergency stash runs and change some things with the plants here, but that didn't affect you. So, on to what does affect you."

Mateo had sometimes been short with David in the past when he was in a hurry or managing many things at once. But

David was slightly taken aback by his demeanor that day. He tried not to let Mateo's sharp tone get to him. The men started digging into the financial side of the business after each taking a shot of tequila. David answered Mateo's questions as simply as possible, trying not to sound like he was hiding anything. But in the back of his mind he was already contriving plans to ensure Belladonna's finances did not end up under Mateo's control.

"Everything sounds great," Mateo affirmed after David finished his synopsis of the current money flow systems. "Now, we have one change that needs to be made. As I mentioned, there are some new situations at hand, and we've done a little reorganizing. What Belladonna needs now is a new bank account for the company. Instead of depositing the money back into her personal bank account, we need a neutral bank account here in Mexico— one not specifically under her name. It should be a business account I have access to, so I can move money around. How do we do that?"

David tried not to show any concern, but his mind was now racing to digest the implications of what he had just heard. Mateo's directives were in complete opposition to Belladonna's previous plans.

"Uhhh ... sure. I'll take care of it," David answered slowly in regards to the request. He didn't want to question too much.

"Good," replied Mateo, "but I'd like to hear all the ins and outs so that I understand the details."

David turned over one of the papers to begin drawing an outline of the details, purposely leaving out a few he decided Mateo didn't need to understand. He was beginning to feel the need to hold a few cards to be played at a later time.

"Sounds good; thank you," Mateo finalized after asking a few more questions. "Now, go ahead and get that other bank account set up as soon as possible and leave the details of the account in an envelope under the mat."

With that, David stood as Mateo stretched out his arm for a handshake. They exchanged a firm grip and stare in an effort to assert their confidence. David jumped back in his car and left. He ran over their meeting in his head while driving into town. There was a piece of the puzzle he was missing from his previous conversation, but he couldn't quite fit it together.

David had never been one to depend on others or risk his neck for just anybody, but he suddenly felt that his life of performing duties and taking his pay without getting too involved was about to change. Something was wrong, and he suspected that Belladonna was in serious trouble. Strange, he thought, that he could suddenly feel worry for a woman he had never met.

One and a half weeks up in the north had been plenty for him. It was time enough to rearrange some financial accounts and make an appearance at each shell and front business. Many meetings and miles later, he was closing up his tiny Guaymas apartment. Some federal representatives had been snooping around many of the business's financial matters in the Sonora area, and it had sent him into a few days of panic. Now, David felt he had it all under control—evidence free. He was ready to get back down south to his little piece of paradise. Grabbing a few bags of churros and a bottle of soda, he figured it would be enough sugar to give him an energy boost for at least the first half of the journey.

Puerta Vallarta had really become home for David. His Spanish was close to fluent and he was still learning local dialects. Happy to have finished with the long day's drive and the last week and a half of hard work, David pulled immediately into Mission Trece for a cold beer. He had become good friends with the owner, Paolo, who was a self-proclaimed "Brazilian import." They clinked their beer bottles, and Paolo jokingly asked him how his mysterious business ventures had been coming along the last week and a half. "Don't tell me. I don't want to know," he would always tease David.

Countless beers later and well into the morning, David had abandoned his car down the street from the bar to walk home instead. He was awakened only a few, entirely too short, hours later by a harsh knock on the door. He pulled his face off the pillow, wiping a touch of drool from the corner of his lip. A few more pounds on the door let him know that he wasn't just dreaming. "Un momento!"

He gave both eyes a hearty rub with the palms of his hands before reaching to open the door. As the door creeped open, it slowly revealed two men with Policía Federal badges and uniforms. David wasn't quite sure what the appropriate response was to two federal officers. They weren't tattooed, scarred, grim-faced, and bulky like typical drug lord minions. Their presence was intimidating in a different way. As he always did in the face of fear, David told himself to act calm and with confidence.

"Señor Davis?" the smaller of the two men inquired.

"Sí?"

"We have evidence of your involvement in drug sales and money laundering. We've come to place you under arrest here in Puerta Vallarta until the judge makes an initial decision on your case. At that time, if the evidence seems to hold solid, you will be transported to Mexico City for a trial."

"Wha …uh … wh … What is this evidence?"

"Everything will be explained to you down at the station. For now, we ask that you cooperate and come with us so we don't have to use force."

"There's no reason an innocent man can't comply," he responded, hoping to instil some faith in his character.

"Señor, here in Mexico, you are guilty until proven innocent."

"Well that's a bit dismal," he mumbled under his breath as he grabbed his keys and wallet to follow the men out the door.

David was still in shock after arriving at the station. He went through all the steps wide-eyed, taking in the process. He thought it was best not to give any statements as requested before finding out the exact details of the evidence and his charges. How in the world had they traced him? David took pride in his lack of any evidence trail, so it must have been a rat. Someone had to have given the police something. But what? And who? The interesting encounters with Mateo on the last visit replayed in his mind. Hopefully, there wasn't enough for a conviction, but if there was, he might be able to trade information with the police to dodge a sentence. That was the trouble with working for multiple drug lords; there was a greater chance of getting ratted out. He would just keep his lips sealed until he knew.

Someone a few cells down had kept him awake through the night with their long, drawn-out snores. As David walked down the hall to be transported to see the judge, he eyed each cell in search of the loud sleeper. He had spent most of the night dozing in and out when he could, hands behind his head for a little extra cushion, running through the possibilities of what evidence they might have for a conviction.

An attorney assigned to the case had shown up to meet with him first, quickly running through the file. David did his best to keep up with the legal jargon while simultaneously getting a good grasp on the details of his arrest.

"This is just the first step," his attorney explained. "If the judge finds the evidence sufficient, then you'll be subject to a longer trial."

"How long, exactly?" David had the feeling he would end up in Mexico City.

"Well, for a case like this, it could take up to a year or more."

"A year?!" David exclaimed in disbelief.

The judge looked over the evidence of false account statements that had been reported, and it didn't take long for him to declare the evidence sufficient. He even raised an eyebrow as he reviewed the papers, leaving David nervous about the trial's outcome. The best bet to save his skin, he thought, was to play a rat in return. If he gave them the bigger cat, they should let the mouse off the hook.

David couldn't believe that he had gone from celebrating with friends all night in a bar, to sitting in Mexico City's federal prison, all within seventy-two hours. Speaking of friends, he needed to get someone to mail him some clothes. His reclusive lifestyle had come to haunt him. Could he count on one of his few friends in

Mexico? He looked to the little window outside. A bummer of a way to visit Mexico City, he thought. The sun seemed to be beckoning him outside for an afternoon of cocktails on a street café. At least, the sunshine brought comfort while he settled for water in the prison courtyard.

He tried to find the positives in his situation and shift his focus from what lay ahead. The afternoon dwindled away, minute by minute, as he sat outside doing one of his favourite pastimes: people watching. Pleasantly surprised by some of the other company, he ended up in some interesting conversations that gave some insight to prison life. The conditions left much to be desired, but at least he had the ability to purchase necessities, wear his own clothes, and, as it turned out, socialize with the ladies on Sunday afternoons. There were also some interesting characters to help pass the days, and he was especially curious about the patched-eye gentleman who appeared in the courtyard every hour.

The conversations he had with fellow prisoners left him feeling slightly dismal about the trial process. If he couldn't post bail, it sounded like he could be there for months. One guy had been waiting ten months already, in and out of several court sessions, awaiting what he expected would be a verdict of "not guilty." The story he explained to David, at least, made it sound like he was framed.

Maybe David had a chance to convince the judge he, too, was

framed. His lawyer had informed him that a new attorney would be arriving the next day to discuss the case with him. David wondered who had obtained the new lawyer. Perhaps word of his arrest had gotten back to Mateo or Belladonna and they had hired him.

A mental checklist had already been started to see what kind of arrangements he could make to get out of there as fast as possible. With the exception of bad food and uncomfortable sleeping conditions, he was finding this to be quite an adventure. Nonetheless, he didn't really want the adventure to last too long.

***

A robust Mexican who did not speak English soon joined the group of prisoners in David's cell. David had not paid much attention to him, not wanting to invite any hostilities. Another man named Luis, a wiry man of undecided age and missing several teeth, had become tentatively friendly toward David and was always offering advice on how to stay out of trouble.

"Choose your friends wisely and watch your back, especially if you left any unfinished business behind," he whispered to him shortly after the large man was placed in their cell.

David told Luis that he had not considered himself in any danger from outside the prison and that he was doing his best to avoid conflict with anyone on the inside.

"The big guy," whispered Luis, nodding at the big Mexican, "he is said to be what we call a silenciador, a silencer. He's been here as long as I have, over a year. They say he worked for some very tough hombres on the outside and continues, still, to do work for them in here."

"A silencer?" asked David.

"They are cartel thugs who are loyal to their bosses; loyal enough to spend time in prison in order to help the cartel maintain silence among prisoners who might know too much."

"Wait," said David shaking his head. "You're telling me there are guys who will spend the rest of their lives in prison just to help the cartel? I don't believe that."

"They are usually only here for a while. They spend a tour of duty like a soldier, and then they are freed and greatly rewarded."

"But this guy's been here for over a year?"

"They say he is still on the payroll of a drug cartel. When someone involved in the cartel gets put here, they say he makes sure they say nothing."

"How does he do that when he's stuck in a cell with only a few guys?"

"Money opens many opportunities, and he is able to move about in the prison walls. Some of the guards help to move him into different cells, and it's said he's also allowed into areas that are off-limits to the rest of us."

"That sounds like a story to scare little children. If he had that kind of support from outside, why is he still in prison?"

"He may be trying to prove his loyalty. His value is much greater within the walls than outside of them. I have heard stories of prisoners suffering great injury and even death because they knew things that were dangerous to men outside."

That night, after head count, David was lying on his bunk making notes for his lawyer, using a small penlight to see. Before he realized it, the big Mexican was standing over him, a look of utmost contempt on his face.

"Atún."

"Sorry," replied David as the sudden appearance had startled him, but did not understand what the big man had said. The big man lifted David from his bunk and tossed him into the middle of the cell.

The other men in the cell stared, but no one made a sound. Even Luis covered his embarrassment by looking away from the scene. David scrambled to his feet, not sure if it was the right thing to do, but he was certain that lying on the floor, where he could be kicked to death, was certainly not. He looked around for help of any kind. Standing beyond the bars were two guards, but they didn't move.

Just as he thought he was about to be killed right in front of witnesses, one of the guards said, "I think he gets the point, Javier, don't you?"

"Sí, I think so," replied the other guard.

The door to the cell opened, and the silencer was escorted out. Luis walked slowly to where David stood and looked him in the eye.

"I am sorry, my friend, but there was nothing anyone could do without risking their lives."

"Don't worry about it, I understand. But why would a cartel think I had any information about them? My associations are with small businesses, mostly dealing in local marijuana."

"The big man must have mistaken you for someone else. He accused you of planning to provide information on a member of the Gulf cartel in exchange for your freedom. Take that as a warning."

The Gulf cartel? Was Ignacio involved in some way with a cartel? David thought about the financial records he had worked on. Maybe he was being used by Ignacio to launder cartel business disguised as small-time local drug dealers. His urgency to get out of Mexico had increased dramatically.

CHAPTER 31

"Months Gone By"

David's new lawyer said that he had been hired, at an apparent great cost, by an anonymous person. He didn't know nor did he care who hired him as long as the fees continued to be paid. This left David wondering who was involved from both sides. Someone seemed to want him in prison while someone else seemed to want him out. Where did Belladonna, Mateo, Ignacio, or anyone else fit in to this?

Getting out of the charges was no longer a viable option. Three months and four court dates had already passed, and the attorney had told him the chances of winning the case were slim to none. Whoever had turned him in had submitted plenty of damning evidence. His lawyer told him to settle in, use money for bribes of comfort, and get a prison job to shorten the sentence. His lawyer also arranged for a bit of David's cash holdings to be transferred to an account so the lawyer could draw any funds David might need to live a bit more comfortably while detained.

He had taken his advice, quickly learning the trading system amongst prisoners. He found the small job he had managed to get in the kitchen somewhat enjoyable. At least it was something interesting to do, and he was learning about Mexican cuisine. Maybe he could impress a lady with his new culinary skills one day, although the words, "I learned how to make this while in prison" didn't sound too romantic

During the first week in the kitchen, a new employee named Raphael was assigned to work with him. David figured that he had bargained his way out of another obligation by agreeing to take the job, because he had no aptitude at all for cooking. In fact, he often disrupted David with small talk while he was trying to prepare meals. David didn't mind; he enjoyed the work, and any conversation was usually welcome. David had already learned to keep details to a minimum when discussing anything with anybody, especially since his encounter with the big Mexican, who thankfully had not made a second appearance. David decided it had all been a case of mistaken identity and began to focus again on making a deal with the court.

Since his lawyer had told him his case was nearly hopeless, David had asked him about the possibility of ratting out someone else. He was hoping to get off the hook completely for giving up one of the tops: Mateo, if they were interested. He didn't trust him, and he had no qualms about trading places with him if it meant freedom. It had to be expected as part of the lifestyle that every man had his price, and nobody was more valuable than one's self. Certainly, Mateo would take steps to protect himself. What if Ignacio had turned him in? He was a big fish and might be worth a deal to the federals. For some reason, he couldn't justify giving up Belladonna. There was something about her he thought he would like if they ever met one day. Besides, he didn't really have all that much information about her. The lawyer had told him it would be some weeks before they knew if the federal police were willing to make the deal and what the deal would be. This gave David time to try to figure out who he was going to deal away.

David was trying to make the best of his situation with a light attitude. He had already lost most of his laundering jobs, save one operation for a client in Chihuahua which he could manage entirely with a phone call each week. At least he hadn't been greedy about spending his money, establishing a couple of smaller accounts at local banking institutions and leaving a very large sum in reserve. He had already started to formulate a plan for when he was out.

There were a few other international prisoners waiting out their time for smuggling charges and the like. He stayed away from the Russian accused of murders. He claimed innocence, but David didn't like the look in his eyes. His imagination dreamed of other places as he listened to them talk about their homelands. Western Asia in particular had become the target on his radar once freedom was achieved. He loved to hear his prison mate, Mehmet, from a few cells down talk about the exotic foods and street life. His time in Mexico had only whet his appetite for more international travel.

The female prisoners were allowed to come over to the men's side to visit in the courtyard for two hours each Sunday. David had even heard that they allowed conjugal visits, but he hadn't yet taken advantage. He almost always attended the Sunday afternoons but rarely interacted with the women. Instead, he found it to be prime people-watching time and therefore his favorite day of the week.

Maria had a light spirit that intrigued Sarah. The first day she moved onto the new floor, Maria was quietly reading in her top bunk bed. The moment the guards left, Maria began a conversation with something other than the conventional question, "What are you here for?" This question was an indirect way to size others up and determine what crime category they were in and how long they might be staying.

Instead, without even peering over her book and looking at Sarah, Maria asked, "If you would say that you're one character from *Little Women*, which one would you say you are?" Her voice and demeanour were both calm and even-keeled. A small smile immediately forced itself on Sarah's lips, and from that moment forward, the two women had a bond that they were more than grateful to share in the grey, dismal prison surroundings.

Maria had claimed nothing but innocence from the beginning. Of course, proving innocence was an entirely different matter. Maria's optimism didn't miss a beat, though. "It's all in how you place it in the universe," she always repeated. "I'll earn my freedom. That's all there is to it. If you put out negative energy, then you're already allowing the possibility that something negative could happen."

Sarah had tried to follow along with her theory: repeating in her mind that the only possibility was for her to be free. She knew in her heart, though, that a shadow of doubt existed. She wished she had total optimism like Maria; it worked for her. After seven months of trials, Maria had come back from her last with a wide smile spread across her face. She was heading back out into the world. All charges had been dropped. Bittersweet was indeed the perfect word for Sarah's feelings. Happiness for Maria's freedom was clouded over by feelings of sadness that a close friend would be gone. Of course, there were promises to see each other again. Though those promises were said with good intentions, there was no certainty that they would be fulfilled.

Just the week before Maria's innocent verdict came through, a tragedy had swept over the prison. Perhaps it didn't shake the long-term prisoners quite as much, but it was enough to make Sarah want to stay in her cell the entire day. Four men masquerading as law enforcement officials delivering a new prisoner had made their way inside the heavily-guarded walls. Sarah had been sitting in her cell when she heard what she thought were gunshots. Maria and two of the other cellmates ran into the room moments later in a wide-eyed panic with orders to get under the beds.

Afraid to peer out from the bed, Sarah only listened to the chaos that followed: gunshots, shouting, rushes of vehicles, screams, and Maria whispering Hail Marys next to her. She was afraid to even crawl out once silence had fallen. Hours later, after lockdown was released, word of mouth had spread amongst the prisoners that the disguised officers were members of the drug cartel who had come in to take care of a rivalling business. They had taken over the prison until hoards of federal reinforcement arrived. Four prisoners and three guards were left dead—at least that was the passed-down version of the story. How much was true didn't matter. It was traumatic nonetheless—whether there was one person dead or twenty, whether it was the drug cartel or some anarchists. It was something she didn't care to experience again; therefore, she tried that much harder to instil Maria's "positive energy" theory following the incident.

After those last weeks, the atmosphere felt a bit heavy, and Sarah needed a change. She had never gone to the Sunday afternoon male-female mingling time before, but it seemed like a good time to start. Women often came back from the afternoon throwing around the word "chingar" and the phrase "me la clavaron," boasting of their afternoon sexual encounters. With the impression that these afternoons turned the courtyard into a meat market, she had been largely uninterested, not exactly intending on finding her "principe azules" in prison.

The hot afternoon sun left David positioned in a corner

under the small shade that the building offered. His hat was pulled down slightly over his eyes, his legs stretched out and crossed in front of him. With his vision obscured by the brim of his hat, he had a whole new perspective this afternoon, marked by the movement of feet and legs rather than bodies and expressions. It was like watching the floor of a dance: pairs of feet moving about amongst each other, between each, towards and away. Some pairs stayed together the entire few hours, while others moved to and fro, bouncing across the courtyard.

Dozing in and out of his state of shaded relaxation, one pair of shoes had caught his attention for more reasons than one. First, they were unusual. The vintage style was certainly not common in Mexico. He found the brown, leather, laced-up boots with the small heel to be interestingly sexy. The top of the boots met with the hem of long, light-pink material; certainly highly unusual. Instead of lifting his hat to take in the full figure of this unusual outfit, he watched the feet move about the courtyard. The movement of these feet didn't meet with those of a male pair. Instead, they moved about independently, almost never meeting any others, and resting for a while, crossed and tucked under one of the benches.

The horn blew, and the guards began their round-up, systematically checking to be sure all prisoners returned to their respective areas. David watched the mysterious pair of shoes file into the women's line before turning the opposite way to head back to the men's side. It was the first time he had noticed the unusual outfit, and he assumed she must be new behind the walls. The picture of the shoes stayed in his mind for days, gradually increasing his curiosity about the person who filled them. They even appeared in one of his dreams.

He decided that the following Sunday, he would look for the shoes, this time taking in what stood above them as well. His mind had drawn different versions of what such a woman might look like. Maybe he would even talk to her.

CHAPTER 32

"Something in Her Eyes"

Sarah slipped the light pink dress over her long, cotton slip. For spending some hours outside, it was her favorite one to wear: the flowing material and short sleeves allowed breezes to keep her cool. Even though she hadn't really mingled with any of the male prisoners the previous week, she decided to return the following Sunday. It was a much-needed change of pace to counterbalance Maria's departure and the stress of that week's upcoming court appearance. The guards whistled to begin the line-up and check-in of prisoners who wanted to attend the afternoon visit. Sarah grabbed her hat on the way out to join the others.

Sarah felt like a young schoolgirl again—unsure of how to interact with the opposite sex. Scanning the crowd in the courtyard, she scouted out men who looked like they might have an interesting conversation to share. Giving herself some time, she decided to sit down in some shade to have a look around, her legs crossed out in front of her. The heat radiated up from the courtyard, and she tipped her hat slightly to wipe her brow.

David entered the courtyard for his weekly Sunday afternoon of people watching. Standing by one of the guards at the entry door, he looked over to his usual shady location. There was only an hour of limited shade that existed in the courtyard as the sun hit just the right location for it to cover most of his body. As he took a few steps that way, however, there was already another body occupying his block of shade. He walked a little closer. It was her—with the shoes—and the dress. She wasn't looking his way. Her face was mostly hidden by the large brim of a hat. He observed what he could at a distance: her slender figure, milky skin, and some brown waves peering out in the form of a pony tail. He moved a little closer, debating whether he should talk to her, sit next to her, or just find another spot.

How could he not be mesmerized? What could she have possibly done to offend the Mexican government? He tried to imagine. Maybe she was a spy.

The hat rose slightly. She had caught him staring, and he froze in his tracks. His mind, his heart, and his body all seemed to be in disagreement: none of them moving together. His mind told him to divert his eyes quickly, but they didn't listen. He was already caught for too long. His heart told his feet to move towards her, but they wouldn't.

As her gaze rose, their eyes eventually met. Locked. David was now swimming in her violet eyes, and he couldn't look away. These eyes were captivating. Bright. Luring. Familiar. He searched his mind for a memory. His steps began to slowly move backwards, their eyes remaining on each other until he finally turned to find another location to sit.

Another court date had come and gone with what seemed like only an inch of progress. This time, the state brought more information to add to the case: additional numbers, calculations, and biological evidence about the pests that Sarah's marijuana crops had supposedly brought across the border. But that was all. Everything seemed to go in baby steps, just crawling along. Now, the judge declared they meet again in three weeks to discuss the new information. This would give the judge more time to review it further, as well as give the defense time to come up with a counter argument. Sarah couldn't believe that six months had already passed without a verdict.

At least her mind had been positively occupied that week with thoughts of the mysterious man from the last Sunday afternoon. Ordinarily, she would have been left with a hopeless feelings about anyone staring at her, but there was something strangely comforting about this man. It couldn't be any connection to someone that she knew in Mexico, and she hadn't interacted with any Caucasians in Mexico. His stare was more than that of a curious stranger. It stirred her. Was he a lover in a previous life? Did she even believe in that?

One Sunday passed and another came. Even though she had the trial to break the week in half, the days felt much longer. Even the hours that morning seemed to pass at a painfully slow pace. Sarah had decided to put the same light pink dress back on, hoping that she would see the mystery man again and he would recognize

331

her. She had imagined the scenario a million times in her head, but was still unable to pick an opening line that sounded appropriate. And what language would she use?

As the women filed into the courtyard, Sarah's pulse quickened. She hoped he would be there again and that he would recognize her.

David caught his reflection in a glass door, combing his fingers through his mid-length hair. Whether he was washing dishes in the kitchen or lying in bed at night, he hadn't stopped thinking about the girl all week. Her friendly eyes and familiar presence was more than just a coincidence.

The women had already arrived in the courtyard. David couldn't seem to set his feelings straight as he stepped out into the glaring sun. Standing just where he had been the previous week, he looked over to the small corner of shade. There she was; this time without a hat, her wavy locks dancing around her shoulders. She looked right at him, and he was afraid that he might freeze in his tracks again. "Move your legs," his brain demanded of his body. Their gaze remained on each other as he moved over to her and sat down.

"Do you mind?" he asked, hoping for the right answer.

She gave him an appraising look. "Alright," she said, not sure if she could go through with the entirely bohemian ritual.

Neither felt comfortable discussing their situations, so they stuck to small talk.

"So, how long are you planning to vacation here?" he said, breaking the tension with humor.

"Well," she replied, "my room is only booked for two weeks, but I have every intention of extending my trip."

They exchanged niceties about the perfect weather, the first class treatment, and all of the amenities of the Mexican resort, including their hosts and many of the other guests. Strangely enough, giving one's name under those circumstances didn't seem like normal protocol. Since they were discussing an imaginary resort, it seemed only appropriate to assume imaginary roles.

"You must be some billionaire world traveller spending your time basking in the sun of a new getaway every month," quipped Sarah. "I think I've heard of you. Aren't you the Count of Monte Cristo?"

"You got me," David joked. "But although your beauty is legendary, I'm afraid I can't place you."

Sarah wore a wry smile until it faded into neutrality.

"I'm not sure who I am anymore. I've been playing a role for so long, I've lost my identity."

David, sensing sadness in her voice, attempted to recapture gaiety with quips and facetious conversation. "Now I recognize you. You're Mercedes, the elusive lady of great fortune."

A smile spread across Sarah's countenance and a comfortable, familiarity soothed them both. Each held a respect for the other's personal secrets and steered their conversations toward lighter, happier thoughts.

They sat for the rest of the period discussing what their lives would be like if they should be freed from their current situation. Finally, the fateful sound recalled them to their miserable realities. He gave her hand a squeeze. "See you next week, Mercedes?"

"Definitely, Monte," she smiled back at him as he took in her violet eyes one more time. They both pushed themselves up to their feet and headed in their respective directions. She gave one more wave before turning to join the crowd of women. Later that evening, music could be heard from a radio as it echoed through the empty hallways. One of the guards had apparently tuned in to a rock and roll station some distance from the prison, the music fighting to penetrate static from the weak signal.

David lingered somewhere between sleep and his thoughts when he became aware of the tune as it floated past his cell. It was Conway Twitty's hit song *Lonely Blue Boy*. His mind summoned the memory of the girl at the Huntington Library and he wondered what life she led.

As the American DJ filled the interlude between songs with trivia a similar version of the song began to play as the first one began to fade.

"You're listening to a tribute to Elvis on this fifth anniversary of his death. That was Conway Twitty's big hit from 1958, Lonely Blue Boy, first recorded by Elvis for what was probably his best movie role, but later dropped when the title of the movie was changed to King Creole. Here is Elvis' version of the original song entitled, Danny."

Sarah listened from her confine as the song passed by the cell door. Her thoughts also returned to that summer day in California and the boy she called as Danny. She wondered where he was and what he was doing at that moment.

CHAPTER 33

"A Rose by Any Other Name"

He looked over at the spot where they had met the previous weeks, only to find it vacant. His mind began to race. "Did she not want to see me again? Was she released? Did something happen to her?"

"Did you think I wouldn't come?" He heard the playful tone of her voice and smiled, gently reaching for hand to lead her to a place to sit. Without any thought or words they sat close to each other, their arms brushing against each other and his hand resting on her knee.

David had managed to procure a desert lily through one of the guards, at great expense. He had been captured by the flowering beauty held hostage for some deep, dark crime that he felt she would rather keep hidden. He held it out to Sarah.

"Its beauty pales next to yours," he said in his most gallant personification, bowing in an exaggerated movement.

Sarah felt both flattered and embarrassed by the effort, having wondered if this man would still want to be with her if he knew what her life had become.

"Perhaps the Deadly Nightshade would be a more appropriate representation of your affection," she said, turning away from his gaze.

David attempted to lighten her mood, not wanting to see her fall into unhappy thoughts.

"And how could one possibly associate such a name with something as beautiful as you?" he asked.

"Are you familiar with the Deadly Nightshade? Rumor has it that the wives of Emperor Augustus and Claudius used the toxic plant as a murder weapon. It was first used to make poison arrows, and since then, its main purposes have been medicine and revenge."

"Wow. A rose and its thorns; a deadly nightshade and its poison. I would like to give you my own nickname, if you don't mind. It's a night-scented flower whose color reminds me of your eyes."

"The Petunia?" she guessed, smiling up at him.

"You guessed it. I think they're a majestic flower—timid and bold all at once."

"You know, the two flowers are actually related."

"Well then, it suits you even better."

David never could find the right point in conversation to reveal to her how he had been involved with the illegal drug business over the last few years. She wondered why he hadn't yet asked her what she was in prison for, but she wasn't volunteering the information until he did so. Instead of all the obvious conversation—"What are you in for?" "How's your trial going?" "What about your family?" They spoke instead about people, philosophies of life, cultures, art, food, and drink.

Those were their chosen topics week after week. They cut through the surface, deep into each other's soul. These souls had been introduced that day at the library. Now, without being aware, they had become reacquainted.

Sarah couldn't believe there was such a silver lining to her imprisonment, and both knew it was destiny. Their hands stuck to each other with a layer of balmy sweat. Her legs were tangled with his in various positions as they went on talking about everything other than their personal lives. They didn't care that it was uncomfortably warm. These were the only two hours a week they had with each other, and David noted by the angle of the shadow that it was almost the end of their time. He reached over to pull a piece of hair away from her face, and s closed her eyes upon knowing his touch. As she turned her face up to look towards his, it was the first time their lips met. Goose bumps crept up her spine and erratic pulses overran his heart. Their lips remained in contact for what seemed like hours but must have been only seconds, the moment interrupted by the cell return siren.

Their ritual remained the same each week; David and Sarah

sat in each other's arms, cherishing those two hours of Sunday conversation without getting personal. . This week, however, Sarah decided to bring up the undesirable topic of time. Her body language became such that David knew she was uncomfortable.

"David ... we've never talked about our trials. How long do you think you'll be here?"

"You probably understand as well as I do that it's hard to tell. I've been trying to make a deal with the federal police to negate my case in exchange for information, but it's moving slowly."

Sarah didn't ask what kind of information. She didn't want to mix that in with their relationship. "Is it just that it's going slowly, or do you think there's any chance that you'll end up staying for some years?" The energy of the conversation had taken on a more serious tone.

"I can only hope they'll let me go. My attorney says they're thinking about it." There was silence. "And you?"

"My trial should close within the next one to three months. It actually doesn't look so good for me. I think I'll have to serve some time. I'm hoping with my job, reputation, and maybe a little bribery I can make it very short, though. I'm willing to get out any way I can. I want to go back to Europe."

"Europe."

339

"Yeah. Who knows, I may be forced to go back there anyway. "I'm having the same problem. I have a large savings. I was thinking of heading over the Atlantic myself."

"What if we requested a private meeting next Sunday?" David nervously asked.

"You mean a conjugal visit?" she giggled. "Call a spade a spade, my dear."

"Well, yeah, but I mean we don't have to—I didn't mean that—I just thought it would be a nice change for some alone time."

It had become a Catch-22. They both wanted out of prison as soon as possible but this would mean separation. Being released at the same time seemed too much to ask of destiny. They tried to stay in the present, savoring each meeting, each Sunday afternoon, and each thought that the other was just across the way. Each meeting with their attorneys became more ridden with anxiousness.

CHAPTER 34

"Deals"

Their kisses slowed, his lips brushing against hers as they worked their way over to her ear, down her neck, and stopping on her shoulder. His palm had a firm grip around her waist, and his warm breath aroused a passion unlike any she had known.

"This is love," she whispered in his ear.

He responded with a caress of his hand across her chest and down to her navel. Their moist bodies remained entangled as they relished the moments of feeling each other: skin to skin, as close as they could be. The moments of holding each other afterwards were just as precious as those while making love. During the week, they spent their nights dreaming of when they could hold each other again; replaying memories of the previous visits over in their heads many times in an attempt to infuse the events into their dreams.

Each week seemed better than the last, and the time became more precious as they understood that those visits were limited. They had managed to get their request granted for a conjugal visit nearly every week. On weeks they weren't able to get one of the private rooms, they settled for their usual spot in the shade, holding each other with talk of the future.

It looked like Sarah's trial was coming to an end, and all signs pointed to a guilty verdict. The main goal of her attorney now was to keep the sentence as short as possible. Things were looking brighter on David's end, since the Policía Federal had agreed they would be interested in a deal. The next meeting with his lawyer would reveal what the deal would be.

David's emotions were a mix of nervousness, curiosity, tension, and relief. After months of waiting, it was supposed to be the day he got a date: the final news on his deal. He followed closely behind his lawyer into the small, white, barren room where the officials were already waiting.

"Señor Clay," they motioned for the men to sit down, not wasting any time.

David took a brief look around the room: the four white walls, the two men with neatly-combed hair sitting in front of him, and the guards surrounding. One of his chair legs was uneven, rocking slightly every time he moved. The rustling of papers filled the silence of the room.

The officer directly in front of him finally reached the page he was looking for. "We are prepared to dismiss your charges for the exchange of valuable information that leads to the arrest of one, Mateo Hernandez, who has been primarily running out of Hermosillo. You will be released as soon as the information you give has proven both valid and useful. Are you in agreement?"

David wanted to give an immediate and emphatic "yes," but looked first to his lawyer, who gave him the nod of approval. The officer once again flipped through some papers until he got to a blank, lined set of sheets. He turned the papers towards David, along with the pen. "The more you write, the better it is for you."

David wrote down every helpful detail he could think of. That meant it would be a matter of days or weeks before his prison vacation was over. He never thought that leaving prison would be bittersweet. Going out into the world seemed pointless if it was without his sweet Petunia. He didn't want to leave without her, but they had promised to wait for each other.

That Sunday, they had been granted their request for one of the conjugal rooms. It was one of the few times they used it only for privacy instead of making love, as Sarah wasn't feeling well that day. Realizing that she had probably been negligent with the amount of water she was drinking, she had tried to drink a lot that morning in hopes that the nausea would ease by the afternoon. Trying to tell herself and her body that she was just fine, she couldn't feign well-being once she sat down on the bed in the dimly lit room. She didn't have to say anything, as David could sense immediately that she wasn't feeling well. Instead of embracing her in a strong, passionate, and fiery kiss as he usually did, he instead sat her down next to him, then gently eased her head into his lap so he could stroke her hair. Sarah gratefully closed her eyes and urged him to tell her about his meeting. As happy as he was to receive the news, he didn't want to tell Sarah about it.

"You first," he urged, knowing that she was also supposed to have had news that week.

"Truthfully, I don't want to tell you," she answered in a quiet voice.

David continued to run his fingers through her dark waves. "Yeah, I understand. That's why I told you to go first. We both knew it would get more difficult at some point, though."

They stayed in silence for a few moments until David decided to go first. "So, it looks like I'll be out in a few weeks. The federal police agreed to a deal, and I wrote out a statement for them on Thursday. Once they've verified the information, I'll be out."

She pushed herself up out of his lap and propped herself against his side, head on his shoulder. "My news isn't so bright. My court date this week was left looking like I'll get five to six years. The final ruling is three weeks."

"What—but", he began to try to find a solution

immediately, but she held her hand up, asking him to wait.

"Yeah, it looks pretty dismal, except that I may have a way out. There's a Russian Mafioso on his way out who, according to my lawyer, promised that he could get me out with him for a fair price. Apparently, his connections are good enough that he can take a lady out with him. I don't know all the details of exactly who he's connected to, or how he might be bribing them, but he said if I can get him 60,000 pesos, he guarantees I can walk out with him. He would get me to Europe, where I would then go as I please."

"Do you think it could be dangerous?"

"No more than taking care of myself in the presence of drug lords," was her response after some thought. David thought to himself, that's the first time she had mentioned anything about her past.

"Why do you think he asked you?"

"I think he probably threw the deal out to a few women who are rumored to have money. I think it's my best shot."

"What if I could break you out?" He found his macho side starting to swell.

345

"Funny enough, I've been thinking through such plans. But listen, what if we do come up with a way for you to get me out, and we get caught. Then we're both back here again—without a doubt—and without a chance of freedom. I think the 60,000 pesos would be money well spent."

They continued to talk through all the "what ifs" and "maybes," making plans for all scenarios.

CHAPTER 35

"Twists and Turns"

David was working in the kitchen when Raphael entered, thirty minutes late. David could tell he was a bit frustrated, not an unusual state for him to be in. Several times over the course of their working together, he had seemed to be overly anxious. When he got in that mood, he tended to get nosy, asking David questions about his case, prying incessantly until David finally let slip some details about his involvement in the financial side of drugs. Raphael would hound him about how much money he must have made and how much he might have hidden in safe bank accounts. He even suggested David might have skimmed a bit from the top, hiding it as well, and wanted to know where someone might hide that kind of money. David had decided Raphael thought he could get at his money if he could find out where it was, but he had tucked it well away from any prying eyes.

This particular day, Raphael seemed desperate for answers. Even his weakly masked effort to appear casual was missing. When David insisted that the conversation was pointless, Raphael became violent. He grabbed a large knife and pressed it into David's throat until it actually drew blood.

"Look, asshole," he shouted, "you have information and I need it now! Tell me where your money is and how to get to it, or I swear I'll kill you!"

David was leaning back as the knife pushed deeper into the flesh of his throat when his hand found the handle of a frying pan. He turned to disengage the knife from his throat and struck out at Raphael's face. The impact knocked Raphael to the floor, but he immediately jumped up. He leaped and caught David by the shoulders as David ran toward the kitchen door, dragging him to the floor. David had never been in a situation where he knew his life depended on him overpowering someone, much less a crazed lunatic who seemed intent on murdering him. He grabbed the legs of a small table and pummelled Raphael, who was clawing his way toward David's throat.

As Raphael fell back, David bent both knees and hit Raphael with both heels, kicking as hard as he could. Raphael seemed undaunted in David's efforts, however. He was on top of David again before he could get to his feet. He began to beat David fiercely, David doing his best to protect against the blows. Raphael stood and began to kick and stomp until David felt himself beginning to fall into a deep black hole. He was sure he was about to be killed, unable to make out anything around him. In the distance, however, he heard voices yelling.

David regained consciousness without any indication of where he was. At first, he thought he was still lying on the kitchen floor but soon realized he couldn't be because the kitchen floor was cold and hard; this was warm and soft. He seemed to be blind in one eye and struggled to raise his arms, finding both of his hands to be bandaged. He put them to his head and found more bandages including a large patch over one of his eyes.

Someone entered the room, but David had trouble making out who or what it was. A friendly voice made its way through the bandages, and David picked up a few words. "Contusions," "fractures," "blood loss," and "internal bleeding" were the ones that stuck. He tried to speak but found he couldn't; his mouth felt swollen, and his tongue felt as though he had bitten it.

"Don't worry, you'll survive," the faceless voice said. "But you had better plan on being here for quite a while."

David wasn't sure how long he had been in the infirmary before regaining a sense of reality that had not been completely numbed by medication. He had just found the strength to raise his upper body and check for any missing parts when a doctor entered.

"Well, I see you are back among the living."

"How long have I been here?" asked David, looking around the room.

"Four days," replied the doctor, "and I expect you'll be with us another week or so."

Four Days! David thought of his Violet Petunia. "Has anyone been to see me?" he asked.

"No visitors allowed, I'm afraid. This is still a prison, you know. Is there anything I can get you?"

David requested writing materials. His sudden brush with death filled him with a need to assure his mystery love that he was still alive and open up to her about who and what he truly was. She would be leaving if the plans hadn't changed, and he didn't want her to go not knowing where he was and how he felt about her.

When the doctor brought a lined tablet and a pen, David started to write a simple note and try to put everything he was feeling into a few lines. He also decided to write about everything he had done, deciding that it would clear his conscience and give her details she needed to know if they were going to attempt a life together. He could not face being apart from her for who knew how long without confessing his true love and identity.

***

It had been two weeks since Sarah was told of the beating and realized who the victim had been. She had still not heard anything from David, nor had she been able to find a way to communicate with him. Struggling with the thought of leaving without saying good-bye, she gathered her few belongings onto the bed in preparation to leave the prison and her newfound love. It suddenly dawned on her that she didn't even know his name.

She wasn't sure if she ever wanted to ask all the details of who Andrei bullied to get her out with him, but the money had been paid through her lawyer and she was due to walk out at eleven that morning. Her stomach turned at the thought of walking through those doors without her love, but a few weeks were better than a few years.

He was due to be released the next week, and she kept reassuring herself that everything would be fine. Her side was the risky deal, and she had confidence in her abilities. All he had to do was get a ticket to Stockholm once he was out. It shouldn't be more than two to three weeks' time.

She sat on her bed waiting for the minutes to tick by. Each set of footsteps put her on alert, looking for a guard coming to release her. Finally, she heard the sound of double footsteps accompanied by a clanking of keys.

"Listo?" The guard handcuffed her before unlocking the door. His partner came in to pick up her belongings. Her cell mates had changed so often after Maria left that she didn't put much effort into forming any relationships; only pleasant acquaintances. She had written a note to David giving him an address of where to meet her in Stockholm. As she was being led from her cell, she gave the letter to Rita, one of her cell mates, entrusting her to get it to her "Count." She waved a few goodbyes on her way out, but only really cared about one person—in an entirely different building—to whom she was unable to say goodbye.

***

The discussion between Sarah and her cell mate had not gone unnoticed. A pair of loathsome eyes observed the note being handed to the young woman. As Rita made her way to breakfast the next morning, she found her path blocked by the belligerent woman who had previously attempted to take Sarah's locket. The note was snatched from her hand and a threat issued … David would never receive Sarah's note.

***

Andrei was waiting for her in front, already checked out. She hadn't anticipated what it would feel like after nearly one year to have the last handcuffs removed and her freedom returned, breathing the fresh air on the other side of the walls. She took one look at Andrei and forced a smile. He looked ridiculous, she thought, wearing all that jewellery. *He must wear his clothes a little too big so he can act as though he might actually be muscular.* He didn't even offer to take her bag.

"Let's go, my doll. We have a five o'clock flight to Geneva."

A guard suddenly rushed out. "Wait, señorita, you have a letter."

Sarah took the letter, but before she could look at it, Andrei gripped her upper arm and lead her forcibly to a waiting taxi.

Sarah ducked into the taxi, and Andrei closed the door

behind her. While Andrei stood outside giving instructions to the driver, she opened the letter and began to read. She read a few sentences and suddenly felt confused, as if in a dream. As she read David's narrative of his life in California, her heart rate increased. What was this? Could it be that David was the boy so many years ago, the boy she had not been able to forget through all these years? She shuffled through the pages, her eyes desperately searching the facts in disjoined pieces. High school, college years, and … how could this be? Her David? The face of the employee she had never met. A pain filled her chest, and she had difficulty breathing as tears began to stream down her face. She turned to look back at the prison where he still remained.

Her eyes remained glued on the prison as they pulled away. She couldn't help but feel a piece of her heart was torn off and left there. "Three weeks," she told herself as she closed her eyes for the remainder of the journey to the airport.

She had been gone several days, and David did not even know if she had received his letter. The doctor had promised to give it to a guard for delivery, but David knew that things didn't always get done without money to motivate most of the staff.

David slipped his lucky penny into his loafers as he dressed for the last trip to see his lawyer. Everything was settled with the police, and he assumed he just needed to sign a few papers before his release was official. Entering the large meeting room full of tables and chairs, David looked around for his lawyer. A wave from the corner gave him guidance.

There were no papers on the table. Perhaps there were no final papers—just a verbal update. David just wanted to know exactly what day he would be packing up.

"David," his lawyer began in the matter-of-fact tone he always carried. "The federal police have denied your release at this point. Unfortunately, they took the information you gave them, but it proved to be unhelpful. Mateo has disappeared. He seems to have moved his operation. Since your information provided nothing for them, they will not authorize your release in return."

David blinked once, twice. "But—I gave them what they asked for, how can they do this?!" The conversation at the table next to him paused as his voice rose.

"But your information led them nowhere."

"Then I'll give them more information! Someone else!"

"That may very well be a good solution. Why don't you write down the names of some others, and I'll take it back to them?"

"We don't have to start this whole process over again, do we?!"

"Not from the very beginning, but it will take a bit more

time and money."

"I've given you money, and lots of it. How will more money help?" asked David in a heated tone.

"Trust me; money will buy anything if given enough time. A few days ago, your lady friend stood no chance of freedom. But enough money to the right people, and the Russian underground was able to work a deal."

David was stunned. A Russian underground involvement; what interest would the Russians have in this woman? What secret had she kept from him? How could they share intimate moments together when he knew so little about her? His head was spinning as he pondered which question to ask first.

"Why would the Russian underground be interested in a simple woman like ..." he paused, embarrassed that he didn't even know her real name ... "like her?" he managed to mumble.

"She was a woman of apparent importance, or the Russians would not have gotten involved. I'm not sure how important or to whom. To me, she was just another drug pusher, but she must be someone very special. But why are you asking me these things? I would think you would know more about her, having worked for her so intimately.

"What do you mean by having worked for her; why would I know about her?"

The lawyer gave David a look of derision. "What did you and Belladonna talk about after your lovemaking?" David didn't answer.

"We'll talk again soon when you've had time to think about your situation," he said as he closed his brief case, nodded once to David, then turned and walked away.

Belladonna! David was in a state of shock. If his conclusions were right, his lovely Violet Petunia was actually Belladonna … his drug dealing employer. Of course! She had admitted to having dealings with drug dealers in an offhand statement, but David had never considered her background to be even remotely tied to his. Deadly Nightshade was just another name for Belladonna. It all made sense now.

David could only think of one thing: one person. It wasn't about him. It was about her. He had to get to her and would do whatever it took to get out as soon as he could.

CHAPTER 36

"The Truth"

Everything about David's time in prison suddenly took on a completely different appearance. David's lawyer had never mentioned his other clients, but that wasn't unusual considering that, even in Mexico, there would be some form of lawyer-client confidentiality. But if he knew that his client was Belladonna, he must also know that David worked for her, even though David had never disclosed her identity to anyone. And if he was representing Belladonna, he must also be working with Mateo. David suddenly had a sickening feeling that his money and efforts to give up Mateo had been wasted if his lawyer was also working for Mateo. David decided that one thing was certain … money could get you what you wanted, but it had to be spent in the right places.

Luis knew as much about the inner workings of the prison as anyone, so David decided on a plan. He offered Luis money to discriminately bribe anyone who could provide him information about his lawyer. He needed something to use as leverage if he was going to turn the odds in his favor. The bribe money paid off, and David had enough information to make his move.

David's next meeting with his lawyer followed just a few days after his previous court appearance. David wasted no time getting to the point.

"You've probably guessed that I've figured out a number of things about you," he said as he stood from the chair where he had been sitting and approached the lawyer.

"You would have to be a fool not to," replied the lawyer.

"Tell me when I get something wrong," David said in his most sarcastic tone.

"I have nothing to hide. My business matters are known quite well by those within this prison. I have treated you no differently than I have many others," replied the lawyer in a very offhand manner.

"Since you represented Belladonna, you obviously knew she was the client I worked for."

"One of them … you had several."

"So you know of my other clients, as well?"

"Of course. I'm a very good lawyer."

"I guess the more corrupt you are, the better a lawyer you'll make," said David, not intending it to be much of a compliment.

"We are each entitled to our opinions. I use my abilities to help my clients, but I must also look out for myself."

"It seems to me your only interest is in looking out for yourself at the expense of your clients."

"That's not true. My record will show that most of my clients avoid paying for their crimes in the end. I just make them pay financially for their unjustified freedom. It is a bit of poetic justice in my mind."

"The big Mexican who was let into my cell to rough me up, and our friend Raphael who tried to kill me, do you know who set them on me?"

"Yes, the big Mexican was a message from one of your clients … Ignacio … just to let you know you could be gotten to. I had no role in that. Raphael, on the other hand, was indeed a poor choice on my part. I knew you must have much more money at your disposal than you had indicated to me. He was supposed to gain your trust and find out where it was. Unfortunately, he could be a bit unpredictable when he managed to find a source to feed his habit."

"And Mateo, how much did he pay you to protect him from my efforts to turn him over in exchange for my freedom?"

"Yes, he was very nervous when both you and Belladonna were arrested. He invested a great deal to slow down the process, but his finances were beginning to dwindle. I would have left him to fend for himself eventually."

"And the Russian, what was your angle getting him released and how did Belladonna tie into the whole thing?"

"The Russian was not one of my clients. He had all the help he needed. I was simply able to work out a financial arrangement to gain the release of Belladonna under his care."

"Who was paid for her release, and where is she now?"

"That was purely an unexpected financial windfall. Mateo paid me to get her out of the country before she could turn over any evidence on him. Ignacio offered me money to get her to give evidence against Mateo to eliminate competition. Belladonna paid me to get her released, and some foreign interests paid me to convince Belladonna to go with the Russian. So you see, everybody plays the same game for money. As for where she is, I have no idea."

As David sat quietly thinking and evaluating his options, his lawyer rose from his chair and picked up his briefcase. "If that will be all, I'm sure you will want to begin looking for a new lawyer."

David stood for a moment trying to sort out everything in his mind.

"Wait," said David as his lawyer started out the door, "I don't want another lawyer. I need someone who can get things done for money."

His lawyer turned his hand still on the door handle. "What is your proposal?"

"What is your proposal?"

"Mateo paid you to keep him from being found. I'll pay more to make sure he is found. It is my only hope to make a deal with the court."

"That is easily taken care of, but can I trust you to deliver the money?"

"Believe me, money is no object. Mateo's funds are dwindling because I put all of Belladonna's funds in a few very safe places. You make sure that Mateo is found, that I get freed, and that you arrange transportation for me out of the country; I promise you will be very well paid. But I do the transferring of funds, not you."

"And if you skip out on me?"

"I won't, but even if I did you wouldn't have lost a thing since you already said you were going to let Mateo fend for himself and you weren't expecting any further business from me."

"You plan to chase down this Belladonna?"

"Yes."

The lawyer shook his head slowly. "Call me a hopeless romantic, but I'll trust you to fulfill your part of the bargain. I've known men to do stranger things for love. You should be free within a week … I know exactly where Mateo is hiding."

***

Two federal police cars pulled into the dirt driveway. Mateo saw them coming and had already taken the cash from its hiding place, prepared to make the customary payment for being transparent to the law. As he reached out to hand the cash to one of the uniformed men, he found his wrist secured in a pair of handcuffs.

Mateo Colmenares, you are under arrest for producing and trafficking of illegal substances. Please ... if you would accompany us?"

***

Sunday came, and David decided he needed to be where the memory of his Violet Petunia, or Belladonna, would be the strongest. He went out into the courtyard where men and women were beginning to mingle. As he sat in the same shady spot where he and Belladonna had spent so much time together, he noticed a young woman; or more accurately, he noticed the necklace she was wearing. He rose and approached the woman.

"That necklace! Where did you get it?" asked David.

"I did not steal it," she replied in broken English. A guard took it from the gringa woman in my cell and gave it to me for being nice to him."

David could hardly believe it. What were the odds that another necklace exactly the same as the one he had seen around the neck of the young Sarah, Pinkie, would show up in this particular place?

"I've seen this necklace before. Where is that woman?" David asked in Spanish.

"She is gone. She was set free along with a foreign man a few days ago."

David almost fell to his knees. His mind was reeling, and he was having trouble breathing. This just could not be; Belladonna and the girl from years before? Sarah!

CHAPTER 37

"Final Letters"

My Darling,

I don't know where else to send this letter. I'm sending it to the prison in desperation that even if you're not there, someone will deliver it. I've sent another to the address I gave you in Stockholm, as well. I'm praying it finds you, wherever you may be.

I thought by now you would be holding me in your arms; that we would be waking up next to each other at dawn each morning. It has now been five weeks since I left Mexico with the hopes of seeing you weeks later in my homeland.

My love, I am in trouble. You weren't wrong to question my safety in the hands of Andrei. It did not go as he promised. I write now, quickly, while he is meeting with some other mafia members. Please forgive me that I cannot write more.

He has taken control of me with great force—he's a monstrous man. I can hardly leave the apartment without supervision and one of his thugs following me. I need you. I hope you haven't thought that I abandoned you. My heart is yours. And we should be sharing in the experience of the physical proof of our love. This is so hard to write because I should be telling you in person. I'm pregnant ... with twins. I can feel the flutters of two beautiful lives within me—lives you and I created. They need the loving arms of two parents who will show them the world through love's eyes.

Please come for me! We are in Geneva, on the north side of the river. My heart waits for you. Until then, I'll continue to visit with you in my dreams.

With all my love, from three beating hearts,

Your Loving Sarah

***

Sarah—Love of My Life,

My heart aches. The wet stains of my tears dot the pages as I write. I am here, in the Mexican prison where our souls were re-united. I am trying to rationalize everything I have learned over the past few days, hardly believing that fate has reunited us after so many years only to have us separated again. I will find you, no matter the cost or how long it may take.

Draw all your strength from within and feel that I am there with you. You are not alone. We will meet in our dreams until we meet in flesh again.

With all my love,

Your David

He carefully folded the letter and slid it into an envelope. Warped sections of dampened paper wore the proof of David's heartache as he licked the adhesive and folded over the flap. He wrote her name then paused. As his pen hovered over the area of the envelope where he should be writing the recipient's address, he resented how the blank space taunted him.

About the Authors

Who is The Holy Ghost Writer? The identity of the author is part of an international contest. The first person to correctly name the HG Writer from the clues found in the Count of Monte Cristo sequels will receive a reward of $5000. Visit the Holy Ghost Writer's Amazon Author Page for Details and see if you can discover the real identity of the author being heralded by fans as the new Stieg Larsson for The Anonymous Girl, the successor of Alexander Dumas for The Sovereign Order of Monte Cristo and the next Ray Bradbury for The Boy Who Played With Dark Matter. Contact the author c/o books@illuminatedpublications.com

Sadia Barrameda is a fashion designer and an early investor in, and advocate for the legalization of all aspects of industrial hemp, medical marijuana and recreational cannabis. She also holds 4 utility patents pending involving the hemp, cannabis and honeysuckle plants. Piroz The ISIS Slayer was her debut novella.

www.ingramcontent.com/pod-product-compliance
Lightning Source LLC
Chambersburg PA
CBHW061512020726

47502CB00006B/2040